Eight Skilled Gentlemen

BARRY HUGHART

Eight Skilled Gentlemen

A MASTER LI

主

NOVEL

A FOUNDATION BOOK

Doubleday

F
HUG

NEW YORK LONDON TORONTO SYDNEY AUCKLAND

A FOUNDATION BOOK

PUBLISHED BY DOUBLEDAY
a division of Bantam Doubleday Dell Publishing Group, Inc.
666 Fifth Avenue, New York, New York 10103

FOUNDATION, DOUBLEDAY, and the portrayal of the letter F
are trademarks of Doubleday, a division of Bantam Doubleday
Dell Publishing Group, Inc.

BOOK DESIGN BY LINEY LI

Library of Congress Cataloging-in-Publication Data

Hughart, Barry.
Eight skilled gentlemen / Barry Hughart. — 1st ed.
p.   cm.
"A Master Li novel."
"A Foundation book."
I. Title.
PS3558.U347E37   1991
813'.54—dc20   90-19271
F   CIP
ISBN 0-385-41709-8
ISBN 0-385-41710-1 (pbk.)
Copyright © 1991 by Barry Hughart
All Rights Reserved

Printed in the United States of America
January 1991
FIRST EDITION
1   3   5   7   9   10   8   6   4   2

*For Derk Bodde, Göran Aijmer,
and all the other pioneers
who almost got it right*

Eight Skilled Gentlemen

1

I have no intention of setting down the disgusting details concerning Sixth Degree Hosteler Tu. I will only say that I was half dead by the time we caught him, and Master Li had been so sorely pressed that he actually volunteered to serve as imperial witness to the execution. This was unprecedented because the old man hates to dress up in formal First Rank attire, even though he's still entitled to wear it, and he cannot tolerate the noise.

Executions in Peking are public occasions, held at the Vegetable Market that forms the western boundary of Heaven's Bridge, the criminal area of the city. A large audience always attends, and this particular Execution Day was certain to draw a larger and louder crowd than ever because Devil's Hand was going for the record. "Devil's Hand" is a generic name passed from one Chief Executioner of Peking to the other, and several centuries ago the executioner managed 1,070 consecutive clean decapitations without needing a second swipe of his great sword. Our current Devil's Hand had 1,044 consecutive clean kills, and since thirty condemned criminals were scheduled for execution the old record could fall before the day was done.

It was the first day of the fourth moon in the Year of the

Horse 3338 (A.D. 640) and every gambler in the city was packed into the square, besieging the bookmakers' booths, and Master Li said he hadn't seen so much money tossed around since Emperor Yang bet the city of Soochow on a cricket fight. (The bookmakers were facing ruin since they had originally offered astronomical odds against the record being broken. I had a small wager myself, but against Devil's Hand. The pressure on him was tremendous and would get worse with every falling head, and all it would take to miss would be a bite of a bug or a slip in a puddle of blood, and anyone who thinks it's easy to hit a stationary target in the exact same spot again and again with a heavy blade is advised to try chopping down a tree.) That meant every pickpocket and confidence man in Peking was on hand, and with the audience in an unusually festive mood it was to be expected that every vender who could cram his wares into the square would do so, and the result was the shattering of uncounted eardrums. Like this:

"*Sha la jen la!*"

"*Hao! Hao! Hao!*

"*Hao tao!*"

"*Boinngg-boinngg-boinngg-boinngg-boinngg!*"

"*My purse! Where is my silver necklace!*"

Meaning Devil's Hand roared the ritual, "I've got my man!" and the mob howled, "Good! Good! Good!" and connoisseurs spread credit where it was due by screaming "Good sword!" and a dealer in household sundries crept up behind me and took aim at my left ear and unleashed the traditional sound that advertised his wares: wooden balls at the ends of strings smacking viciously against brass gongs. The last agonized wail speaks for itself, and it was really very interesting to look down from my vantage point and see the victim being divested of his valuables by Fu-po the Ferret.

I was seated beside Master Li on the dignitaries' platform, sweating in the uncomfortable junior nobleman's uniform he makes me wear on such occasions and which will land me in boiling oil one of these days since I am scarcely entitled to the badges of rank. Master Li was letting an underling handle the honors until it came time for Sixth Degree Hosteler Tu to receive the sword, and was passing the time by catching up on his correspondence. He leaned over and yelled in my ear, trying to shout above the ghastly din.

"Something for you, Ox!"

He was waving a missive that seemed to consist of tracks made by a chicken after gobbling fermented mash.

"A literate barbarian!" Master Li yelled. "Fellow named Quintus Flaccus the Fourth, writing from a place called the Sabine Hills! Somehow or other he got his hands on one of your memoirs!" He swiftly scanned the chicken tracks. "Usual critical comments!" he yelled. "Clotted construction, inept imagery, mangled metaphors, and so on!"

"Nice of him to write!" I shouted back.

"Sha la jen la!"

"Hao! Hao! Hao!"

"Hao tao!"

"Who has taken my bronze belt buckle and my python skin belt!"

"Whangity-whangity-whangity-whang!"

That was a cobbler who had taken aim at my right ear and was advertising by smashing his metal foot-frame with a hammer. The head just chopped off by Devil's Hand, I noticed, was rolling like a ball across the cobblestones toward two little girls who were seated facing each other, playing the handclap game: clap opposing hands, clap left hands, clap right hands, clap own hands, and so on, while singing an ancient nonsense rhyme. They watched the severed head approach with large eyes, lifted their stubby legs in unison to let it roll past, and resumed clapping. Shrill happy voices reached through a momentary pause in the din:

> *"Kuang kuang ch'a,*
> *Kuang kuang ch'a,*

Miao li he shang
Mei yu t'ou fa!"

Did barbarian children in the Sabine Hills chant something like that while clapping hands?

"Cymbals a pair,
Cymbals a pair,
The old temple priest
He has no hair!"

Master Li leaned over and began yelling again. "Ox, this barbarian is a remarkably sound critic! Listen to this. *'Inceptis gravibus plerumque et magna professis purpureus, late qui splendeat, unus et alter adsuitur pannus, ut proicit ampullus! Parturient montes, nascetur ridiculus mus.'* A bit prolix, but beautifully phrased, isn't it?"

I have no idea why he asks questions like that. I continued to sit with my mouth slackly ajar in flycatching position while another prisoner received last words from the junior official and was dragged to the chopping block. Master Li placed his lips back against my ear.

"A rough translation might be: 'Often on a work of grave purpose and high promise is tacked a purple patch or two to give it color, but throw away the paintpot! Your mountains labor to give birth to a laughable little mouse.' "

"Very nicely phrased," I said.

"That's not all," said Master Li. "He gets better, except he still uses more words than he should and like all uncivilized writers his prose is strangled by unnecessary punctuation. I'm half tempted to send friend Flaccus a manual on Chinese Poetic Shorthand. Do you know Li Po's 'Short Song'?

'Earth too big
Sky too far
Ride six dragons

> Around North Star
> Crazy dragons stinking drunk
> Enjoy self!'

"Think, my boy, of the benefit to the barbarian's style if he studied Li Po's technique and altered his missive accordingly.

> 'Purpose grave
> Promise high
> Mountains labor
> By and by
> Out creeps mouse with purple nose
> Throw away paintpot!' "

"A vast improvement," I said.

I forgot to mention the venders of soft drinks. These fellows are almost alone in advertising their wares with their own voices, and the reason is that each and every one is convinced he's but a temporarily undiscovered star of Peking opera, and one of the bastards had crept up behind me and was pointing his gaping maw at both my ears. Along with the rest of it, the result was like this:

"*Sha la jen la!*"
"*Hao! Hao! Hao!*"
"*Hao tao!*"

> "*Soothing syrups chilled with ice!*
> *Try mine once you'll try them twice!*
> *Ten cash a cup to beat the heat*
> *With a taste like snow, but sweet-sweet-sweet!*"

"*Who has made off with my costly silk trousers! My pure velvet loincloth!*"

"*Clang-clang-clang-clang-clang-clang-clang-clang!*"

That last was a scissors grinder. They advertise by clashing rows of metal discs sewn into the linings of their long, wide sleeves, and the sound has the peculiar quality of cracking the porcelain of your teeth. The latest severed head rolled to the little girls, who didn't even look up as they automatically raised their legs, and the sweet childish chant continued as the head joined the row of its bodiless colleagues, and I suddenly leaned forward and started to count: ". . . twenty-four, twenty-five, twenty-six." Twenty-six meant Devil's Hand had just tied the record, and the next would set a new one! I was going to lose my bet unless a miracle happened, but I didn't mind. In fact, for the first time that day I felt a glow of well-being, because I knew the next prisoner in line all too well. How delightful that the record should be set by Sixth Degree Hosteler Tu!

"Ox, here's a very interesting comment from Flaccus the Fourth!" Master Li was yelling. "He begins by bemoaning your excessive sensationalism, and then writes, *'Ut turpiter atrum desinat in piscem mulier formosa superne—'* "

I nudged his arm and pointed, and Master Li arose and adjusted his robes. He stepped to the front of the platform as the bailiffs dragged the prisoner forward, and I could see the old man compose himself and begin formulating suitably dignified Confucian comments to help the hosteler resign himself to his imminent demise. Unfortunately Master Li couldn't quite attain the proper tone of serene gravity since he had to contend with the mob, the venders, the gamblers, and two little girls clapping hands, and the result was something like this:

"Sixth Degree Hosteler Tu—"

"Six to five! Last chance at six to five! Money-money-money!" howled Gold Tooth Meng.

"Your crimes are debased beyond belief—"

"Whap-whong! Whap-whong! Whap-whong!"

That was a peddler of combs and hairbrushes who advertised by bashing a drum and a gong simultaneously.

"And were it in my power to do so—"

"Soothing syrups chilled with ice!"

"Stop, thief! Bring back the lint from my navel!"
"I would sentence you to the Thousand Cuts—"

> *"Kuang kuang ch'a,*
> *Kuang kuang ch'a,*
> *Miao li he shang*
> *Mei yu t'ou fa!"*

"Beginning with your polecat prick and baboon balls, you miserable turd!" Master Li yelled at the top of his lungs.

Further words would be redundant. He waved to the bailiffs, who hauled Sixth Degree Hosteler Tu to the chopping block and kicked his legs out from under him. Devil's Hand began his breathing exercises and prepared to hoist his sword for the record-breaking attempt, and that was when the first of the extraordinary events that were to entangle us in the affairs of the Eight Skilled Gentlemen occurred.

I wouldn't have believed anybody could scream loud enough to make the mob in the Vegetable Market shut up and pay attention, or make the Chief Executioner of Peking come to a halt with his sword raised high, but that is exactly what happened. All eyes turned to six figures that were racing into the square through the Gate of Prolonged Righteousness. The five men in the lead had wide staring eyes, faces bleached white with terror, and mouths gaping like coal bins as they emitted one earsplitting scream after another. The sixth figure was the cause of the commotion, and one look was enough to freeze my blood. I had heard tales of vampire ghouls from Auntie Hua since I was five years old, but I had never expected to see one, and this *ch'ih-mei*, as Master Li later confirmed, was a specimen so classic it could have been used to illustrate the famous scientific study by the great P'u Sung-ling, Recorder of Things Strange.

It had long greenish-white hair growing all over it, tangled and rank, dripping with decaying fungus from a tomb. Its huge red eyes glared like charcoal fires, and its vulture claws dripped with somebody's blood, and its huge tiger teeth glittered in the sunlight. The terrible thing moved with immense powerful strides and would surely have caught the fleeing men in no time if it had run in a straight line. Instead it weaved and stumbled, clawing the air with impotent fury, and when it ran into one of the vender's carts I finally realized what Master Li had grasped instantly. The monster was blind and dying. That was what Auntie Hua had always told me: "Number Ten Ox, if you are chased by a ch'ih-mei, run to daylight! The sun is poison to the living dead!"

The old lady had been right. The vampire ghoul stumbled around in circles, and when it started toward the chopping block Devil's Hand almost twisted himself in half. Instinctively he had started his great sword down toward the block, and then he tried to stop in mid-swing and arc the blade toward the monster, and the result was that he missed the neck of Sixth Degree Hosteler Tu by three feet and the sword shot up a shower of sparks as it struck the cobblestones.

"Ten thousand blessings!" screamed Gold Tooth Meng, and every bookmaker in Peking joined in an earsplitting howl of *"Money-money-money-money-money!"* because Devil's Hand had just missed his chance to break the record and the bookmakers had been saved from bankruptcy. They immediately took off after wealthy bettors they'd given credit to, joining the howling mob battling to escape from the square through the Gate of Peace and Harmony. I saw a young mother snatch up the little handclapping girls, one under each arm, and kick severed heads out of the way like calabashes as she galloped for safety. Venders' carts and stalls were flying every which way, and showers of shattered bamboo poles and brilliantly painted canvas awnings joined goods of every description that covered the square. In an astonishingly short period of time the only occupants of the Vegetable Market were Devil's Hand, Sixth Degree Hosteler Tu, bailiffs who couldn't flee because they were chained to the hosteler and had dropped the keys and couldn't find them in the litter, Master Li,

a monster, and me. Master Li hopped down from the dignitaries' stand and trotted over toward the monster just as it ran into the Wailing Wall behind the chopping block and fell on its back. I ran after Master Li. Just as I got there the vampire ghoul hissed horribly, clawed the air one more time, shuddered, and lay still. Slowly the terrible fire died in its staring blind eyes, and I didn't need a medical examiner to tell me it was dead.

"Fried internally by sunlight, which penetrates putrid flesh to the vital organs," Master Li said matter-of-factly.

Putrid flesh indeed. It stank horribly of decaying matter, and its own body was just as responsible for the reek as were the bits of flesh and gristle from the person it had recently eaten sticking to its claws and teeth.

"Absolutely lovely," Master Li said reverently. "A specimen this perfect hasn't been seen in Peking for a thousand years, and I would very much like to know why it left the safety of a grave to commit suicide in burning sunlight."

The answer wasn't long in coming, because seven more figures were running slowly and exhaustedly through the Gate of Prolonged Righteousness. I recognized the one in the lead, Sergeant Hsienpo of the City Guard, with six of his men behind him. They were panting like a pack of winded hounds when they reached us, and dripping with perspiration. It was clear that the sergeant was delighted to find the monster dead, and almost equally delighted to find a First Rank official to take responsibility. He saluted Master Li smartly.

"Sergeant Hsienpo, sir, from the Coal Hill Watch," he said. "Got a report that suspicious men were at the Lin family cemetery. Found five grave robbers at work in broad daylight, as bold as you please."

The sergeant made no attempt to disguise his admiration for the thieves, who had avoided the guard dogs that patrolled at night by forging a work order for a drainage ditch and marching up the hill with picks and shovels over their shoulders, whistling cheerfully. They could tunnel like moles, and by the time the sergeant and his men had been alerted by the head gardener (he was suspicious because he hadn't received his customary kickback for Coal Hill contracts) they'd already cut two side passages from the central ditch and removed the jewelry and jade burial pieces from two coffins. They were starting on a third when the soldiers tiptoed up behind them.

"So this fellow lifts the lid and freezes solid like a chunk of ice, and these god-awful *claws* come crawling out around the edge, and this horrible *thing* sits up in the coffin and lets out a roar of rage—"

The sergeant told a vivid tale. The grave robbers had taken to their heels with the ch'ih-mei behind them, and the sergeant had rallied his men and given chase. The monster had hurled something at the robbers, but it had bounced harmlessly off the back of one of them, and then it had been a footrace which the vampire ghoul would easily have won at nighttime, but the searing sunlight had done its work and allowed the robbers to escape.

"And a smart piece of work, Sergeant!" Master Li said admiringly. "There aren't many men who would give chase to a ch'ih-mei, and if a promotion isn't forthcoming I'll be the most surprised man in Peking."

I could see that the sage was wrestling with temptation, and for once temptation lost.

"Actually, Coal Hill isn't my district," he said regretfully. "That's the responsibility of Magistrate Han-shan—you'll never find a better audience for your tale than Han-shan, whose grandmother was eaten by a weretiger—and a shortcut to his yamen would be to retrace your path through the Lin family cemetery."

He had something in mind, of course. The soldiers made a litter for the dead monster from pieces of venders' stalls while Master Li confronted an unfortunate fact concerning a fortunate gentleman. Sixth Degree Hosteler Tu could not now be executed.

Devil's Hand had swung his sword and missed, which meant that official soothsayers would have to ascertain that the phenomenon had not been caused by the will of Heaven, and the emperor would have to sign a new death warrant, but the emperor was off on another bandit-hunting expedition in Korea. So Devil's Hand and the bailiffs dragged the horrible hosteler back into the dungeon at Executioner's Tower, and then Master Li and I accompanied the soldiers and the dead monster back to Coal Hill.

We climbed the long path all the way to the top where the Lin family estate was. The grave the monster had occupied yielded a great number of gnawed bones, and some fresh bloodstains which seemed to interest Master Li.

"You say the creature hurled something that struck one of the robbers in the back?" he asked.

"It looked like it," Sergeant Hsienpo replied. "Right over here."

They searched through the tall grass until one of the soldiers let out a high sharp yell, and Master Li leaned over and took out his large green handkerchief, and when he straightened up he was carrying a man's half-eaten head.

"No wonder the monster was annoyed. Grave robbers interrupted his dinner," the sage said mildly.

The head had been ripped right from somebody's body, and a nasty tangle of tendons and part of the vertebrae dangled down, making it look like some kind of obscene sea creature. Nobody was going to identify the poor fellow. The vampire ghoul had devoured the face, and I have seldom seen a nastier mess. Master Li had the soldiers look around on the odd chance that the body might be nearby, and then he added the head to the litter and sent the soldiers on toward the yamen, with a note to the magistrate praising the sergeant's work.

Coal Hill is the domain of the wealthiest families of Peking, and when Master Li walked to the edge of the cemetery he was enjoying the most expensive view available. All the city opened up below us, and almost directly down I could see the rosy walls and emerald foliage and blue and yellow and crimson roof tiles of the Forbidden City. The old man was rocking back and forth on his heels with his hands clasped behind his back, whistling tunelessly, and I realized with surprise that he was as happy as a flea surveying the imperial kennels.

"Ox," he said, "the gods have decided to reward us for our ghastly encounter with Sixth Degree Hosteler Tu."

"Sir?" I said.

"Get plenty of brushes, ink, and notebooks," he continued cheerfully. "It might be a nice gesture to send Flaccus the Fourth an account of what's about to transpire."

"Sir?" I said.

He reached inside his elegant robes and pulled out his odorous goatskin flask and removed the plug, sending an alcohol reek in my direction that caused me to choke.

"Ox, something about that half-eaten head is almost as unusual as the creature that ate it," said Master Li. "The last criticism from our barbarian friend had to do with fish stories, and unless I am greatly mistaken a great white whale of a case is headed in our direction."

"Sir?" I said.

He swilled a pint of the stuff, and I briefly wondered if a vampire ghoul could have survived it.

"A livid leviathan," he said. "My boy, the spout reaches toward the stars, and the wake rocks offshore islands as it swims toward us, circumnavigating sacred seas with the awesome inevitability of an iceberg."

"Oh," I said.

2

E arly on the following morning a palatial palanquin draped with white cloths of mourning and trailing plumes of smoke from sacrificial incense burners proceeded up the Imperial Way toward the Gate of Correct Deportment, with a bonze and a Tao-shih marching in front banging a gong and a wooden fish. I had no idea why I was riding in the thing with Master Li, both of us dressed for an aristocratic funeral. My experience with the old man has taught me to keep my mouth shut when the wrinkles around his eyes squeeze up in tight concentric circles, so I waited until his mind relaxed along with the wrinkles, and then he shook himself and turned toward me.

"Ox, have you ever visited the Forbidden City?"

Of course I hadn't. I was scarcely a mandarin or member of the imperial staff, as he knew very well.

"That's where we're headed. I have reason to believe something very peculiar is going on," said Master Li.

He reached into his robe and pulled out a Fire Pearl. (I don't know what barbarians call them. They're convex pieces of crystal or glass used to focus the sun's rays and start fires, and they can also greatly magnify or diminish the image of things. In my village they're "Big-Small Stones.") Then he reached into another pocket and extracted his handkerchief, and when he unfolded it I discovered I was staring at somebody's left ear.

Where had he picked up an ear? It was neatly severed and there was no trace of blood. Then I remembered Master Li the previous afternoon picking up a half-eaten head in the Lin family cemetery, and I remembered how he had been alone when the rest of us went searching for the body.

"Yes, I took the liberty of acquiring a piece of the ch'ih-mei's victim," he said calmly. "Take a look and tell me if you see anything unusual."

I gingerly took the handkerchief and held the Fire Pearl close to the ear.

"The skin is so smooth it shouldn't be real, except it is," I said after a pause. "There's something filling the pores. It's like butter, but not quite, and there's a strange kind of glow to it." I ventured to touch the thing. "It's soft and slick, almost like soapstone, and the stuff filling the pores is just a little bit greasy."

He reclaimed the Fire Pearl and the ear.

"Excellent," he said. "I saw traces of the substance caught in the monster's claws when we examined its body beside the chopping block, and the discovery of the victim's head confirmed my suspicion. The slick stuff is an incredibly expensive compound made principally from rendered goose fat. It's called Protocol Soap, and it has the peculiar property of causing human skin to acquire a soft glow. The stuff is used almost exclusively by eunuchs and ministers in daily attendance upon the emperor, the idea being to suggest a reflection of the radiance that emanates from the Son of Heaven."

It took a moment for that to sink in, and then my eyes widened.

"Sir, do you mean that one of the ministers of state has been killed and eaten by a vampire ghoul?" I said in a shocked voice.

"So it would appear," Master Li said mildly. "Even more extraordinary is the fact that no hint of anything amiss has escaped the pink walls. There isn't a place on earth more addicted to gossip and rumor than the Forbidden City, but I checked every source I could think of last night and all I could learn was that something is going on and it's top secret. My boy, it isn't possible that a state minister can vanish without causing an uproar, and keep in mind the fact that we found not one trace of the victim's bones or body. Do his colleagues have it? If so, what could cause mandarins to cover up the crime of the century?"

What indeed? A scandal on a scale to shake the empire seemed not impossible, and as we passed into the Imperial City and started up toward the Altar of Earth and Grain a line began running through my brain: ". . . monsters, mandarins, and murder . . . monsters, mandarins, and murder . . ." The priests at the altar bowed in reverence to the dead as our palanquin passed, as did their counterparts at the Supreme Temple of Ancestors (". . . monsters, mandarins, and murder . . . monsters, mandarins, and murder . . ."), and dignified Confucian clerks touched their caps respectfully. The Imperial City is the walled enclave of bureaucratic basilicas and aristocratic residences surrounding the Forbidden City of the emperor, but those who assume our funerary progress through such rarefied surroundings was solemn and sedate have never rented palanquins in Peking. I think I may have given a misleading impression, so I will correct it.

"Sheee-ut!" screamed Rat-Scurry-down-the-Street from his front left bearer's pole. *"Why don't the big heavy kid sit in the middle with the scrawny old bird on his lap? This thing's as unbalanced as a raft rowed by a rat and a rhinoceros!"*

Viper-in-the-Grass had the matching position on the right bearer's pole.

"Stop squawking, gong-head! You ain't got the brains to talk and carry at the same time, and when you open your goddamn mouth your shoulders start shaking like tits at a wet nurse convention!"

Chamber Pot Chong and the Worm, at the rear bearer poles, did not approve.

"Eat vinegar, you turds! You think we like having our faces sprayed with spit from a pair of polecats with hoof-and-mouth disease!"

"Ox, from here on we should travel with decorum," Master Li said.

I stopped the palanquin and jumped out and picked up the front bearers' pole along with the bearers still attached to it, and slammed them back to earth in a manner designed to loosen teeth.

"Listen to me, *ming t'e mao tsei!"* (A very useful phrase for visitors to Peking. It means: "You mulberry caterpillar grain-eating grub thieves!") "One more squawk and I'll feed your combined remains to a gnat."

I climbed back into the palanquin and we proceeded in seemly silence between the Phoenix Towers and across the moat. Master Li has been out of official favor for years, but he still has the rank and proper credentials and the guards had no orders to stop him, and we passed without difficulty through the Meridian Gate and the Forbidden City opened in front of us.

"Now I need your sharp young eyes," Master Li said. "If I'm right, one of the senior mandarins made a meal for a vampire ghoul, and for whatever reason his colleagues are doing everything in their power to hush it up. They have to give the fellow a funeral, however, and under the circumstances they can't possibly deny him a pole."

I saw what he meant, but I'm not sure it will be clear to uncivilized readers, so I will briefly explain.

All people have two souls. The higher *hun* soul resides in the liver, and when a person dies a hole is bored in the coffin just above the liver to allow the higher soul to fly in and out when it wishes. The lower *po* soul resides in the lungs, and under no circumstances must it be allowed out. It is the seat of man's animal instincts and behavior, and it can easily go bad and wander the earth as an evil spirit. The *hun* soul must journey back and forth between the liver and the law court of the God of Walls and Ditches in Hell during the forty-nine days in which it is being judged, but when it is away from its familar body it can easily become disoriented, and it is a great tragedy for a higher soul to get lost. It can panic and settle into a totally inappropriate body and become perverted, and when a higher soul goes bad it *really* goes bad. That is how creatures like vampire ghouls are formed, and that is why a beacon is erected to help traveling souls find their way home. It's a tall pole with a bright red flag at the top, placed outside a house where a death has occurred: left of the door for a man, right for a woman. Master Li's point was that the mandarins couldn't possibly take the chance that their colleague's hun soul might get lost and turn into the very kind of monster that had slain him, so they had no choice but to erect a beacon pole.

I kept a lookout for a red pole, and in a way it was a pity. This was my first trip to the Forbidden City and I would have liked to look around and ask Master Li about it, but all I learned that day was that it might better be called the Forbidden Garden. Once we left the central avenue we were in mazes of trees and shrubs and flowers artistically designed to open to delightful or surprising vistas, such as great dragons and phoenixes in ivory bas-relief upon coral walls or exotic birds that appeared to be posing for artists as they settled upon quaint rocks beside tur- quoise pools. It was one of those bright birds that drew my eyes away from pole searching, and it took a moment to realize that not all the brightness came from feathers.

"There!" I exclaimed.

A tall slim line lifted behind a row of pomegranates, and at the top was a crimson flag. Master Li had the bearers turn at the Golden River and pass through the Gate of United Harmony toward the complex where he had spent twenty wasted years— at least he called them wasted—and we passed the Hall of Liter- ary Glory, the Hall of Proclaimed Intellect, the Hall of Reverence for the Master (which is the second-greatest library in the world, the first being in Ch'ang-an), and there in the great courtyard of the Hall of Literary Profundity stood the soul pole, left of the entrance, and beneath the red banner flew the flag of a senior scholar who was entitled to display all fourteen symbols of academic distinction: wishing pearls, musical stone, good-luck clouds, rhombus, rhinoceros-horn cup, books, pictures, maple, yarrow, banana leaf, tripod, herb of immortality, money, and the silver shoe.

"That flag narrows the list of possible victims considerably," Master Li said happily. "Has there been any word that one of the foremost scholars in the empire has breathed his last? No, there has not, and now I'm beginning to think that my suspicion of conspiracy and cover-up is a certainty."

When we turned through the outer gates we saw a courtyard crammed with palanquins and carriages and sedan chairs like ours, swathed in mourning cloths. A mob of junior mandarins bowed deeply to Master Li's cap and badges, for he was wearing the whole works, including symbols of imperial office he hadn't held in sixty years, and the effect was very impressive. He marched up the steps as though he owned the place, and we entered a reception hall that was huge to the point of being grotesque. Several forests had been depopulated of wild animals to provide furs to cover the walls, along with immense tapestries and various hangings. A carpet that seemed to be made of white ermine stretched across an acre of floor to a marble dais, and upon the dais rested a huge coffin.

Senior mandarins were making their way with stately dignity up the carpet to pay their last respects to their colleague. Then somebody noticed Master Li. A sharp intake of breath caused heads to turn, and it was fascinating to see eyes widen in sequence and one elegant robe after another twitch backward as though avoiding contact with leprosy—almost a dance, and Master Li did his part by greeting each flinching fellow with a toothy smile: "Wang Chien, dear friend! How delightful that these unworthy eyes should once more bask in your divine radiance!" And so on. At first nobody else said a word, but then the silence was broken.

"Kao! By all the gods it's Li Kao! Now why didn't I think of calling you in on this mess?"

The man who was painfully working his way toward Master Li with the aid of two canes was dried and shriveled and hunched with arthritis, and older than I could have believed possible. I thought Master Li had reached the limit of a human life span, but this gentleman added a good thirty years to the limit. I noticed that his progress was followed by deep bows, and greeted by Master Li with real pleasure.

"Hello, Chang! How are you these days?" he said warmly.

"How am I? Senile of course," the shriveled antique said. "A few days ago I had a long conversation with my eldest grandson, and I was wondering how he'd suddenly grown so intelligent when I realized he's been dead for twenty years and I was talking to the parrot. Who's the big kid with the muscles and the squashed nose?"

Master Li motioned for me to step forward and bow.

"Allow me to present my former client and current assistant, Number Ten Ox," he said. "Ox, this is the Resplendent Thearch, Supreme Lord of the Eastern Aurora and Grand Subtlety, Bearer of the Cinnabar Scepter of the Highest Mystery of the Great Mystery—or, if you prefer, the Celestial Master."

I honestly think the only thing that prevented me from bouncing up and down upon the floor was the fact that my body couldn't decide whether to topple forward or backward. This was none other than Chang Tao-ling, the highest high priest of Taoism, and the only man in the empire universally acknowledged to be a living saint. In my village he was worshipped both by the abbot of our monastery and by my atheistic Uncle Nung, and it was commonly said that a list of his good deeds would cover four of the five sacred mountains, and here I was standing right in front of him. Somehow I managed a jerky bow without falling on my face.

"Kao, you're just the man we need, and I'm glad somebody had the brains to think of it," the Celestial Master said. "It was one of the weirdest things I've seen in my life, which means it might have been designed for you."

The Celestial Master was partially deaf and didn't realize his voice level was just below a shout. Master Li had to speak loudly to make his words clear, and the effect was quite strange: hundreds of people standing stone-faced and silent in a huge vaulted chamber, listening to two voices bounce between walls until their echoes began playing tag above a coffin.

"You say you saw it?" Master Li asked.

"It happened right before my eyes, and if something that horrible has to happen it's just as well the victim was somebody like Ma Tuan Lin. Awful ass, you know, and a disgrace to scholarship," the Celestial Master shouted.

From the sudden gleam in Master Li's eyes I assumed he shared the Celestial Master's opinion of the late Ma Tuan Lin, but he tried to be diplomatic.

"Oh, I don't know. Ma had some good qualities when it came to research. It was only his conclusions that were idiotic."

"Kao, you're too damn generous!" the Celestial Master shouted. "He was a donkey from the top of his head to the tips of his toes, and his self-esteem was as bloated as was his body. You should have seen them try to squeeze that hunk of lard into the coffin."

The saint swiveled painfully on his canes and glared at the rows of tight-lipped mandarins.

"Damn fools!" he yelled. "If you'd given Ma's corpse an enema you could have buried what remained in a walnut shell!"

He turned back to Master Li.

"All right, this is your kind of thing, not mine. You're in charge, so tell me what you want and I'll try to help," he said simply.

"We'll start with what you saw, but let's get out of this mausoleum," Master Li said happily.

I felt a warm glow as the Celestial Master hobbled toward a side door. What a marvelous stroke of luck! Master Li would have been deader than Ma Tuan Lin if eyes could kill, but all the mandarins could do was glare. We took a corridor to a small office at the end, looking out over a small simple garden. It was a worn and battered sort of room, crowded but comfortable, with mementos from the time of my great-great-great-grandfather, and the Celestial Master gave a groan of relief as he let himself down on a cushioned bench and relaxed his grip on the canes. He went straight to the point.

"It was the night before last, Kao—morning, actually, around the double hour of the sheep. I couldn't sleep, as usual, and the moon was bright and you know how warm it's been. I got up and into a robe and grabbed my canes and made it to the dock and my boat. Rowing's the only exercise I can handle now. I get practice with the canes," he said, making cane-shuffling gestures that really were like rowing. "I rowed to Hortensia Island, where I have a special dock and path I can manage. I was taking a walk through the woods, admiring the moon and wishing my mind could still create poetry, when I heard the damnedest scream. Then I saw Ma Tuan Lin running toward me."

The saint tilted his head so he was looking down the sides of his nose at Master Li, and a faint smile tugged at his lips.

"Here comes the senile part, perhaps. I'm not sure, Kao, I'm just not sure. I can only tell you what I saw or thought I saw. To begin with, Ma was being chased by a little wrinkled man older than you, maybe even older than me, but who was running as lightly as a child, making sharp sounds that sounded like *'Pi-fang! Pi-fang!'* "

"What?" Master Li asked.

The Celestial Master shrugged. "No meaning, just sound. *'Pi-fang!'* Ma was holding something in his hands that looked like a birdcage, an empty one, and he let loose another scream of terror that made a pair of nesting grouse come shooting up through the darkness with their wings going pop-pop-pop! and they flapped right across my face and made me fall backward into some tall weeds, and that's probably what saved my life. The little old man didn't see me as he ran past. He waved his right hand and something started to glow in it, bright red, and then he hurled a ball of fire that struck Ma Tuan Lin square in the back."

Master Li choked and pounded himself on the chest. "A ball of fire?" he asked when he'd recovered.

"I know, I know. The old boy's finally had the last bit of his brains turn to butter," the Celestial Master said wryly. "I'm telling you what I thought I saw. Ma was dead before he hit the ground—I didn't need an autopsy to tell me that—and the little old man ran past him, leaping lightly as a leaf in a wind, and then there was a bright flash that blinded me. When my eyes cleared there wasn't any little old man. Ma was lying there with that cage thing sticking up through tall grass beside him, and his back was smoking, and I looked every which way. No little old man. Then I heard a high distant 'Pi-fang!' and I looked up and saw a great white crane flying away across the face of the moon."

The saint drew a deep breath and spread his hands wide apart. "Think that was crazy? I haven't even started."

"I can hardly wait," said Master Li.

"Kao, beside the pavilion Ma uses on Hortensia Island there's a big pile of earth from some kind of construction project that was canceled, and it wasn't until I saw the pile that I realized I was at the pavilion," the Celestial Master said. "What made me look toward the pile was a small sound coming from it, and I knew I'd lost my mind for certain when a terrible claw came crawling out into the moonlight. Then another claw followed it, and earth fell away and something big heaved up into the moonlight, and when the dirt dropped off it I was looking at the prettiest ch'ih-mei to appear in China in a century or more. A classic vampire ghoul, Kao, and it was looking up at that crane in the sky. Then the crane dwindled to a speck and disappeared, and the ch'ih-mei looked down and saw Ma Tuan Lin. In two strides it had reached him, and I swear it ripped the head right off the body! It lifted the gory trophy and took a big bite, but I didn't see any more. I was crawling backward, sort of pushing with my canes, hoping the creature's chewing noises would drown out any sound I made, and I made it safely back into the trees. Then I got to my boat and rowed back and gave the alarm, and that's all I can tell you."

Master Li nodded appreciatively.

"To whom did you give the alarm?" he asked.

"The emperor has an officer attached to my household staff. A nursemaid, I suppose, but useful at times."

"And you told him what had happened?"

"I had to," the Celestial Master said. "He didn't believe a word of it, of course."

"Well, I do." Master Li grinned and winked. "I didn't say I believe *all* of it, but I'll keep an open mind and who knows? I've come to accept some incredible things in my time."

The Celestial Master grinned back, and then winced and tapped his head.

"Tired, Kao, tired. The time I have left is about as limited as my remaining brains, and if you want anything more from me today you'd better get it now," he said wearily.

Master Li leaned forward.

"What I want," he said, speaking slowly and clearly, "is a written commission to investigate this matter and anything that may be connected with it, with the full authority of, and signed by, the Celestial Master."

Not long afterward Master Li led the way out through a series of side doors, and then around through the gardens to the court-yard and our palanquin. He was clearly depressed when he should have been exhilarated, and I looked at him question-ingly.

"Well, Ox, we can forget about getting a case like a great white whale," he said.

"Sir?"

"I owe the mandarins an apology. They were hushing up the matter and hoping to cram the corpse into a tomb before busybodies like me came along, for the very sound reason that China's greatest living saint has confessed to the murder of Ma Tuan Lin," Master Li said sadly.

3

Master Li was getting weary, and once I had rowed over to Hortensia Island and tied the boat at a dock he had me bend over so he could climb up on my back. He weighs no more than a schoolboy, and his small feet fit easily into my tunic pockets, and I'm so accustomed to carrying the old man around that without him I feel undressed. I took the paths he indicated toward the pavilion where Ma Tuan Lin, according to the Celestial Master, had met his death.

The island has changed beyond belief in the short time since that day. New construction is everywhere, and scarcely an acre of wooded land remains. Then it was almost totally given over to trees and shrubs and grass, and outside of the Yu (much more about which later) there was only the collection of astronomical instruments first established by the great Chang Heng and fewer than twenty secluded pavilions used as retreats by eminent mandarins. It was peaceful and beautiful, and we saw and heard nobody at all as I followed the paths through the trees. Ahead was a grassy clearing and Master Li had me stop and set him down. He reached inside his robe and pulled out his wine flask and swilled moodily, spitting the pulpy residue at flowers. I expected them to shrivel and die beneath the bath of pure alcohol, but for some reason they didn't.

"Ox, I must congratulate you on your self-control. Not one single question," he said with a wink. He knows he's trained me well. "Let's look around. I'm betting the Celestial Master actually did see our vampire ghoul remove Ma Tuan Lin's head, thus greatly improving Ma's appearance, and I'll be disappointed if proved wrong."

We'd already learned that the body had indeed been found and removed from here, and as we walked forward I saw the outline of the pavilion and then I saw a huge pile of fresh earth beside it, and finally I saw something black and moving, sharply outlined against a green background. It was a cloud of flies buzzing around sticky black streaks that had recently been red, matting the grass. We walked to the pile of earth and found signs of a very recent disturbance that might have been caused by a creature crawling out, and I found sandal prints in a soft spot in the path close to the pile. The toes had dug in and sprayed dirt backward, which would be consistent with somebody running for his life, and I soon found another soft spot with a huge print on it that might have been made by a creature like a vampire ghoul.

"The Celestial Master would have no reason to invent an item like a birdcage. Let's find it," Master Li muttered.

We found the cage in tall grass close to the bloodstains. The sage picked it up and whistled appreciatively as he looked at it, and even I could see the workmanship was superb, and very old. It couldn't have held a bird, however. The bars were oddly spaced with at least one gap through which a small bird would have escaped, and a peculiar maze of wires ran across them. A single bead was strung on the wires and with a little dexterity it could be made to slide this way and that, but Master Li said one bead couldn't possibly fulfill enough functions to serve as a primitive abacus. The bars were decorated with a jumble of symbols of every description, from animals to utensils to astronomy, and Master Li shook his head and shrugged.

"I have no idea what it was used for but it's almost unbelievably ancient," he said. "Say what one will about Ma Tuan Lin, he had a gift for discovering valuable artifacts. He was a considerable collector and claimed to be an authority, and maybe we'll find something about this in his papers."

He tied the cage to his waist with his long yellow sash and stood looking around for a moment with his hands on his hips.

"My dear old friend and teacher rowed over here and took a walk in the moonlight," he said in a slow melancholy voice. "As fate would have it, he arrived at this spot just in time to see a monster chasing its dinner, meaning Ma Tuan Lin, and he did indeed see the creature rip Ma's head off. Ox, you've heard the Celestial Master. You know he couldn't stand Ma Tuan Lin. Deep inside he felt guilty for not grieving at a terrible murder, and the guilt worked through a weary mind and projected images, and the result was that he really does believe his story about—pay attention—'a little wrinkled man older than you, maybe even older than me, but he was running as lightly as a child.' All right, what kind of hat does the Celestial Master wear?"

I thought about it. "It's a white hat, tall and conical, tapering to a point," I said.

"It's called Hat of Nine Yang Thunder," Master Li said dryly. "It's meant to resemble the beak of a crane. Did you notice his robe?"

"It was a Taoist robe, except for the First Rank emblem," I said.

"Which is?"

"A crane."

"Yes indeed, and did you notice his ring of office?" Master Li asked.

"Some kind of large red stone," I said.

"It's a garnet called Ball of Retributive Lightning," said Master Li.

"Oh-oh," I said.

"Oh-oh indeed," said Master Li. "Ox, the Celestial Master pro-

912082

jected himself as a tiny wrinkled old man who could throw away his canes and run lightly as a child as he massacred bastards like Ma Tuan Lin, blasting them with his ring of office and then transforming himself into the crane he carried on his robe and hat, flying safely away across the moon, like in dreams. The mandarins feared that the wrong people might take that tale and cause a terrible scandal, but you and I are not going to be the wrong people."

"No, sir," I said.

"We'll go through the motions of an investigation," the old man said. "If nothing else I have the Celestial Master's authentic signed commission to show for it, which is scarcely to be sneered at."

"Yes, sir," I said, and then made something of a point of shutting my mouth. ("That," I added silently, "is the understatement of the decade. After he finishes doctoring a document like that he can present a pass allowing him to wander in and out of the imperial treasury with forty mule carts, eighty peasants with shovels, and a derrick.")

There was nothing more to be found at the scene of the murder, so Master Li led the way into Ma Tuan Lin's pavilion. I was rather surprised to find it was a simple austere place: one large room and a bathing chamber, opening to a small enclosed garden and a vista overlooking the lake. Master Li explained that mandarins like Ma were not allowed to build palatial establishments on the island. All the pavilions were identical, designed for peaceful contemplation, and were the property of the emperor. We looked through the mandarin's papers and collection of books and scrolls, and all we found were notes in scholarly shorthand I couldn't read and Master Li said were pure Ma Tuan Lin: idiotic garbage. The only point to the search was to see if there was any information about a peculiar old cage, so Master Li made it quick. Just as we were about to leave he stopped in the doorway.

"I almost forgot," he said. "Fifty or sixty years ago I took one of these pavilions for a week or two, and since they're all the same . . ."

He let the sentence hang in the air as he turned and walked back to the small wooden altar against the east wall.

"They showed me where to stick jewelry or whatever if I didn't trust the gardeners," he said, and he reached out and pushed a wooden panel and then slid it aside and stuck his hand into a tiny hole. "I'll be damned," he said, because when his hand came out he was holding a small thick notebook.

We sat at the table while he went through it. Not even Master Li could make sense of the entries because they were simply series of numbers and marks indicating percentages, and there was no indication what the numbers represented.

"The total goes up and up, dramatically, and all of a sudden the percentage doubles, and all I can say is if it's Ma's money he was getting rich enough to buy an estate on Coal Hill," Master Li said. Then he turned the last page and pulled something from the notebook. "Ox, look at this!" he exclaimed happily.

There was the cage we had found, in the form of a small ink rubbing apparently taken from an old stone surface. I say stone as opposed to metal because blurred and blotched places indicated a worn chipped surface, but it was clear enough to unquestionably represent the cage. Master Li hoped for some explanatory text when he turned the rubbing over, but instead he found Flying White shorthand, which he translated for me.

" 'Eight! I've found all eight! Now they cannot deny me the principal share, and my bones shall lie on White Dragon Peak!' "

"Sir, do you know what that means?" I asked.

"Not really, but the last part is interesting," he said. "White Dragon Peak is the principal landmark rising above a large and rich valley near Shensi which Ma Tuan Lin—falsely, I always assumed—claimed was once his family's ancestral estate. This sounds as though he hoped to buy it back, and that would take an incredible amount of money."

We soon left and I rowed without incident back to the city. We stopped at Master Li's shack long enough to hide the old cage beneath the platform that keeps our pallets dry when storms send water washing across the floor, and then he had me carry him to the Wineshop of One-Eyed Wong. (I've described Wong's in previous memoirs and it doesn't play a significant role here, so I'll simply say it's a place in the criminal area of Heaven's Bridge where Master Li can find useful people, and he found some now.) He had a couple of forgers make fast copies of Ma Tuan Lin's rubbing of the cage, and then he got a pack of street boys to take the copies to every first-rate burglar he could think of.

"You see," he said when we were eating dinner at his private table, "there's a chance that Ma was referring to cages rather than a hundred other things when he wrote on the back of the rubbing. If so, he had found eight of them. Where are the other seven?"

I shrugged. "His office, his house."

"Keep in mind, Ox, that the cage we have is very ancient and superbly made. It's a remarkable artifact, and if Ma Tuan Lin was holding eight of them he would certainly have made his extraordinary collection the excuse for banquet after banquet, at which he could boast of the infallible instinct and keen trained intellect that enabled him to find treasures where lesser men failed. So far as I know he did no such thing, and let's remember the wording. 'Eight! I've found all eight! Now they cannot deny me the principal share, and my bones shall lie on White Dragon Peak!' "

"Sounds like he had partners in a business enterprise," I said hesitantly. "Sounds like the cages would be valuable to them, so much so he'd get the principal share in whatever the venture was."

"That's exactly what it sounds like, and thus he would give cages to partners in exchange for percentages of the business.

Perhaps the very existence of the cages would be kept secret, perhaps not, and if not, we will consider an interesting possibility," the sage said. "Ma Tuan Lin would never dream of going into partnership with lesser mortals. His partners would have to be mandarins of his own rank or higher, and such men tend to collect rare items and display them in their homes to envious visitors."

From his silence I judged he wanted me to see how far my sieve-like brains could carry the thought, so I said, "If Ma Tuan Lin gave cages to his partners and his partners put them on display, the burglars of Peking can tell you exactly where the cages are."

"Good boy," said Master Li. "Every mansion in town has been scouted again and again by burglars using inside help. It would be asking too much to find all seven, but if we can find even one I'll satisfy a bit of curiosity by questioning the owner. If not, I think we'll just forget about cages and worry about what sort of a report we can give to the Celestial Master."

Within an hour we had a visit from a gentleman with shifty eyes and an interesting pattern of knife scars where his nose used to be, and an hour after that we were back inside a palatial palanquin, being carried up Coal Hill.

It was night, with a huge round moon that had orange circles around it, and Coal Hill was just starting to come to life. I never cease to be fascinated by the spectacle of the wealthy arranging to be seen seeing people who have been seen seeing people worthy of being seen seeing, if that's the proper way to phrase it. First it's a glow of light approaching, and then a rhythmic *"Hut-chu, hut-chu, hut-chu!"* and the foreman appears leading an army of jogging grooms carrying torches. Another glow follows, and another chant—*"Mi-chi, mi-chi, mi-chi!"*—comes from trotting servants dressed like royalty who surround aristocratic palanquins and carriages, carrying brilliantly colored lanterns. *"Yi-cha, yi-*

cha, yi-cha!" chant yellow-gowned eunuchs who mince beside the principal palanquin swinging censers of smoking incense, and one may be lucky enough to see a flash of emerald and turquoise, glittering gems and glowing jade, gold-stitched silk and embroidered satins, a crimson gleam from a long lacquered fingernail, a liquid glance from a languid eye, and then trumpets blast *"Ta-ta-taaaaa! Ta-ta-taaaaa!"* and heralds puffed like peacocks in their pride prance forward and turn down the awaiting lane where other trumpets answer *"Tum-teeeee! Tum-teeeee!"* and lights appear as if by magic, a thousand paper lanterns illuminating trees that in winter have artificial leaves sewn to them, and an orchestra in a clearing plays a hymn of welcome, and dancers leap and vault ahead of the heralds, and a flock of pink geese hiss and squawk and cackle, and those gorgeous butlers in the courtyard are not spreading yellow sand to receive the illustrious footprint of the eminent guest—oh no, that's real gold dust forming a path to the door.

I have a cousin who works on Coal Hill. He's a professional and proud of his mastery of the craft. What he does is dress in black clothes and blacken his face and hands with soot so he won't be seen at night. Then he takes a long sharp pin—much longer than a knitting needle—and crawls into the pen where the geese are kept, and just at the right moment when guests arrive he jabs the geese in the ass. The hissing and honking of geese is considered a lucky omen, you see, and the trick is to get a chorus of squawks just as wealthy people descend to the lowly cringing earth, and he's very good at it. I once asked him if he considered expanding his trade to include dyeing the geese pink (also a lucky omen) and he was furious. He's a master *bird-butt jabber*, and lowly *pinion painters* are scarcely in his social class! Besides, they have a closed guild and the only way to qualify is through heredity.

The lane our palanquin turned into wasn't lit up for guests but our informant had been certain the owner was home. Master Li put on his grandest air of Neo-Confucian superiority and sneered lesser servants out of the way until he got the major-domo, and a flash of the commission from the Celestial Master was sufficient to send the fellow bowing and cringing upstairs to seek the master of the house. We waited in a very elegant room where ancient artifacts were displayed, but Master Li was not impressed.

"Nine tenths," he stated flatly, "are palpable fakes, and the tenth that isn't is of little value. The one exception is this toad dropper, which is done in the earliest example of the glaze called Pretty Girl Sky-Clearing I've ever seen."

Toad droppers are little ceramic toads with a chamber to hold water and a built-in dropper. You use them to moisten an ink-stone with just the right amount of ink for a perfect stroke, and Master Li has a very nice collection of them. When he bent over and slipped aside the false heel of his left sandal I turned pale.

"Sir . . . ah . . . Venerable Sir, don't you think it would be unwise to . . . ah . . ."

He came up with his lock picks, and a moment later the case held one less toad dropper. I mention this to explain why I was already unnerved when we heard the screams. They were high strangled screams, clearly from somewhere in the house, and I automatically bent over for the old man to leap upon my back.

"Quick! We'll make a run for it!" I cried.

As soon as I felt his weight I galloped to the hall and out the door, and I was halfway across the outer courtyard before I realized that Master Li was pounding my head and shoulders and yelling, "Stop, you idiot!" I skidded to a halt and he twisted on my back, and then a gnarled finger shot past the side of my head and pointed. "There!"

It finally dawned on me that I was supposed to run toward the screams, not away from them, and in a way it was fortunate that I'd panicked and run outside. Master Li was pointing to an upper story where the silhouette of somebody who seemed to be fighting could be seen behind a gauzy curtain, and I made a mental note of the location and charged back inside and started up the stairs.

The screams were coming from the majordomo, but I doubt he was aware of the noise he was making. His eyes were wide and glazed with shock and his mouth opened and closed automatically as he stood petrified at an open doorway on the second story. I shoved him out of the way. Master Li slipped down off my back and I heard the sharp click as the rattan coil inside his right sleeve shot the throwing knife from the sheath strapped to his forearm up into his hand. I dove through the door low and fast, hitting the floor and rolling left and jumping up braced for an attack, but there was no attack. I stood there rather like the majordomo had, frozen in place with my mouth gaping foolishly, and from the lack of motion behind me I assumed Master Li was also standing and staring. The scene was complicated, and took a bit of sorting out.

In the foreground, meaning the center of the elegant room, stood a man whose face was covered by the hood of a big old-fashioned cloak. He was methodically using a stone striker to bang the most ancient of all instruments, a set of stone chimes. He was standing on one leg because that's all he had: one single leg, growing squarely from the center of his body. In front of him a man in elegant mandarin dress was dancing to the chime music, but it was a dance of death.

His robes whipped wildly through the air as he leaped and capered across the floor, twisting and jumping with manic energy, kicking his legs high above his head, whipping his feet down to pound the floor as though attempting to drive holes through it. His eyes were quite insane, driven mad by pain, and he would have been howling if he had the breath. I gasped and jumped back instinctively when I saw white splinters of bone thrusting from his silk-covered thighs, and blood dripped down his knees. This mandarin had danced until both thighs shattered, and he was dancing still, and now blood was bubbling from his mouth and nose and I realized his insides had been pounded to jelly. He leaped even higher. His feet struck the floor even harder as the stone chimes thudded monotonously, and the bone splinters thrust out farther and farther, and then a great gush of blood came from his mouth and the light of insane agony died in his eyes.

When the one-legged creature continued to pound on the old stone chimes he was making a corpse dance for him. That mandarin was dead. I knew it as surely as I knew I was still alive, but I also knew the body was dancing like a doll of straw around the room, head lolling and bouncing lifelessly on his shoulders, arms and hands flapping around without guidance, both broken legs bending almost double where they shouldn't bend, between knee and hip, blood from the gaping mouth spraying around the room in a fine pink mist.

That, mind you, was only the scene in the foreground. Simultaneously my brain was trying to accommodate the background as well, but it was difficult because with an overdose of grotesque images they tend to cancel one another out. Everything was getting blurred, and I shook my head vigorously—the first motion I'd been capable of—and decided I really was looking at another weird creature. It was a man, yet the face was that of a hideous ape with a silver-gray forehead, a scarlet nose, bright blue cheeks, and a yellow chin. I can't explain why, but I knew in my bones this wasn't actor's makeup. This was real, and the man-ape bared strong white teeth in an expression between a grimace and a smile as it looked at Master Li and me, and then in one powerful bound it was at the wall, and with another effortless leap it was out the window and down into the garden and gone, vanished into the night, but not before I'd seen that it was carrying something.

The weird creature had been carrying a cage precisely like the one Master Li had.

Master Li had stepped up beside me, and now he whirled back toward the center of the room just as the stone chimes stopped playing and the dancing corpse collapsed limply to the floor, as though someone had cut the strings operating a puppet. The one-legged hooded figure stood motionless.

"Careful, Ox."

As if I needed the warning. I moved forward cautiously, scooping up a heavy bronze figurine as a weapon, and Master Li made a flanking movement with his knife cocked beside his right ear. The chimes player still made no motion. I was at an angle where I could look straight him—or it—and in the dark shadows behind the opening of the hood I thought I saw the gleam of a single eye in the center of a forehead.

Suddenly there was a bright flash that blinded me. I gasped and stepped back, covering my eyes, and gradually the orange haze and black spots cleared, and I stared at the room. So did Master Li, blinking and rubbing his eyes, and there wasn't any one-legged chimes player. He wasn't in the room, and he wasn't in the hall outside, and the wind whipped the curtains away from the window and we gazed out and up at the night sky, where a great white crane was slowly flying away across the face of the moon.

4

"Well, Kao, have you found anything interesting?" the Celestial Master asked.

"Mildly so," Master Li replied. "To begin with, another mandarin—I assume you know, or knew, Mao Ou-Hsi?"

"Revolting fellow. Third-greediest man in the empire, the Celestial Master said disgustedly.

"The fourth-greediest will be interested, because he's just been promoted," Master Li said. "Mao bade farewell to the red dust of earth last night in a rather spectacular manner. Ox and I happened to be there at the moment, and the creature who killed Mao then disappeared in a bright blinding flash, and the next thing we saw was a white crane flying away across the moon."

The Celestial Master paused with a teacup halfway to his lips. Briefly, in an instant in which his eyes sharpened and hardened, I glimpsed the brilliance and sureness of long ago, when he had been considered to be the finest mind in the empire.

"How convenient," he said dryly. "Did it carry a sign in its beak saying 'Save the Celestial Master from Mother Meng's Madhouse?' "

Master Li tossed his head back and laughed. "Believe it or

not, this actually happened," he said. "As soon as we'd looked around and found nothing we summoned the magistrate to take over, and at the moment the gates opened at dawn we entered the Forbidden City and chased the honor guard away from the remains of the late Ma Tuan Lin, and I had Ox open the coffin. You tell it, Ox."

I gulped nervously as the bright eyes of the saint flicked toward me.

"Most Reverend Sir, the corpse was lying on its back, of course, but I managed to lift it upright—"

"That must have been a hell of a job," the Celestial Master said, with real concern in his voice.

"Yes, sir," I said. "The body was covered with Dragon's Brains (Borneo camphor), which made me choke, and after I scooped it away I started to choke from the smell of the corpse, and there wasn't any head and it looked horrible." I started choking again, just at the memory. "The body was stiff as a tree trunk and I almost got a hernia trying to lift it."

"Ghastly tub of lard, wasn't he?" the Celestial Master said sympathetically.

"He hadn't missed much rice," I said diplomatically. "Master Li had me prop him up so we could examine the back."

"And?"

"Reverend Sir, it was just as you told us!" I said excitedly. "The entrance mark of the fireball was very small and the folds of robes covered it up, but Master Li cut through the clothes and skin, and just beneath the outer flesh there was a great big hole! Everything inside had been burned to a crisp."

The saint sipped his tea and put the cup down, and then he leaned back and rubbed his eyes.

"How odd," he said. "Kao, I'd just discovered what caused me to hallucinate about that old man and his ball of fire, and now you tell me I wasn't hallucinating."

He leaned forward, and his eyes were clear and keen. "I'm going to show you what might have stimulated a senile imagination, but first I'm interested in a matter of symmetry. You say Mao Ou-Hsi died spectacularly. Was a monster involved?"

"Yes."

"Tell me about it."

Master Li told what we had seen, simply and clearly, and as he talked I saw wonder and speculation form in the saint's eyes.

"Well, Kao, I said at the beginning this was your sort of case, but I didn't know how right I was," the Celestial Master said. "Before I tell what I know, is there anything else you want to add?"

"Indeed yes. Beginning with this," said Master Li, and he pulled the cage we'd found from beneath his robes and placed it on the table.

"Pretty, and it looks like the thing Ma was carrying, but what is it?" the Celestial Master asked.

"Damn. I was hoping you could tell me once you got a close look at it," Master Li said. "It is indeed the cage you saw and we found it where you said it was. The interesting thing is that Ma Tuan Lin had made a rubbing of an old stone carving depicting a cage like this. On the back he indicated he might have found as many as eight of them. A plausible inference is that he gave cages to partners in some sort of enterprise, and I had traced one to Mao Ou-Hsi, which is why we were there. Simultaneous with the murder the cage was being stolen, and the burglar was another monster. It was a man resembling an ape like the one the emperor takes such pride in at the imperial bestiary: silver-gray fur or skin on the forehead, bright blue cheeks, a crimson nose, and a yellow chin. The eyes are deep and shadowed, and the gaze is highly intelligent."

The Celestial Master nodded. "A mandrill, if one excepts the intelligence. Why do you say 'man-ape'?"

Master Li shrugged. "So far as I could tell, the body was that of a medium-size but very powerful and acrobatic man, and both the body motion and eye contact were human."

The saint nodded and said, "The creature means nothing to me. He got away with Mao's cage, you say? Another crane?"

"No, he simply leaped out the window to the garden before either of us could move. Speaking of monsters, the vampire ghoul who decapitated Ma Tuan Lin is dead, in case you haven't heard, and I haven't the slightest idea what its connection to the rest of it is. I'm trying to track down the owners of the other cages, and until I can find out why monsters would want them I'm at the end of a blank alley."

Master Li leaned back and the Celestial Master leaned forward, taking a sheaf of papers from a lacquered box lying on the table.

"I can't tell you why the cages are valuable, but I can give you something to think about concerning monsters," he said. "When I was a young student—long before you were born, believe it or not—I went through the normal period of fascination with ancient shamanism. That means shamanism of the aborigines who originally inhabited China, of course, practiced by priests of beliefs and rites that to some extent evolved into our own, and I found repeated but maddeningly unspecific references to a small group of shamans who seem to have been greatest of all: Super Shamans, if you will, aloof and mysterious, to be appealed to only as a last resort. I was never able to prove this, Kao, but I became convinced that they're the mysterious hooded figures depicted on the walls of the Yu."

"Really?" Master Li appeared to be very interested. "Any specific reason?"

"One specific, one not. The nonspecific is simply the fact that they were spoken of with awe as always being silent, always performing mysterious rituals with mysterious objects beyond the grasp of man—the general atmosphere of the Yu, if you will, and the Yu and the shamans would seem to date from the same period. The specific is that there were eight of them, like the eight Yu figures, and indeed they were known as *Pa Neng Chih Shih.*"

" 'Eight Skilled Gentlemen,' " Master Li said thoughtfully. "Sounds like they may have practiced alchemy or engineering or astronomy in addition to their priestly and magical duties." The Celestial Master shrugged. "I never found a clear reference to their exact function, and I doubt anyone did. There was, however, one extraordinarily interesting fragment concerning them that I put down at the time as primitive myth, but peculiar enough to make notes of."

The saint picked up the sheaf of papers and shook his head wonderingly as he looked at them.

"So long ago," he said softly. "It had completely fled what's left of my mind, and then suddenly, after you'd left for Hortensia Island, I remembered, and at least I keep good files. Long, long ago, the Eight Skilled Gentlemen were said to have enlisted the aid of eight very minor demon-deities, siblings although physically dissimilar. What they wanted them for was no longer known, but a brief description of each was provided. You can see why I planned to show you the origin of a hallucination."

He slid a paper across the table. It was old and somewhat faded, but still clear, and I caught my breath. Years ago as a young scholar the Celestial Master had sketched a little old man who carried a glowing ball of fire, and beneath it he had written, "Third demon-deity: *Pi-fang*, kills with something like a tiny comet."

Master Li whistled sharply.

"Save your whistles," the Celestial Master said with a smile, and he slid another sheet across the table. This time I uttered a distinct yelp, and then turned bright red as the Celestial Master winked at me.

We were looking at a one-legged creature who was playing something like stone chimes, and beneath it was neatly written, "Fifth demon-deity, *K'uei*, the Dancing Master. Kills by forcing victims to dance themselves to death."

Master Li's eyes were gleaming. He seized an ink stick and a stone and a brush and some paper and went to work, swiftly copying each sketch and brief descriptive comment. Each of the eight creatures was very odd in that it was a killer whose ability to kill was limited to a specialty that couldn't possibly massacre large numbers of people, such as our modern crossbows and exploding charges of Fire Drug—but then, I had to admit that the very limits and peculiarities made violent death seem real and terrible, like strangling hands around one's throat as opposed to a random missile that strikes by accident on a battlefield.

"I said there were these eight and they were siblings, but later in a passing reference too insignificant to lead anywhere an anonymous commentator said there was a ninth child, a boy," the Celestial Master said.

"Could he possibly have had a face like a painted ape?" Master Li asked sharply.

The Celestial Master smiled. "Not a chance, Kao. I said he was a boy, and I meant it. He was human, which implies one of his parents was mortal and one divine, and he was said to possess extraordinary beauty." The saint shrugged. "That's why I never tried to follow up on a ninth child. It reeks of a thousand fairy tales."

"If not a million," Master Li muttered.

I looked at the sketch he was making. It was of the fourth demon-deity, a huge snake, and it was very strange. Part was terrible: two human heads with fangs, a great crushing constrictor's body—but it wore two silly little hats and a jacket far too small for it, and somehow it seemed lost and lonely, and beneath it the Celestial Master had written, "The *Wei Serpent* has known greatness and sorrow. It cannot abide noise, and when a carriage rattles past it raises its heads and hisses."

Apparently the Celestial Master was reading my expression, and he said, "I know, Ox. There's something sad about these creatures as well as terrible. They seem ancient to us, but they had to be among the last recognized by the aborigines, and gods—even minor demons like these—of a dying race are often creatures of pathos. You must ask Master Li about it sometime."

Master Li had finished. He folded the papers neatly and put them in his money belt and reclaimed the cage.

"I've told all I know. Do you have anything else?" he asked.

"If I did I've forgotten it," the Celestial Master said. "What's next for you?"

"Ox and I are going to pay our respects to Eight Skilled Gentlemen," he said. "Meaning I'm going back to Hortensia Island, and I want to show Ox the Yu. After that—well, I have a theory worth testing. I'll report when I have anything worth talking about."

The effort to maintain mental clarity had been exhausting. The Celestial Master managed only a wink and a wave as we bowed our way backward and then out the door, but Master Li was as full of energy as he'd been in a year.

"Ha!" he exclaimed as we walked out into the sunlight. "What a delightful development! I take back everything I said about white whales turning into minnows. What kind of case did I originally predict this would be?"

I thought about it.

"The spout reaches toward the stars, and the wake rocks offshore islands as it swims toward us, circumnavigating sacred seas with the awesome authority of an iceberg."

"Slightly over-alliterative, but not bad," said Master Li.

5

We stopped at Master Li's shack in the alley and changed into comfortable clothes and replaced the old cage in the hiding place beneath the pallets, and I boiled some rice and went out and found a vender of the strong fermented fish sauce we both like. We hadn't slept in thirty hours, but the excitement of the case was keeping us wide awake, and a short time later I was at the oars again, rowing back to Hortensia Island.

I'd never seen the Yu. The island is mandarin territory, and the visit I've recounted was my first, but before I can describe the Yu I have to explain it.

The history of China is punctuated by more Great Floods than scholars know what to do with, and one of them a couple of thousand years ago left the Peking Plain covered with thirty feet of mud and silt. The city that was to become Peking was built in many stages on the hardened crust, and geomancers decided that in the process too much attention had been paid to male yang influences and too little to the female yin, and the imbalance must be corrected. The fastest way to strengthen yin is through water, so the North, Central, and South lakes were created by digging down through the crust and filling the holes with water drawn by canals from the Hun and Sha rivers. (Actually the lakes are called "seas," but that's confusing, so they'll be lakes on these pages.) The earth from the lake beds was heaped up and tamped down to form Coal Hill, thus creating the world's costliest pile of dirt, and while digging the bed for North Lake workmen ran into a mass of nearly solid rock, which was left as it was. Water filled up around it, and eventually it was covered with a layer of earth and planted with pretty pink-and-blue-flowering shrubs imported from the Cannibal Coast (Japan), and thus Hortensia Island was born.

One day when the water had risen to a certain level an extraordinary thing happened. A great burst of sound suddenly arose from North Lake: hauntingly beautiful, but without apparent theme or musical form. It was like the sound of a huge horn except it had a husky hollow undertone as it swooped between *huang-chung* and *ying-chung*, the low and high notes of the untempered chromatic scale. The eerie sound lasted only a minute or so. Then it died away and wasn't heard again until six months had passed, at which time excited scholars announced that the sound seemed to be occurring at the precise moment of the winter and summer solstices.

The phenomenon was tracked to a cavern on Hortensia Island, in a crag jutting out over the water's edge on the southeast side facing the city. The cavern had been notable only for ancient wall carvings and statuary, but now a brilliant young musical student announced that in uncovering the island the workmen had uncovered a cave that was actually a musical instrument devised by aborigines to work as a solstice-sounder, although he had no idea why they wanted such a thing. A hole in the floor of the cavern seemed to lead down through a hundred feet of solid rock to an unreachable lower chamber, and the musical student theorized it was some sort of wind-chest. When the water reached a certain level, and the temperature and humidity—perhaps even the intensity of sunlight—were just right, pressure was created that caused great amounts of air to be sucked inside. The air swooshed up through a network of tiny tunnels in the stone that been thought to be natural but revealed marks of axes and chisels, and exited up through the cavern roof.

"In short, the tunnels out over the lake are mouthpieces for air intake, the lower cave is a wind-chest, and the upper holes are pipes. It's an organ, except it operates primarily by inhaling rather than exhaling," said the musical student, but nobody paid him the slightest attention, so he went away and built a miniature model and made enough money to buy a dukedom.

(His organ was the *sheng*, which has been a standard orchestral instrument ever since. It's a little hard on the lungs because it works by inhaling, so a totally false legend has grown around it to the effect that no great sheng master has lived past the age of forty. This allows a player to win wild applause and be pelted by bouquets hurled by lovely ladies, who often hurl themselves as well, simply by pausing to cough during a performance and then wiping his lips with a handkerchief daubed with blood-red rouge, and when the other members of the orchestra can bear it no more they toss away their instruments and set upon the bastard with fists, feet, and fangs.)

The cavern became known as the Yu, first in popular reference and then officially, because Yu is a legendary emperor who is said to have invented all the musical instruments Fu-hsi didn't. It continued to sound the solstices with incredible accuracy, but since nobody knew the point of it the phenomenon had long ago settled into the peculiar atmosphere of Peking, like sweet-sour wells and red brick dust and blowing yellow sand and the Mandarin dialect, and that was how things stood when I tied at a dock in the shadow of the crag that held the famous cavern, looming above us like a giant hand lifting from the water. Master Li led the way up a path that wound through thick shrubbery toward the entrance tunnel. He stopped and pulled reeds aside, and I jumped backward with a sharp yelp.

"Striking, isn't it?" he said.

"I think the word is ghastly," I said when I stopped gulping.

It was only an old stone statue, but it had seemed alive when the light first struck it. It depicted a creature that was half man and half lizard, crouched and hissing, with a jagged edge at the open mouth where a long stone tongue had broken off. The face was contorted with rage, and hatred exuded from it as naturally as the odor of fermented fish sauce exuded from me. The old man kept uncovering more of the grotesque statues as we climbed, ten in all, and even the most human of them was ugly beyond belief.

"Oddly enough, Ox, there are art lovers who consider these to be very beautiful," Master Li said. "Whether those who created them thought they were beautiful or ugly cannot be determined, but the terms really aren't relevant. These are carvings of minor gods, demon-deities, and unless we and the Celestial Master have been taken in by extraordinary illusions we've seen creatures that may be of the same breed."

I thought of the one-legged chimes player and the ape-faced burglar and the Celestial Master's little man hurling fire, not to mention a lowly monster like a vampire ghoul. "Sir, can such creatures really be beautiful?" I asked.

"Beautiful and terrible," he said. "Our distant forefathers swept across this land exterminating a people and a culture, seizing and reshaping whatever interested them. Theologians will tell you that simultaneously an invasion was taking place in Heaven, with old gods being ruthlessly overthrown and new gods taking their place, while the most dangerous and powerful of the old deities were placated by titles and duties and honors and absorption into the pantheon."

I had nowhere near enough knowledge or experience to feel the same excitement that was making Master Li look forty years younger, but something of his intensity was being transmitted to me.

"Ox, here on Hortensia Island and in a few other scattered places the last of the great artists of an expiring race took up their chisels one more time. One assumes they were starving, since famine was the principal weapon our ancestors used," Master Li said sadly. "One assumes they were half mad, and they honored their gods by carving deities in death agonies. You're looking at an unparalleled psychological self-portrait of an exhausted race, teetering upon the edge of extinction, but don't you see the wonder of our recent experiences? Some of the old gods were sure to survive. They're stirring, my boy! They're awakening from their long sleep, yawning and stretching, and you and I are right in the middle of it! Damn it, Ox, I feel like a boy whose been bemoaning the fact that he was born too late for the age of giants, and then one day he hears a snore that rocks the sky, and it's accompanied by an earthquake that knocks down his house, and he discovers that the valley his village is sitting in bears a very strong resemblance to an immense navel."

There was power mixed with the twisted pain of these stone idols, I had to admit it—still, my conservative peasant taste has definite limits. I pointed ahead through a gap in the bushes.

"Venerable Sir, look at that," I said.

A hideous head was just visible, rising above leaves. It was as though a sculptor had molded a man's face in soft clay, and then reached out and cruelly dug his fingers into the surface, poking and twisting.

"Isn't it possible that the artists carved at least a few evil creatures along with the gods?" I asked. "I can't for the life of me see how anyone could find beauty in that."

The hideous head gazed back at me. Then the mouth opened, and a resonant baritone voice said, "Be it known, boy, that legions of lovely ladies have praised these features."

"Yik!" I said, or something like that as I leaped backward into a tangle of rose thorns.

"Ha!" said Master Li, who seemed to be enjoying this.

Unless I was going crazy there was a twinkle of amusement in the eyes of the grotesque face, and bushes parted and a middle-aged strongly built man stepped to the path. He made a superbly graceful gesture that was like an exaggerated shrug, and added, "Of course, that was before the God of Beauty went quite mad with jealousy, so I shall forgive your impertinence."

For the first time I saw a smile I was to see often, as warm and brilliant as the sun rising, and it was accompanied by a bow so superb that no opera star could have matched it.

"This humble one is called Yen Shih, and his insignificant occupation is to manipulate mannequins upon a stage, and he is honored to recognize and greet the legendary Master Li, foremost among truth-seekers of China."

He turned to me.

"You would be Number Ten Ox, and you really shouldn't feel as uncomfortable as you look at the moment." The extraordinary man offered a wink that absolved me of guilt once and for all. "I told my daughter just the other day that when I die she can spare the expense of a funeral by propping my corpse beside these statues, since nobody will notice the difference."

The God of Beauty had been jealous indeed. What I had taken to be an artist's depiction of torment was in reality the ravages of smallpox, and rarely have I seen such destruction to a human face. It was a miracle that his eyesight remained, and as for his craft—who hadn't heard of Yen Shih, greatest of puppeteers?

Master Li's bow wasn't quite so graceful, but it was very good.

"The honor is mine, for Yen Shih is said to be puppeteer to the gods on temporary vacation from Heaven, and Yen Shih's daughter has also earned the jealousy of mere mortals." Master Li dropped the artificial air and accent of formal speech and switched to the people's vernacular. "I've seen you perform three or four times. If you got any better you'd be accused of witchcraft, speaking of which I've heard your daughter is absolutely the best."

Master Li turned to me. "No, she isn't a witch," he said with a laugh. "She's a female shaman, a shamanka, who specializes in the old rituals, and nothing but good is said about her." He turned back to the puppeteer. "Ox has never seen the Yu, so I'm taking him inside for a look," he added casually.

That was a subtle way of inviting information without demanding it. Yen Shih might be famous and respected, but as a puppeteer his social rank was precisely at the bottom. He had absolutely no right to set foot upon aristocratic premises like Hortensia Island—even less right than I would have if I hadn't been with Master Li—but on the other hand he wasn't being pressed to explain his presence. He decided to do so voluntarily.

"I come here often just before the seasonal sacrifices. The purpose is to steal something," he said matter-of-factly. "I've offered to buy the stuff time and time again but I always get turned down, and I would be honored to have witnesses to my crime."

"The honor shall be ours," Master Li said graciously.

So there were three of us as we continued up the path. Master Li was perfectly content to let Yen Shih take the lead, and the puppeteer pulled weeds aside and ducked low and stepped into the opening of a natural rock tunnel. Inside the entrance was a barrel holding a stack of torches and Yen Shih and I each lit one, and then we followed the tunnel on and up into the heart of the famous Yu.

I really don't know what I was expecting. I do know that I was disappointed. There was practically nothing to see. It was only a cavern of stone worn smooth by water, with a small round hole in the center of the floor and a maze of little tunnels leading up and out through the roof. Even the ancient altar was no more than a large stone blackened by fires of thousands of years ago, and I have to admit that I found the modern touches more interesting than the ancient ones. The modern part was simply the stack of crates holding ceremonial material for the rites of the next moon, since the Yu cavern was traditionally used for such purposes, and Yen Shih walked over to one of the crates and lifted the lid and smiled down at the contents.

"What thief could resist it?" he asked.

I stared at the stuff. "Clay?" I said.

"Very special clay," said the puppeteer. "It comes from the bank of a river near Canton, and it's used to blend with incense and form fragrant figures of sacrificial animals. I've been trying without success to buy it, because it's perfect for modeling puppets I'll eventually carve in permanent form."

I watched with awe as his fingers swiftly kneaded a ball of the clay. A marvelously funny laughing face appeared, a merry woman, and then with a flick of fingers it became the sorrowful image of a weeping old man.

"I don't need much, but it's fragile stuff and several times a year I have to steal a bit more of it," Yen Shih said with a shrug, and then he neatly wrapped some clay inside a piece of oilskin and tied it around his waist beneath his tunic.

"I'll see if I can get you a permit," was Master Li's only comment. Then he changed the subject. "Let's show Ox the wall carvings. A friend of ours has an interesting theory concerning who they're meant to represent, although he hasn't the slightest idea what they're supposed to be doing."

Again Yen Shih led the way with his torch, and I must honestly report that again I was disappointed. The famous frieze was in a long side tunnel that tapered to a tiny hole looking out over the lake, and at first I didn't see anything at all. It was only when Master Li had me hold my torch close to the wall that the figures appeared, and even then I could barely make them out.

Eight hooded men were seen over and over, apparently performing different stages of some sort of ritual. The stone was worn almost smooth, and no details were visible. Each of the shamans—if that's what they were—seemed to be carrying something, but no trace of the objects remained. So far as I could see they could have been doing anything from sowing a field to celebrating a marriage, and the few surviving symbols above them that Master Li identified as birds of some sort didn't mean anything either.

"It's a real pity there isn't a clearer record," Master Li said regretfully. "One would expect to find more carvings of the eight figures, but so far as I know none have come to light."

I realized that Yen Shih was standing very still with his eyes fixed on Master Li's face. I could see he was weighing various factors, and then he came to a decision.

"I haven't been totally truthful. I come to the island to steal something else as well, and I think you may be interested in looking at it," he said.

We followed the puppeteer back into the sunlight. He turned left and began to climb a small winding trail to the top of the crag and the row of astronomical instruments that were used to confirm predictions of eclipses in the annual imperial calendar.

"Incredible waste," Yen Shih said, pointing at the huge metal base the instruments rested on, glinting dully in the sun. "That's partially high-grade bronze and partially Dragon's Sinew, meaning an alloy of a small amount of copper, twice as much antimony, and a great deal of tin. It costs a fortune, relatively speaking, and I need a lot of it to make nearly invisible wires for my puppets. Fortunately, I could keep digging this stuff out for several centuries."

A long flat rock lay beside the platform, and when Yen Shih lifted it I saw a deep hole, big enough to slide into. He did so, taking the torch he still carried, and when he climbed back up the torch was still below, illuminating a small cave.

"There isn't space for two, but you may find my Dragon's Sinew mine rather interesting," he said cryptically.

Master Li went first, and I heard a sudden sharp exclamation, and then his voice lifted happily. "Yen Shih, everything I have is yours!"

Some minutes later he had me lift him out, and then I squeezed down through the hole myself. The torch was stuck in a crevice, burning brightly, and the first thing I saw was the puppeteer's "mine." The workmen had poured Dragon's Sinew with lavish abandon, leaving large congealed pools of the stuff, and Yen Shih had been very neatly chipping away at the edges.

As I followed the glinting path of the metal I saw it run into a shelf of solid rock.

"I'll be the Stone Monkey!" I yelped, and I heard Master Li laugh up above.

Yen Shih had led us to his private gallery as well as his private mine. "Eight! I've found all eight!" Ma Tuan Lin had written before a monster burned a hole in his back, and here carved in stone were the eight hooded shamans of three thousand years ago, and the details had not worn away. They were carrying eight cages precisely like the one concealed beneath Master Li's pallet.

6

A short time later we were seated on the bronze platform beside the astronomical instruments sipping wine—meaning Yen Shih and Master Li were emptying the latter's wine flask while I drank plum juice with vinegar from my own flask. The puppeteer appeared to have insides of solid copper. Alcohol didn't seem to affect him at all, and he was getting on splendidly with Master Li, who was in an expansive mood.

"Yen Shih, my friend, when you come to this island you scarcely announce your presence," Master Li said. "By any odd chance did you happen to be here two nights ago, about the double hour of the sheep?"

"No, I was sound asleep in my house at the time," Yen Shih said.

Master Li pointed in the direction of Ma Tuan Lin's pavilion. "Something peculiar has been going on down there," he said. "You've heard about the vampire ghoul who caused Devil's Hand to lose his chance for the record? Well, a few hours earlier, around the double hour of the sheep, that ch'ih-mei was unquestionably right where I'm pointing, at one of the pavilions."

The puppeteer looked where Master Li pointed, and then raised his eyes to the water of North Lake lapping at the bank beside the pavilion, and his eyes continued to lift to the opposite shore and Peking and the Vegetable Market, where the ch'ih-mei had fallen and died. The terrible smallpox craters deprived the puppeteer of normal facial expressions, but his right eyebrow was eloquent as it lifted toward the top of his head.

"But how . . ."

"Ah! You see it. I thought you would," Master Li said happily. He turned to me. "Ox, that's the most important reason for coming back to the island. We're now absolutely certain that the vampire ghoul was outside Ma Tuan Lin's pavilion a few hours before it crawled into its coffin on Coal Hill. All right, how did it get from the pavilion to the cemetery?"

"Why, I suppose it just—"

I halted with the sentence half formed. North Lake was between the pavilion and Coal Hill, and could a ch'ih-mei swim? The idea of such a monster rowing sedately across in a boat with a ripped-off head neatly stored between its feet was ludicrous, and I seemed to hear Auntie Hua on the subject of monsters: "Ox, if you can't get to sunlight, run toward water! The living dead fear it, and will brave it only as a last resort."

Master Li shared the last of the wine with the puppeteer, and then pitched the goatskin flask to the water below.

"I would assume you have a pick and shovel stored somewhere," he said to the puppeteer. "Our meeting has been so fortunate that I'd like to prolong it, and if you have nothing more pressing to attend to you might like to help track the path of a vampire ghoul."

Yen Shih's eyes could also be expressive, and they were sparkling. "Delighted! If nothing else I can dine on the tale for a month," he said.

Master Li got on my back and the three of us made good time to the pavilion, pausing only to collect Yen Shih's pick and shovel from a ditch where he'd concealed them, and soon we were standing close to the spot where flies still swarmed around grass stained with a mandarin's blood. I thought Master Li was going to have us fan out and search for claw prints, but he had something more specific in mind and he pointed toward the huge pile of dirt the creature had apparently crawled from.

"That's supposedly dirt dug for a construction project that was canceled," he said. "Construction on Hortensia Island is rare, and I hadn't heard of anything scheduled. See if you can find the hole this stuff came from."

We worked around the great pile, hacking through weeds. Then we circled out farther and farther until we reached the limit at which dirt could reasonably be pitched where it was, but still we found no hole. There remained the possibility that the workmen had been terrible amateurs who tossed dirt so that half of it slid back on top of them, and we dug a series of holes down through the pile itself, but always the shovel scraped against solid earth and dead matted grass.

"Venerable Sir, the dirt didn't come from here," I finally said. "It had to be hauled in from some other location."

"That," Master Li said complacently, "is precisely what I expected, and it's a hundred to one that the other location is across the lake near Coal Hill. Vampire ghouls never stray far from their coffins. This one happened to fall into, or was taking a nap in, a pile of dirt near the cemetery, and it was accidentally carried here, and its homing instinct allowed it to find the path the dirt had taken. If a ch'ih-mei can find a path, so can we."

It didn't take long now that we knew what we were looking for. Yen Shih swung his pick at thick reeds against the bank of a low cliff nearby and almost spiked himself in the left leg as the pick met no resistance and whipped around. We pushed reeds down and found a large dark hole, and any doubts vanished when we found dribbles of loose dirt and marks of large sleds that had been carrying heavy loads. I raced back to the Yu and returned with torches, and then we started down the tunnel that was headed east, toward the Imperial City and Coal Hill.

The path dipped down and down, and finally leveled off, and I nervously lifted my torch and studied the stone ceiling. This tunnel hadn't been dug recently. It was old, perhaps as old as the Yu, and I saw black spots on the ceiling that seemed to move like giant spiders, and a slow menacing plop-plop-plop sound announced the dripping of water. We were making our way beneath the surface of the lake now, and I didn't want to think about things like rockfalls. There was no sound except that which we made.

"Hold up," Master Li said.

He had turned aside and was waving his torch around an alcove that opened on the north side. It was about thirty feet long and ten feet deep, and the floor was littered with fragments of rock. I saw a huge scar in the stone wall, recently made, and Master Li found traces of ancient chisel marks on some of the smashed fragments.

"It almost looks as though somebody discovered an old frieze and then smashed it to pieces before anybody else could see it," he said. "Ox, do you remember that rubbing we found in Ma's pavilion? I wonder if it came from here. After all, dirt was carried through this tunnel and dumped right in his backyard, and I doubt that he knew nothing about it."

There was nothing else to be seen, so we continued on. I was very nervous. For all I knew the ch'ih-mei had his whole family down here, and our torchlight was announcing the approach of dinner. I clutched the pick like a battle-ax, but nothing happened. The path began to rise, and far ahead we saw a flicker of light. We finally came to a flight of steps that led up to a stone landing, and a wooden framework and a pair of large doors confronted us, and the hazy yellow light was coming through the crack between the doors, which stood slightly ajar. Master Li signaled for us to extinguish our torches.

"I think we've come up to ground level," he whispered. "I also think we're inside the artificial mound of Coal Hill, and that explains why dirt was removed and carted to the island, where it wouldn't cause comment. This is a cave that was dug recently and secretly, right beneath the palaces of the wealthiest mandarins."

We slipped silently through the doors into a large room that was piled with packing cases, stacked one on top of another almost to the ceiling. Across from us was another pair of doors and the light in the room was coming in through cracks at the edges, but this wasn't artificial. It was sunlight, and when we put our eyes to the largest crack we were looking down at water.

"Ha!" Master Li whispered. "That's it. This is a smuggling operation, and it must involve mandarins of very high rank. That's the canal at the base of Coal Hill. Their barges pass through customs at Ta Kao Tien, preferably at nightfall, and begin inching up toward Export Clearance at Shou Huang Tien. Halfway through they pass here, where well-trained crews are ready: doors are opened, cargoes are switched, and with scarcely a pause the barges proceed to Export Clearance, and stamps will be applied automatically since the cargoes have just been inspected and couldn't possibly have been altered in the middle of a canal."

He paused, and then added, "The point has to be twofold: they pay negligible import duty on cargoes that are practically worthless, and then switch cargoes for goods that are both costly and restricted, meaning forbidden for export. If the goods are coveted by wealthy barbarians they must be making an incredible profit."

He turned from the doors and we tiptoed toward the back of the room where there was another door, a large single one. As we drew closer we could hear voices, and Master Li gently shoved the door partially open. We were looking at an alchemy laboratory where vast numbers of vials and jars were stacked on worktables, along with burners and mortars and a great number of arcane instruments. Five people were visible.

One dominated the room, even though he was the softest-spoken. He was dressed in costly silks and gold-trimmed satin, and his rings and other jewelry could probably have ransomed a king or two. He was immensely fat, and moved with the peculiar dancer's grace that some bulky people possess—probably half in the viewer's imagination, because one expects ungainliness. The next three men obviously deferred to the fat man. Seldom have I seen more unpleasant people than those three, who seemed closer to the world of animals than to that of men. The leader was a man who looked exactly like a wild hog, and Hog I was to call him ever after. The second and third might have been brothers, sneaky, skulking, backstabbing brothers, and I dubbed them Hyena and Jackal.

The fourth man had clerk written all over him. He was on his knees with his hands tied behind him, and a brush was stuck in his topknot and ink stains marked his shabby tunic, and he quivered in terror as the fat man addressed him.

"My agents inform me that in a wineshop you mentioned that I was soon to leave on an important mission," the fat one said softly, and I realized he had a tiny lisp that gave his voice a purring sound, like a cat.

"I said nothing about purpose or destination!" the clerk protested. "Your Excellency, I swear I—"

"My dear fellow, I don't doubt it for a moment," the fat one purred. "Why should you bother to tell what you could show?"

"Show? But I've shown nothing!" the clerk cried.

The fat man took a jeweled pillbox from a pocket and opened it. He extracted something I couldn't make out at that distance and held it up for inspection.

"No? How odd that my agents should pick this up from where you foolishly left it, right on top of your table in that wineshop," the fat man said.

Hog and Hyena and Jackal leaned forward, licking their lips, and I've seen prettier sights at feeding time in the imperial tiger pit.

"Your Excellency, I swear I forgot I had such a thing with me!" the clerk squealed. "It was only an accident, and I have been faithful and hardworking. I ask only the chance to redeem my moment of forgetful stupidity!"

"You shall have your chance, and it shall be more than a moment," the fat man said in his cat-purr voice. "I grant you all eternity for redemption, unless Hell has other chores that take precedence."

He hurled whatever he had taken from the pillbox into the clerk's face and swiveled around and walked gracefully away and through one last door at the rear of the laboratory. The moment he turned the other three had moved forward, and the sounds of the door closing behind the fat man were drowned out by terrible screams. I don't want to go into details. The three were precisely as animalistic as they looked—with the addition of human ingenuity—and they took their time killing the clerk. It was horrible. At the end they had a gory mess on the floor and they laughed about it as they went to a storeroom to get rags to mop up.

Before I knew what was happening Master Li had slipped through the door. He sidled on tiptoe through the mess so as to avoid prints, and pushed and poked through ghastly pieces of the late clerk, and finally came up with something that made him grunt in satisfaction. He turned and tiptoed back and rejoined us, and we silently shut the door and went back into the shipping room. Master Li whispered to us to find an open case and we split up and went through the rows of stacked boxes. From my end it was a futile endeavor. Every case I found was numbered, nailed tight, and sealed with wax symbols bearing customs stamps that certainly looked real to me. Meaning the wax had melted here and slopped over the imprint there, and been chipped and broken, and at times had been stamped in a totally inappropriate spot: real.

Master Li was doing a great deal of swearing under his breath, and when I passed the puppeteer he lifted his eyes heavenward and shrugged. Not one case was accessible, unless we wanted to leave calling cards in the form of broken seals, and finally we had to give up.

Coarse laughing voices were moving toward us. The door opened. Master Li winced and pointed, and Yen Shih and I followed the sage back toward the tunnel entrance, stooped low behind cases, moving like mice. Hog and Hyena and Jackal were too busy joking about the way the little clerk had screamed to notice. We could probably have walked out carrying a case, but Master Li didn't want to deal with an alarm from a careful tally clerk and he signaled for us to keep going. We made it easily back into the tunnel, and then I sensed that Yen Shih was going to ask questions, so I put a hand on his arm and squeezed no-no-no. In the last light before darkness closed around us I had seen the old man's wrinkles twist into tight circles on his face, and I knew he wanted silence for thought.

When we were far enough down the tunnel and I was tired of groping I lit a torch and the sage made no objection. In fact, he took it from me when we reached the place where the wall of an alcove had been chipped away and examined both the wall and the cracked fragments, swearing monotonously. Then he snapped out of his reverie and turned to the puppeteer.

"Well, Yen Shih, I got you into more than anyone bargained for," he said. "At least you weren't spotted."

Yen Shih flashed that gorgeous, astonishing smile. "I enjoyed it," he said openly and frankly. "Can you have them arrested?"

"I would tend to doubt it," said Master Li. "That fat fellow who ordered the murder happens to be the second most powerful eunuch in the empire, commonly called Li the Cat. He holds ministerial rank. I'd need a warrant signed by the Son of Heaven, and by the time I got it the contraband would have vanished and the cave would be a Home for Hapless Orphans and the clerk's dear old mother would swear her darling boy expired from typhoid fever at the age of four."

He reached for wine and realized he'd finished it. "I need to nail them for the smuggling racket, not murder, and that won't be easy. Because of this." Master Li pulled out a tiny object and held it to the torchlight.

"A tea leaf?" Yen Shih said.

"Indeed yes, and it's also a very bad tea leaf," said Master Li. "Good tea is restricted, of course, so fortunes can be and are made smuggling it to barbarians, but this stuff can be shipped out by the ton. It's *ta-cha,* the cheapest of all boheas, and on top of that it's been damaged, probably by a flood. Tea like this is worth no more than ten cash a pound, yet this is what Li the Cat threw in the clerk's face, and apparently it was so important that leaving the premises with a leaf of it in his possession cost the clerk his life. You figure it out."

"No, thank you," said Yen Shih. "I do, however, have a favor to ask."

"If I can grant it, it's yours," Master Li said grandly.

"Consider that I now have a small stake in this affair, and command my services, night or day, when something comes up." Small points of light flickered deep inside Yen Shih's eyes, dancing and glowing, and again his sunrise smile belied the ruins of his face. "One gets bored," said the puppeteer.

We got back to the island, where we left Yen Shih, who had unfinished business, and I rowed back to the city. Master Li still had things to do and wanted to waste no time. He had me rent a palanquin, and then we went to office after office of bureaucrat after bureaucrat, gathering a bit of information here and a trace of a rumor there, and it was long past sundown when we started home. I was starving, but Master Li had at least sated a different sort of hunger.

"It's official," he said firmly. "Li the Cat has arranged to get the protection of the Wolf Regiment, and he's traveling to Yen-men, in Shansi, to confer with the Grand Warden. Ox, I'd give a great deal to be a fly on the wall when they meet. That poor clerk was already condemned to death for having even hinted that Li the Cat might be going on a trip, and what's so secret about a conference with the Grand Warden of Yen-men?"

I had no answers, of course. I concentrated on the rumblings of my stomach until we paid off the palanquin and walked up the narrow winding alley toward Master Li's shack to change clothes before going to dinner at One-Eyed Wong's. Again there was a very bright moon, and old Grandmother Ming from the house next door was waiting for us.

"No big monkeys!" she yelled from her window, leaning out to shake a fist.

"Eh?" said Master Li.

"Burglars you got! Pickpockets you got! Cutthroats and grain thieves and robbers come calling day and night! Drunks and mushroom-heads and whores and pirates and jailbirds and embezzlers—all right, all right, all right—but no big monkeys!" screamed Grandmother Ming.

Master Li was standing very still.

"Would this particular big monkey have a rather gaudy face?" he asked.

"What kind of monkey would come calling on *you?*" the old lady howled. "No big monkeys with red noses and blue cheeks and yellow chins!"

I dove inside the shack, but the damage was already done. The place had been ransacked, and the mysterious old cage was gone.

7

Before, we had seen the Celestial Master at his office, but now Master Li took me to the saint's house just at daybreak, saying that the old boy awoke with the morning star. An old female servant let us in. She knew Master Li well, and led us without question through a simple bare house where tame deer were playing with dogs they had been raised with, and pet parakeets jabbered at cats, and a huge old owl opened sleepy eyes and said "Who?" We stepped outside again at the back into the most famous private garden in the empire. I could see the water of North Lake glinting through gaps in shrubbery in the first rays of the sun, and the little dock and special ramp that allowed the Celestial Master to hobble down to his boat. The garden itself can't really be described, although countless writers have attempted it. The problem is that it's so simple. I counted three small fishponds, a pile of rocks, ten trees so old that even small branches had beards of moss or creepers, one small patch of lawn where a statue of Lao-tse stood, innumerable shaggy shrubs, and flowers beyond counting. That was all, and none of it explains the sense of timelessness that wraps like a blanket around every visitor, the suggestion of continuity without beginning or end. Perhaps the closest anyone has come is Yuan Mei in his popular song "The Master's Garden," and even he admits failure except for the opening lines:

> A wind ancestral sings,
> Soft with scents of summers and springs,
> "Draw near, draw near!
> Ten thousand yesterdays are gathered here."

The Celestial Master was finishing the last of his morning tea when we approached, seated at a table made from a small millstone. "Hello, Kao!" he said cheerfully, but I had the sense that he was forcing his air of cheer through a curtain of immense weariness. "A bright good morning to you, Number Ten Ox. Any more grotesque murders?"

"One, but while it was extremely nasty I can't really call it grotesque," Master Li said, and then he went on to explain what we had seen, step by step, pausing to go back over points when he felt the ancient saint's attention was slipping.

"Li the Cat, eh?" the Celestial Master said at the end. "That's bad news, Kao. He's powerful and he's slippery, and I very much doubt that you can convict him on a murder charge."

"That's what I told our puppeteering friend," Master Li said sourly. "I think our only hope is to find out exactly what their smuggling racket involves, nail them on that, and then put pressure on underlings to implicate the mandarins in murder, true or not, and squeeze the mandarins into involving the powerful eunuch. Messy and probably illegal, but I don't know what else we can do."

"Keep it legal, Kao," the Celestial Master said gently.

"Yes, sir," Master Li said like a schoolboy, and like a schoolboy he had the fingers of his left hand crossed behind his back. "To tell the truth, it isn't eunuchs and mandarins and their rackets and murders that interests me, because I'll bet anything you like that their involvement in really important matters is peripheral, if it exists at all. Old friend and teacher, what can you make out of the reappearance of ancient cages that may have belonged to the Eight Skilled Gentlemen? The simultaneous appearance of minor demon-deities of a destroyed religion? And what about that damned ape-faced creature who may be helping to murder mandarins, and is certainly stealing cages, including mine?"

The Celestial Mandarin scratched his nose and shrugged. "How would I know? Kao, are you absolutely positive that the ape man's gaudy face is real? Not clever actor's makeup?"

"It's real," Master Li said flatly. "Ox?"

"Yes, sir, it's real," I said. "The moonlight was very bright when we saw him, and so were the lamps in the room, and I could almost see the pores of his skin, and that wasn't paint or dye."

The Celestial Master sat silently for a moment. Then he said wearily, "I can't concentrate anymore. I'm like an old tree, dying from the top down, and I'll tell you something: I've had the same dream six nights in a row. It starts with my mother, who's been dead for fifty years, and it ends with me trying to find my father's shoes. I'm not going to see the leaves turn this year, Kao, and I can't think clearly enough to make sensible suggestions. What do you plan to do?"

I could see that the saint's skin was almost transparent, and even the effort to sit up straight was tiring him, and I felt tears burn my eyes. To dream of the dead and then of shoes is an irrefutable omen of joining the former, because "shoes" and "reunion" are homophones: *hsieh.*

"The key to the whole works would seem to be the cages," Master Li said. "Both cages were held by murdered mandarins, and we can assume they belonged to the smuggling ring. It can't be an accident that the tunnel entrance was practically at Ma Tuan Lin's back door, and his note on the back of the rubbing seems to link cages to a business enterprise. A reasonable assumption is that the remaining cages are held by the remaining members, so to find the cages is to find the conspirators, and, I hope, to discover what in hell makes the cages so special. Li the

Cat is traveling to Yen-men to confer with the Grand Warden, and I think it would be a good idea for Ox and me to attend the meeting."

The tired old head lifted. "How?" the Celestial Master said with a trace of revived vigor. "To get to Yen-men you have to pass through three different bandit territories. There's always the sea route, but can you afford a couple of accompanying warships for protection against pirates? And once you get there, how do you join the meeting?"

Master Li grinned. "Li the Cat is indeed taking the long, slow sea route, protected by the Wolf Regiment. If everything goes right Ox and I will leisurely travel overland, enjoying the sights and not losing sleep about bandits."

This was news to me, and I leaned forward intently, and Master Li winked at me.

"You heard Yen Shih, Ox. He's caught the fever and wants to stay on the case, so far as he understands it, and have you ever heard of a bandit insane enough to interfere with a traveling puppeteer?"

He was right, of course. Nobody interfered with puppeteers. They brought laughter and joy to everybody, bandit and soldier alike, and they traveled under the protection of more deities than most priests could count. Master Li turned to the Celestial Master and winked.

"On top of that, Yen Shih's daughter is a renowned shamanka, young as she is. With the protection of a puppeteer and a shamanka I'd travel into the den of the Transcendent Pig," he said. "As for spying on the conference, we'll wait and see what comes up. It all depends, of course, on Yen Shih's decision, and whether or not his daughter will join us."

The saint nodded. "Bring them for a blessing if they wish one," he said. "Ox, too," he added with a nod in my direction. "You won't need one, Kao, because I decided long ago that the August Personage of Jade is reserving your blessing for himself, just as soon as he can stockpile enough lightning bolts."

The following morning there were four of us at the Celestial Master's door, along with the morning star and the first light of the sun. Five, if one counts the gift.

Yen Shih had listened intently to all Master Li said, and when I told him of the pets wandering around the saint's house he wondered if one more pet would be an appropriate gift, and after seeing it Master Li was sure it would be welcome indeed. It was a small bright-eyed monkey with greenish silky fur, and I had never seen such a wonderfully intelligent creature. Once taught it could bring designated objects on command, and it had been trained to pluck out three recognizable tunes on the pi-pa (although it was likely to switch abruptly from one to another), and it was a marvelous mimic of human gestures. Yen Shih led it in by the hand, dressed in a small cap and tunic, and when he touched his own forehead and said "Where are your manners?" the creature bowed quite beautifully to the saint, who was enchanted.

"Yen Shih, eh? I saw you once, incognito of course, because you were doing *Hayseed Hong*. I haven't laughed so hard since Abbot Nu confused one of the newfangled ceremonial vessels with a Sogdian chamber pot and anointed his acolytes with the contents of the latter," the Celestial Master said happily. "And this is your lovely daughter! My dear, Tao-shihs and shamankas have a great deal in common, to the despair of theologians, and if I'm feeling a bit stronger when you return we must sit down for a long talk."

He blessed us and prayed for safety and success, and the old female servant had already learned the list of command gestures and got the little monkey to wave goodbye as we left. I can't describe our leave-taking in more detail because my mind was concentrated on one overpowering ingredient, and that was the puppeteer's daughter.

Her name was Yu Lan. Shamankas learn their craft young, and she had learned from her mother, and I felt very callow and ignorant when I realized that the puppeteer's daughter—no older than I—was already a fully accredited priestess of the ancient Wu cults, and practitioner of shamanistic mysteries and magic I didn't dare dream about. She lived in a world far above me even when we shared the same physical area and conditions, but there was nothing unfriendly about her. When capitalized as a personal name Yu Lan means "Magnolia," but uncapitalized and in a different context *yu lan* can mean "secretly smiling," and that is how I came to think of her: silent, graceful, distant as a drifting cloud, but never haughty, never reproving, secretly smiling.

She worked with everyone else to help her father's puppet shows, but her own personal work could not be shared. I remember when we reached hills where strange wild people still lived in dark ravines. That night Yu Lan suddenly stood up in the light of our cooking fire and walked to the edge of the shadows where a boy had appeared as if by magic. He had brown skin and high sharp cheekbones and an expressionless face, and he silently extended a stripped branch with notches cut in it. Yu Lan studied the notches and then told the boy to wait, and a few minutes later she was dressed in a robe made from bearskin and carrying a case of various sacred things, and she disappeared with the boy into the night.

Her father had said nothing. Only when she was gone did Yen Shih remark, "Her mother would sometimes vanish for days on end, but she always found me when she was ready to." Then he changed the subject.

She hadn't gone far, however. Later when we were preparing to go to sleep we heard wailing and chanting from above us on a hilltop, and then a high clear voice exclaimed, *"Hik!"*

Master Li yawned and muttered, "The next sound you'll hear is *'Phat.'* "

"Sir?" I said.

"Phat!" rang sharply from the hilltop.

"It's Tibetan. Didn't you notice the boy's Tibetan features? Somebody's died and they've asked Yu Lan to guide the soul safely into the hereafter," he explained. "She has to start by freeing it from the body, which is done by opening a hole in the top of the head to let it out. Shamans practice on themselves with a piece of straw."

"Sir?"

"Watch."

He plucked a piece of straw from his pallet and laid it carefully on top of his head, down flat. *"Hik!"* he exclaimed, and I stared with bulging eyes as the straw began to tilt and move, as though one end was sliding down into a hole. *"Phat!"* he cried, and the straw was standing up straight. He made a show of plucking the thing out of the hole in his head, and then tossed it away.

"Neat trick, isn't it?" he said. "Yu Lan now has to guide the soul through wild country populated by demons and beasts, strengthening it by prayers and incantations, and she'll be at it all night. Go to sleep."

He rolled over and soon began to snore, but I stayed up for hours acting like a fool with a piece of straw. I never did learn how it's done.

I'm getting ahead of myself, however. I really wanted to write about our very first evening on the road, even though nothing at all happened. We camped on a hill as the sun was setting. Yen Shih's huge puppeteering wagon was bathed in rosy light, and he and I prepared to fix the canvas awning that served as a dew catcher above our pallets. We were swinging mallets, knocking metal sockets into the ground to hold the bamboo poles that supported the awning, while Master Li chanted the count for the mallets and Yu Lan's clear pure voice lifted to the crimson clouds, improvising on the scene in the style of Liu Chu:

"Five
    perching crows
     four
       low clouds
        three
          wild geese
            two
              rows of willows
                one
                  flame of setting sun."

"Pole!" cried Master Li, and the hand of the puppeteer's daughter happened to brush mine as she helped the sage set the pole in the socket.

"Venerable Sir," I said that night as we lay in our pallets, "is it true that shamankas can't stand presumptuous males?"

"Bllppsshh," he muttered, or something like that.

I searched for omens in the stars. "Sir, is it also true that an angry shamanka is as dangerous as a tigress with cubs?"

He rolled over. "You may be right, my boy," he said drowsily. "Knew a great lusty fellow once. Half rearing stallion, half raging bull. They called him Tong the Tumescent. One day Tong laid his paws on a pretty little shamanka, and she gave him the Eye and spoke words in an unknown tongue."

That seemed to be that. Snores arose from Master Li's pallet, and then I heard a sputtering sound and the old man said between yawns, "Now they call him Yang-wei."

The snores resumed, and it took me a moment to connect Tong the Tumescent to Yang-wei, which means "Droopy Penis."

"Oh," I said.

8

Since Li the Cat was taking the slow sea route we had time to allow Yen Shih to replenish his coffers along the way with puppet shows. I think I mentioned that everyone helped out. Yu Lan played a variety of instruments and sang very beautifully, and Master Li put on magic or fortune-telling or medicine shows, depending on his mood, and I donned a black hood and an evil smile and wrestled the local champions, who had to pay for the privilege and could claim a substantial prize if they won. I'd been tossing people out of rings since I was ten, so I wasn't worried about losing, and I never hurt anyone. I have too much to tell about important things to spend much time describing those days, even though I'd like to, so I shall settle for three brief sketches. For the first, it was a warm afternoon in the market square of a small town, and the puppeteer and his daughter were inside the tent preparing for the show, and I had finished my wrestling act and was pouring dippers of water over my head, and it was Master's Li's turn. He wore a flat hat that looked like a board, with peculiar things on the ends of tassels dangling down, and his robe was covered with symbols representing the 101 diseases and the gods thereof, and he was standing on a platform examining a local dignitary who had a potbelly, a purple nose, and crimson cheeks.

"The kidneys, my misguided friend, are not to be trifled with," Master Li said gently, waving a cautionary finger in the fellow's face. "The season of the kidneys is winter, and their orientation is north, and their element is water; their smell is putrid, their taste is salty, and their color is black; their animal is the tortoise, their mountain is Hang Shan, and their deity is Hsuan-ming; their virtue is wisdom, their emotion is fear, and they make the low moaning sound *yu;* the emperor of the kidneys is Chuan-hsu, they take the spirit form Hsuan Yen—the two-headed stag commonly called Black Darkness—and of all body parts they are the most unforgiving. What have you been doing to these great and dangerous organs?"

The old man has sharp bony knuckles rather like chisels, and plenty of snap in his right arm when it comes to short body punches.

"You have been drowning them in the Shaoshing wine of Chekiang!"

"Eeaarrgghh!"

"The Hundred Flowers wine of Chen-chiang!"

"Eeaarrgghh!"

"The Orchid Stream wine of Wusih!"

"Eeaarrgghh!"

"The Drip-Drop wine of Taming!"

"Eeaarrgghh!"

"The Golden Waves wine of Chining!"

"Eeaarrgghh!"

"The Grain of Paradise wine of Hunan!"

"Eeaarrgghh!"

"The Fragrant Snow wine of Mouchow!"

"Eeaarrgghh!"

"The Old Cask wine of Shanyang!"

"Eeaarrgghh!"

"The Peppery Yellow wine of Luancheng!"

"Eeaarrgghh!"

"The White Double wine of the Liuchiu Islands!"

"Eeaarrgghh!"

"The December Snow wine of Kashing!"

"Eeaarrgghh!"

"The Top of the Cask wine of Kuangtung!"

"Eeaarrgghh!"

"The Spring on Tungting Lake wine of Changsha!"

"Eeaarrgghh!"

"And the Double Pepper wine of Chingho!"

"Eeaarrgghh!"

The sage stepped to the front of the platform and addressed the audience in solemn tones, while the patient held his wounded parts and moaned pathetically.

"My friends, consider the wondrous nature of the kidneys, and the beneficence of the deities who have granted them to us," Master Li intoned. "It is the kidneys that produce bone marrow and give birth to the spleen. The kidneys convert bodily fluid into urine, and give birth to and nourish the hairs. The kidneys are the officers of bodily strength, and thus the top pair are attached to the heart. The kidneys are the officers of intellect, and thus the bottom pair winds through the pelvis and climbs up the spinal cord into the brain. The kidneys store the germinating principle that contains the will, and their song is 'Somber Darkness,' and their dance is 'Engendering Life,' and when mistreated they become swollen, sensitive, and very, very sore."

"Eeaarrgghh!"

"Fortunately," said Master Li, opening a large case to display rows of small vials, "the Academy of Imperial Physicians is allowing me to part with a very limited amount of Pao Puh Tsi's amazing tonic for the kidneys known as Nine Fairies Elixir, and you need scarcely be reminded that this is the very elixir that saved the life of Emperor Wen. The ingredients are cinnabar, flowers of sulphur, olibanum, myrrh, camphor, Dragon's Blood, sulphate of copper, musk, burnt alum, bear's gall, yellow lead, centipedes, earthworms, silkworms, plum blossoms, cow bezoar, toad spittle, white jade dust, borax, tree grubs, and snails, and while some may consider the price slightly steep, the wise will consider the alternative."

"*Eeeeaaaarrrrgggghh!*"

Yen Shih was in charge of the show, not Master Li, and he politely but firmly prevented the old man from shearing the sheep right down to the skin. "After all," he pointed out, "I have to return year after year, and it is difficult to entertain lynch mobs."

I just said that Yen Shih was in charge, and the next sketch requires some expansion on the theme. To begin with, right from our first meeting I had sensed two very powerful elements in the puppeteer's being. (Leaving out the tragedy of smallpox that disfigured him; the shock must have been unimaginable, because his natural movements and gestures were those of a good-looking youth who had grown into a handsome man.) The first was the light dancing deep inside his eyes when danger threatened, and I suddenly remembered the boy we had called Otter in my village, and his glowing eyes when he prepared to do a pelican dive into the shallow water in the quarry pit, far below at the base of Torn Tree Hill—a feat the rest of us didn't dare daydream about. I often felt that staying too close to the puppeteer would be like staying too close to a fire where a thick piece of bamboo is burning slowly and steadily, meaning that at any moment the flames may reach a large air pocket surrounded by soft sap, and the explosion may send you sailing in a ball of fire through the wall of your cottage. That leads to the next fact about the puppeteer. He was an aristocrat, and I don't mean that as a figure of speech.

"From a noble family? Oh yes, or so I assume," Master Li said when I asked him about it. "He practically reeks of a rarefied upbringing. Confucianism mandates a family's continued nobility whether they maintain imperial favor or not, and the empire teems with proud younger sons working incognito as fishermen and gamekeepers, so why not puppeteers? Yen Shih may decide to tell us his story someday, and until then we can at least extend the courtesy of keeping our mouths shut."

The scene I want to describe is this. We had reached an inn on the outskirts of a town and been held up by rain that turned the roads to mud. Yen Shih had started drinking early in the morning in the large common room, seated by himself at a small table in the corner. He was still drinking, slowly and steadily, in late afternoon, showing no ill effects from the strong wine, but sinking more and more into his own private world. Yu Lan (thank Buddha!) was resting in the wagon. Suddenly the door burst open and a party of noblemen strode in. They were dressed for the hunt and drenched to the skin, and the others deferred fawningly to the leader, who had a flushed petulant face and hot hasty eyes. He yelled for wine and a larger fire, ordered us peasants out, and in almost the same breath he turned to the closest peasant and commanded him to sweep the stinking floor clean enough to receive superior feet. The closest happened to be Yen Shih, who leisurely arose and picked up a broom that was propped against the wall. He surveyed the nobleman with speculative eyes.

"Gad, the resemblance is remarkable," he drawled. "Would Your Magnificence perchance be related to radiant Lord Yu Yen?"

The sheer audacity of a worm daring to address a tiger left the lord speechless. Besides, Yu Yen means "Fish Eyes."

"No? How odd. I could have sworn you were brothers," Yen Shih said. "Masters of the hunt, legends in war—Lord Yu Yen, for example, having heroically won high rank, medals, and military command upon the field of primogeniture, was granted the honor of accompanying the Son of Heaven upon a bandit-hunting expedition, and as fate would have it he was granted an early opportunity of displaying his worth when his men encountered a band of marauding Miao-chia."

The nobleman had finally grasped the incredible fact that this low creature was addressing him in familiar language, and he uttered a roar of rage and pulled his sword from the scabbard. I started forward, but Master Li grabbed my shoulder and held me back. Yen Shih was casually balancing the broom on his right forefinger and seemed to be unaware of the shining sharp steel that glittered coldly in the afternoon sunlight.

"What a hero he was," the puppeteer said admiringly. " 'Send forth your champion!' cried valiant Lord Yu Yen. 'He against me! Man to man and hand to hand!' It was seemly said, but one regrets to report that the rabble to which it was addressed was disgustingly drunk."

"That's the Miao-chia," said Master Li.

The nobleman screamed with rage and lunged with a swipe that was meant to remove the puppeteer's head, but Yen Shih casually flicked the handle of the broom and sent the blade flying harmlessly aside so that it chopped a candle in half and knocked a tin bowl from a table.

"Indeed yes," the puppeteer said sadly. "The swine clung together, laughing and giggling in drunken disarray, pointing greasy fingers at Lord Yen Yu. Then they sent their cook."

The nobleman screamed and swung again, and the broom handle sharply rapped his wrist. Yen Shih appeared not to see the fellow dive to the floor and scramble to pick up his sword.

"The cook was a rather large woman," he said mournfully. "Fat mottled arms and the evil eye. 'I'll not fight a female!' roared gallant Lord Yu Yen, and the bitch grabbed his lustrous locks and jerked his head forward and bit off his noble nose."

"That's the Miao-chia," said Master Li.

The nobleman tried a thrust to the heart. The parry spun him around, and then a small amount of blood sprayed into the air as the broom handle rapped his nose.

"Lord Yu Yen," said Yen Shih, "decided to unsheathe his sword—a bit late, some might say—and the harridan treated his fingers most foully in the process of taking it from him. Then she hacked off his aristocratic arms at the elbows."

"That's the Miao-chia," said Master Li.

The nobleman's savage swipe swung him around in a circle when Yen Shih leaned back. The blade swished harmlessly through the air and then the broom handle flicked out and the nobleman yelped and grabbed both elbows, and his sword again hit the floor.

"Valiant Lord Yu Yen was somewhat handicapped, but still undaunted!" the puppeteer said proudly. "He stepped forward and attempted quite a savage kick, and might even have essayed another had not the hag chopped off both legs at the noble knees."

"That's the Miao-chia," said Master Li.

The nobleman straightened up and tried to fend off the broom handle with his sword, and then he hopped around the floor clutching both aching knees.

"What a champion was Lord Yu Yen!" Yen Shih said emotionally. "He magnificently managed to wriggle forward on his stomach and inflict a very painful bite upon the lady's left ankle, and would surely have wounded the right one as well were it not for the slattern's total disregard for the rules of civilized warfare, which became apparent during the process by which she removed his lordship's teeth."

"That's the Miao-chia," said Master Li.

The nobleman wasn't a complete idiot. When the broom handle pointed at his head he jumped four feet backward, raising his left arm protectively in front of his mouth.

Yen Shih wiped a tear from his eye. "Although deprived of teeth, legs, arms, and nose, gallant Lord Yu Yen was still magnificent in battle. He went on the offensive with some genuinely harsh language, and was even contemplating spitting when the hussy made such action academic. I regret to report that details of her subsequent behavior are quite unsuitable for circulation in any country other than Tibet."

"That," said Master Li, "is the Miao-chia."

The nobleman raised his sword again, and then paused to think it over.

EIGHT·SKILLED·GENTLEMEN

"We scoured the field of battle, searching for a piece of our hero large enough to place in a sacristy at the Military Academy, from which valiant Lord Yu Yen could inspire generations yet unborn. Alas! All that remained was a greasy spot on the grass," Yen Shih said mournfully. Then his eyes lit up. "But wait! Possibly a twin would suffice, and all we need is a piece!"

His teeth bared in a small tight smile, and he twitched the broom back and forth like a cobra's head as he stepped forward, and the nobleman uttered a small shrill shriek and ran out the door and disappeared, leaving his sword behind him.

The minor noblemen of the hunting party had remained absolutely still throughout this. The puppeteer turned and looked them over, and then he growled. That's all. Just the low snarling growl of a bear about to lose its temper, and in less than five seconds there wasn't a nobleman to be seen. I was paralyzed, but Master Li was not.

"Ox, pack up. We're leaving fast," he said. Then he turned to the puppeteer, and his voice was sharp and hard. "Pretty, but self-indulgent. I sincerely hope you wouldn't have done that yesterday, and we had better be where I assume we are."

Yen Shih's eyes slowly changed as the dancing, leaping light died down. He took a deep breath and bowed his head in apology that seemed to be half mock and half real.

"You're right, of course, and I'm not quite enough of an idiot to have done that yesterday," he said. "We're at the border of bandit country, and inside of two hours no nobleman would dare follow us with his private army."

Master Li grunted, and the affair was never mentioned again, but I would be less than truthful if I didn't admit that when I gathered firewood I spent part of the time swinging a stick in my hand, fencing imaginary noblemen.

The third scene is not so tidy and not so triumphant, and I wouldn't describe it at all were it not for the fact that it turned out to be important.

We had no trouble at all going through bandit territory, just as Master Li had predicted. Everybody welcomes a puppeteer, and in addition there is superstitious awe in outlaws where magic-makers are concerned, and that includes beautiful young shamankas. I soon learned not to worry about Yu Lan, and certainly her father never showed that he did. On the fifth day through the bandits' domain (which officially doesn't exist) we ran straight into one of those coincidences that people who know nothing about life insist happen only in books. The guest of honor at the camp of the bandit chief we were to perform for turned out to be the man we were traveling to see, the Grand Warden of Goose Gate (Yen-men).

We soon learned he had every reason to be there, because he had recently wed the bandit chief's daughter, which showed intelligence, according to Master Li, and we also learned that the bride, who was back at Yen-men, was suffering from a mysterious illness that no physician had been able to cure. We were able to split up and enter the camp as two separate groups traveling together for companionship: Yen Shih and Number Ten Ox as puppeteer and assistant, Master Li and Yu Lan as shaman and shamanka who specialized in healing. They had no trouble impressing the grand warden, and it was arranged that they should try their hands at treating his young wife.

The scene I want to describe is very humiliating. I had to warm up the audience without the help of Master Li and Yu Lan, so I pretended to be on the verge of defeat a couple of times, and then pretended I was losing both temper and judgment when I doubled the wager, and the crowd got quite excited. The noise drew distinguished visitors. I looked up to see the Grand Warden of Yen-men sneering at me, with a party of noblemen and one fellow dressed as a commoner.

"Professional wrestler, eh?" the warden said jovially. "Bill yourself as Muck-Muck the Mule, or some such, eh? Buddha, look at all those bulging things! Muck-Muck the Muscle-bound Mule, eh?"

His entourage treated that as the apex of humor, but I happened to notice that the warden's shifty little eyes didn't laugh when his mouth did, and there was something cowardly and cruel in his voice when he volunteered to provide a friend of his as my next opponent. The friend turned out to be the commoner, and a minute later I reached two decisions. The first was that the commoner's familiar manner suggested a relationship with the grand warden that was far more than friendly, and the second was that he wasn't human.

He was a good deal shorter than I was, but I guessed he was actually heavier. His head seemed to be rammed down on his shoulders without benefit of neck. I've been told I look like that too, but this creature also had little in the way of discernible shoulders, waist, hips, or thighs. The bastard was all of a *piece*, one solid tube of sinuous muscle from his jaw to his knees, and then tapering only slightly from his knees to his feet. As he stripped to his loincloth a bee landed on his left shoulder, and instead of brushing it away he simply shuddered his flesh donkey-style, the entire hide twitching effortlessly, under total muscular control.

"Number Ten Ox," I said silently, "you are in bad, bad trouble."

The creature stood surveying me with glittering, expressionless eyes, and when a smooth ripple of muscles sent him gliding to the challenger's place in the ring I dubbed him the Snake. The warden had claimed the judge's flag as a prerogative of rank. He suddenly dropped it to catch me off guard, but that's exactly what I'd expected him to do and I was ready. I decided there wasn't any point looking for weakness in a snake, so I was airborne the moment the flag started down, twisting in midair to aim a vicious leg whip at the reptile's ankles. He hadn't expected it. He simply dropped a hand and slapped my extended foot so hard that I spun around like a cordless kite and crashed to earth in a cloud of dust. I managed a backflip and landed crouched in a defensive position, but he wasn't bothering to attack me. He was waiting for me to come and entertain him again, and this time he was so contemptuous he didn't try to stop me when I went for a waist hold. That's when I discovered the slick shine of his flesh wasn't an optical illusion. My hands slipped helplessly over oil, and with another effortless donkey shudder he'd sent me spinning harmlessly away.

What kind of creature walks around covered with oil? I didn't get a chance to think it over. The Snake stepped forward and the next thing I knew I was sailing up toward the clouds, and then I was looking at them upside down, and then I returned to earth with a crash that knocked the breath from my body. He could have finished me then and there, of course, but he was gliding snakelike around the ring as he bowed to the applause of the warden and his entourage. I used the opportunity to dig up handfuls of dirt, and I lunged when his back was turned and managed to smear the stuff around his waist. Now my hands had dirt to cling to, and before it became oily mud I got a full grip and heaved, harder than I ever had in my life, and I managed to get full extension. The Snake was poised in the air above my head as I strutted around the ring, and then I tossed him down at the warden's feet with everything I had.

I sometimes wonder how I've survived this long with a couple of plover's eggs masquerading as brains. There I was bowing to the bandits, swollen like a blowfish in my conceit, but since when do you incapacitate a reptile by tossing it to the ground? You annoy it, that's what you do, and when I was able to think again I had a dim impression of having been struck by a cyclone. I flew this way and bounced that way and flipped over and over, and then I was lying flat on my back and the Snake was seated comfortably behind me. He had my arms pulled backward and pinned, and his legs were wrapped around my neck, and slowly, very slowly, he was squeezing them as a constrictor tightens coils around its dinner.

The Grand Warden of Goose Gate was leaning over me, watching. His tongue flicked out and licked his lips, and he was making little snickering sounds as he waited for me to perform a song for him. It was to be the drumming of my heels against the ground as breath left me, faster and faster and then slower and slower, and then silence. I couldn't hear anything except a muffled gong sound in my ears, but suddenly the pressure lessened and allowed me to breathe a little, and I realized the warden had looked away and up, and then I saw a beautiful and terrible figure looming above me. It was Yu Lan, and she had wrapped the aura of her priesthood around her like shining armor, and her eyes flashed with anger.

"Would you arouse the sickness demons that are attacking the body of your wife?" she said to the warden, snapping each word like the crack of a whip. "You have asked aid of the Mysteries of Wu, and taken vows of purity until a cure is accomplished, and now you dare to kill?" Her hair was actually rising like cat's fur, and if I hadn't been in my current position I would have cringed like a whipped dog. "Know you not that you run the risk of angering the Three Corpses and Nine Worms inside your own body, and of visiting upon yourself the very Death Spirit you incite? Release him, and pray to the gods for their forgiveness."

She made a commanding gesture. The Snake looked to the warden for guidance, and the warden looked at the Snake—very much the gaze of bedmates—and then the warden nodded. The pressure relaxed completely and my arms were freed. I managed to sit up and massage my neck, and the warden and the Snake and the entourage strode away. Yu Lan also turned and walked off through ranks of bandits who nervously jumped aside to let her pass.

Master Li had arrived when Yu Lan did, and in case awe and moral superiority needed some support he'd taken a crossbow from a bandit and had the Snake in the notched sights. Now he bent over and examined my bruises.

"Nothing broken," he said cheerfully. "The only thing damaged is your pride, and I wouldn't lose sleep over that if I were you. That fellow simply isn't human."

"Soivnzd," I wheezed, which is as close as I could come to "So I've noticed."

So the stage was set for our arrival in Yen-men, with Master Li and Yu Lan invited to enter the palace walls to treat the grand warden's sick bride, and Yen Shih automatically welcomed as a puppeteer, with me as assistant, and also arriving would be Li the Cat, and waiting for us would be the Snake, and I had a powerful premonition that the combination was going to be interesting.

9

The palace at Yen-men was a great gloomy place complete with a drawbridge and a moat, built to withstand sieges during the wars of the Three Kingdoms many centuries ago. I was interested to see that Master Li and Yu Lan looked the place over, came to some sort of unspoken agreement, and arranged to see the grand warden's sick wife immediately. When they emerged from the bedchamber Master Li said "Parasites?" and Yu Lan said, "Almost certainly." Then they closely questioned the lady's maids, following which they examined some ornamental ponds that were scattered here and there in the gardens. They prepared a vial of some odorous liquid and made sure that the sick woman drank it, and Master Li said, "That should do it."

"You mean that's all?" I asked.

Yu Lan looked at me with a faint smile tugging at her lovely lips, and Master Li laughed.

"Ox, in terms of conventional medicine the answer would be yes," he said. "In shamanistic terms we've barely begun, and I think you'll find the next two steps to the cure to be rather interesting."

That turned out to be an understatement, although I was disappointed at first when it seemed that I was excluded. They huddled with Yu Lan's father. Yen Shih rapidly wrote out a detailed script of some sort, adding a few suggestions of his own, and they announced that the warden's wife was being attacked by exceptionally vicious demons who were trying to steal her higher soul, and they set sunrise the following morning as the time for the decisive battle with the Agents of Darkness. I was told to collect a bag of rice and a sack of bees (I had no idea what they were for) and to ride out into the hills and gather huge amounts of poppies. Yen Shih let me help him fix various puppeteering equipment in the grand warden's audience chamber, but after that all I was allowed to do was play the drums, and I was forced to admit they were right. I would have lost my head and done something foolish if I'd been in a more responsible position, and in my defense I will offer the following description.

The Doctors and the Demons

SCENE: *The palace audience chamber at dawn; curtained, almost airless, heavily shadowed. Torches flank a table placed upon a dais at the end of the room, with heavy hangings on three sides. Incense burners send thick fragrant smoke into the air, and the smell of poppies is overpowering. A bat wobbles erratically through the air and collides with a burner, flaps upside down around the room, and lands on the floor—under the impression it is the ceiling—and clings to a chair leg, giggling. A drum begins a slow monotonous beat, and a parade of dignitaries led by the Grand Warden of Goose Gate enters. Silence, except for the drum. Coughing and shuffling of feet. More silence. More coughing and shuffling. The drum slows: da-dum, da-dum, da-dum . . . dum . . . dum . . . dum . . . Dead silence, then the grand warden and the dignitaries leap three feet into the air.*

VOICE FROM NOWHERE: Bring . . . the . . . afflicted . . . to . . . me . . .

Dignitaries leap aside to form a path as the grand warden's wife is carried in on a silken litter. She is a young woman, not bad-looking, powerfully built, with a commanding presence but clearly ill. The litter is carried up the steps to the dais and placed upon the table facing the audience. The carriers bow and back away through the side curtains. Silence.

VOICE FROM NOWHERE: The Demons of Sickness, in the days when they lived as men and women of this world, committed the 9,999 Offenses. For their sins they are linked to the Nine Darknesses. Their foul souls have fallen into the sufferings of the Thousand Ages, and to gain warmth and light they seek pure souls to serve as lantern and hearth in the Domain of Eternal Night. Ye who would steal the soul of this woman, I command thee, show thyselves!

Silence. Then a snickering sound is heard, malicious laughter, and points of bright light flicker in the shadows to the right of the litter. A child's face appears, but an evil child with teeth like those of a rat, and horrible eyes. More children appear until there are seven of them. They laugh as they approach the litter, menacingly.

VOICE FROM NOWHERE: The Hag of the Nine Hollow Hills sends her grandchildren, but fears to show herself? So be it.

A blinding flash of light is followed by a loud bang and a cloud of smoke, which clears to reveal Master Li standing to the left of the litter. He wears a tall winged hat covered with stars, indicating the path he takes when consulting the gods, and in his right hand is the Horse of Night he rides to visit the underworld. When not in use the horse takes the form of a cane with an iron horse head at the top and an iron hoof at the bottom. In his left hand is the Magic Tambourine: top side shows sunrise, two blackbirds, two horses, and the bear's tooth; bottom side shows the birch tree, two frogs, seven nests, seven maidens, and the Mother of Fire. His long white robe is covered with bells, dolls, bones, icons, and the twenty-

eight metal discs symbolizing the Palaces of the Moon. He levels his cane at the demons.

MASTER LI: In the name of the Supreme Born-of-Chaos Lord of the Tao of the Five Transcendents and Seven Luminaries, I bid thee begone!

The evil children laugh at the shaman. Their mouths gape wide, wider, impossibly wide, and great clouds of poisonous bees pour out and buzz in a deadly cloud toward Master Li. He opens his own mouth wide, and as bees buzz in he transforms them into grains of rice and spits them back out. More and more bees attack. Piles of rice cover the shaman's feet, but suddenly he must fight on two fronts at once because there is another blinding flash, another loud bang, another cloud of smoke, and beside the demon children stands the Hag of the Nine Hollow Hills. Her face is blue, her wings are black, her arms end in raptor's claws, and she hurls the poisoned arrows that form her feathers. Master Li catches arrows on the shield of his tambourine, but he cannot also defend the patient on the litter as the demons move closer.

MASTER LI: O Lady Immortal of the Mysterious Supreme, Flower of the Middle Original, Bearer of the Sword and Girdle of Supreme Purity, heed this cry of your servant and come in thy anger and glory!

A third flash, and a third bang, a third cloud of smoke, and Yu Lan stands behind the litter. She is absolutely breathtaking. Her hair is woven like a cloud over the silver tricorn Night Moon Crown in the Primal Daybreak, and then allowed to flow freely down her back like an ebony waterfall. Her cape of kingfisher feathers bears the Seven Sapphire Flowers. On her vermilion silk caftan is the Grand Ribbon of the Phoenix Pattern, and around her waist is the Fire Jade Girdle of the Six Mountains. Suspended in a silver scabbard is the Sword of Fluid Yellow and Pulsating Phosphors, and her boots are embroidered with the steeds she rides into shadows or sunlight: Blood Horse of Day, Pearl Horse of Night.

YU LAN: Back to your hole, Hag! No innocent soul shall light the blackness nor warm the bone-chill of the pit to which you were sent by the Celestial Venerable of the Sacred Jewel and Nine Breaths!

HAG OF THE NINE HOLLOW HILLS: O Winged Ones! Fanged Ones! Clawed Ones and Horned Ones! Fly to me! Fly! fly!

A horrible horde of demons with edged wings like swords and beaks and horns like spears shrieks down upon Master Li and Yu Lan, who counter with sword and iron cane, and the clash-clatter-clang-bang sounds like six simultaneous blacksmith conventions. The creatures swoop high out of range and then dive in sneak attacks, and Master Li holds out his cane at arm's length and shakes it as he shouts words in an unknown tongue, and suddenly a great horse is standing there. He leaps on its back as Yu Lan stamps her left boot and cries out in arcane language and lo! her foot is bare and the Blood Horse of Day receives her lithe leap. The shaman and the shamanka ride up into the air, and the battle rages overhead. Master Li's tambourine releases the carnivorous Horses and the terrible Bear, the eye-pecking Blackbirds and the poisonous Frogs. Yu Lan battles the demons swarming around her with the Sapphire Flowers that turn into blue tigers, the Grand Ribbon that becomes a dragon, and the Fire Jade Girdle that explodes with sheets of flame and bubbling lava.

HAG OF THE NINE HOLLOW HILLS: Fight, my lovely ones! Fight!

The Hag is wiser than her advice. She slips from the fray and swoops down toward the litter where the patient lies, and when she flies up and away she has something warm and shining in her claws. Master Li is routing the demons by reversing his tambourine to release the Trees, the Nests, the Maidens, and the Mother of Fire, and Yu Lan wheels her great horse around and sees the Hag. The shamanka jerks her tricorn crown free and hurls it, and it is the whole glorious moon that spins toward the Hag, who screeches in fear. The small shining light of a soul slips from her claws and flips and flops wildly away, and then disappears. Master

Li and Yu Lan pursue the Hag and the last of the demons, and then they too disappear, and their voices are heard here, there, and everywhere.

MASTER LI: O soul, come back!
In the east are giants a thousand fathoms tall,
And ten suns that melt metal and dissolve stone.

YU LAN: O soul, come back!
In the south the people have tattooed faces and
blackened teeth;
There coiling snakes devour men as sweet relish.

MASTER LI: O soul, come back!
In the west the Moving Sands stretch for leagues;
You will be swept into Thunder's Chasm and
dashed
to pieces,
And beyond lies a desert with red ants huge as elephants.

YU LAN: O soul, come back!
In the north is the Frozen Mountain of the Torch
Dragon,
Its eyes glaring red, with serrated teeth and wild
mad laughter,
And the sky is white and glittering and rigid with
cold.

MASTER LI: You cannot climb to Heaven above, O soul,
For leopards and tigers guard the gates,
And slant-eyed wolves pad to and fro.

YU LAN: You cannot descend to the Land of Darkness,
For there the monster lies, nine-coiled;

Three eyes has he in his tiger's head, and his body
is a bull's.

Smoke rises around the litter. When it clears Master Li and Yu Lan are
flanking the patient, heads and hands lifted toward the stars.

MASTER LI: O soul, we call to guide you, standing by your body
to lead you back in.
The quarters of the world are full of harm,
But here in your old abode are high halls and deep
chambers,
Stepped terraces, storied pavilions.
Warm breezes bend the melilotus, and set tall
orchids swaying,
Sending scents through chambers of polished stone
With ceilings and floors of vermilion.

YU LAN: Many a rare and precious thing awaits in your
chamber;
Braids and ribbons, brocades and satins,
Bedspreads of kingfisher feathers, seeded with
pearls,
While damask canopies stretch overhead
Lit by bright candles of orchid-perfumed fat.

MASTER LI: O soul, the food is ready.
Rice, broomcorn, early wheat mixed with millet,
Ribs of fatted ox, tender and succulent,
Stewed turtle and roast kid, served with sauce of
yams,
Geese cooked in sour and bitter, casseroled duck,
fried flesh of the great crane,
Braised chicken, tortoise seethed in soup of Wu,
Fried honey cakes and malt-sugar sweetmeats,

And jadelike wine, honey-flavored, fills your cup,
Strained of impurities, cool and refreshing.

A tiny twinkling light appears high overhead, in the deepest shadows of the vaulted ceiling.

YU LAN: Hear the musicians take their places, O soul,
Set up bells, fasten the drums, sing the latest popular songs:
"Crossing the River," "Gathering Caltrops," and "The Sunny Bank."
Dancers await you, attired in spotted leopard skins.
Bells clash in their swaying frames, the zither's strings are swept,
Pi-pas and lutes rise in wild harmonies, the sounding drum sonorously rolls.

The shining light glows larger and brighter as it sinks down toward the dais; Master Li and Yu Lan guide it to the liver of the grand warden's wife, who has been observing all this with eyes like soup bowls.

Your household awaits you, O soul!
MASTER LI ⎫ Lovers await you, O soul!
YU LAN ⎭ Life awaits you, O soul!
Come back! Come back! Come back!

The light disappears as the shaman and shamanka ease the soul back into the patient's liver. Master Li closes her eyelids and has her lie back and softly tells her to sleep. Yu Lan steps to the front of the dais and speaks in the general direction of the grand warden, while still maintaining the distance of the Mysteries.

YU LAN: The sickness is gone. Life and love await, but forget not the Tao. Take great care in your sacrifices and prayers, for evil influences seek to return where once they have sported, and to the Three Venerables should be offered nine lengths of green embroidered silk. The Servants of Wu ask nothing, being content with the thrill of battle and the joy of triumph. Return now to the red dust of the world.

Doors are flung open, and sunlight pours in, and the audience stumbles out. The litter is carried back to the lady's bedchamber, while poppy fumes carry their thick sweet fragrance toward the clouds.

I picked myself up from the floor (I was lying beside the giggling bat) and gasped deep lungfuls of fresh air. Yu Lan and Master Li were pouring pitchers of water over their heads, and Yen Shih descended from his perch on the rafters, grunting and gasping and practicing eye-focus as he stretched his arms and legs.

"That went rather well, considering we didn't have time for a decent rehearsal," said Master Li.

"I've seen worse," Yen Shih said.

Yu Lan, as was her habit, made no comment. She walked out past me: silent, graceful, distant as a drifting cloud, secretly smiling.

"You see, Ox," said Master Li some time later as we were walking through the palace gardens, "to a shaman the identification of a medical problem and its appropriate treatment is merely the beginning. In this case the problem was easy to identify. It was tadpoles."

"Tadpoles?" I said.

"Precisely," he said. "You've had a rather unfortunate encounter with the grand warden, so perhaps you can sympathize with his bride. She's a bandit chief's daughter, my boy, practically born on horseback and happy out in the hills where she grew up, and here she is in a gloomy pile of stones where she's supposed to spend her time sewing and gossiping with maids. On top of that it's her duty to present her husband with children, and one can imagine what she thinks of that shifty-eyed cowardly creature as the father."

Master Li stopped at one of the decorative ponds in a courtyard close to a high gray wall, where a balcony ran beneath tall windows.

"Tadpoles," he said, pointing down at the green water. "One of the oldest of old wives' tales holds that a woman who swallows fourteen live tadpoles on the third day after menstruation, and ten more on the fourth, will not conceive for five years, so the poor young woman has been swallowing the creatures. They're harmless. What isn't harmless is the parasitic flatworms that transfer from the tadpoles to the swallower's stomach and make her sick as a yellow monkey. Yu Lan and I gave the lady a powerful vermifuge and forbade tadpoles until further notice, and since she's basically as healthy as a horse she's already recovered in a physical sense."

He thoughtfully regarded the tadpoles, and reached into a pocket and took out a small vial with a stopper in it.

"That," he said, "is where conventional medicine stops and shamanism begins. What good is it to cure the body when the real damage is to the spirit? Think of the humiliation to a bandit chief's daughter forced to swallow tadpoles, the destruction to her self-esteem! So Yu Lan and I—with the invaluable assistance of Yen Shih—made the lady feel she was the most important person in the whole world as the forces of good and evil battled for her soul. The final step to the cure is eliminating the need for tadpoles, of course. She'll find the obvious solution to the problem of proper parenthood in due course, but no respectable shaman would take the chance of a relapse while she's figuring it out."

With that he removed the stopper from the vial and pulled out the front of my tunic and dumped a live scorpion down inside. Until an official disrobing contest is held in all the major provinces, the record belongs to me. I was out of my clothes and into the pond in three seconds flat.

"Wha-wha-wha—" I said, or something equally intelligent as I splashed scorpions away.

"Sorry, Ox. I assure you that I'd first removed the venom

from the thing, and I thought it would be funny. I must be farther on the road to senility than the Celestial Master is. Dear me, dear me," he said as he sauntered happily away.

The pool turned out to be less than two feet deep, so I was not in a modest position as I tried to untangle my clothes and get them back on, and while I was trying to squeeze my left foot into my right sandal a very elegant footman appeared and informed me my presence was demanded inside. He turned me over to a maid who did a great deal of giggling as she led me upstairs, and I was ushered through elegant doors into a luxurious bedchamber with tall windows opening to a narrow balcony that overlooked a shallow pool where tadpoles swam, frolicking through the thongs of my missing left sandal.

"Tee-hee!" said the warden's wife.

That wasn't really her style, so she dropped the coyness and crooked a commanding finger.

"Come here, you," growled the bandit chief's daughter.

I subsequently learned that nine months later she gave birth to a son (thirteen pounds eleven ounces) and chose the milk name Liu Niu. The assumption was that she was thinking of a minor deity called Liu-hai, so the milk name meant "Lucky Calf," but if she happened to be thinking of another minor deity called Liu-lang the milk name means "Sexy Ox," and I will leave it at that.

10

When I passed the tadpole pond again that night I had Master Li riding on my back, and this time I slipped silently behind bushes and then began to climb. Away from us, at the drawbridge, trumpets were blaring and soldiers were standing at attention. The sage had wanted to get the matter of the grand warden's wife out of the way before we got down to serious business, and the timing couldn't have been more perfect, because Li the Cat was just entering in a sedan chair decorated with imperial dragons, escorted by the elite Wolf Regiment.

The climb was ridiculously easy. The huge stones that formed the wall were set irregularly, giving all the foot- and handholds I needed, and it was possible to swing back and forth so I could reach the grand warden's private suite without once leaving the shelter of overhanging parapets and balconies. When I crawled up over the edge of the last balcony we could look through a window into the corridor and outer offices and see just where guards were stationed, and another window let us into the warden's private sanctuary.

"Why don't they hang out a sign: 'Rob Me!' " Master Li whispered disgustedly.

It got even better. There was a five-panel decorative screen in a shadowed area away from lamps and moonbeams, but still close to the low jade-covered conference table surrounded by silken sitting pillows, and a cabinet provided Master Li with a jar of excellent wine and me with a jar of the finest pickled seaweed I have ever tasted. We settled down to wait, and we didn't have to wait long. Within an hour the sounds of guards' boots clicking together and weapons being grounded announced the arrival of the grand warden, and it was only the warden and Li the Cat who entered, along with two servants, and when the servants had prepared a brazier and placed a pot on it for water to boil they bowed backward from the room and the door shut firmly behind them.

"I can't wait for the palate of a connoisseur to evaluate this batch," Li the Cat said unctuously. "To my taste it's an improvement of fifty percent, at least, but I don't pretend to be an expert."

"Neither do I. I'm just facile with experts' clichés," the grand warden said with a mock bow, and they both laughed heartily.

Li the Cat opened his money belt and extracted a small round object that seemed to have the imperial seal stamped on it. It was pale green with light purple shadings, and apparently as hard as a hunk of wood. Master Li's fingers dug into my shoulder.

"Ox, that's Tribute Tea," he whispered. "How in hell did that slimy eunuch qualify for Tribute Tea?"

The question was rhetorical, of course, so I said nothing. The eunuch shaved thin pieces from the little hard cake with a silver knife, and the grand warden used a silver pestle to powder the shavings in a silver mortar. With great ceremony they passed the powder three times through a silver sieve, and then poured equal amounts into two wide, shallow *chien* saucers. The water in the pot (actually it's not a pot but a "soup bottle") was boiling, and the grand warden carefully poured it into the chiens. They briskly stirred with bamboo whisks. At first the liquid was white, then it turned bluish gray, and then bluish gold, and the aroma that reached my nostrils was the delicious subtle scent of tea of the very highest quality. They bowed to each other and raised the saucers to their lips and sipped, and then the warden grimaced and spat the stuff into the fire.

"It still tastes like camel piss," he said petulantly.

"Well, I didn't claim perfection, and it really does taste better," the eunuch protested. "Try another sip, and don't expect miracles."

The grand warden cautiously tried again, and this time kept it down.

"All right, it is a bit better," he said grudgingly. "It still wouldn't fool a baby, however."

"Who's in the business of fooling babies? We're fooling barbarians," the eunuch said with a chuckle. "Look at the uncompressed leaves and tell me there's something wrong with *them!*"

He extended some tiny things from his money belt, which the warden viewed admiringly.

"Buddha, that's marvelous. You used the same batch?"

"Exactly, and some of the worst of it at that. We have the technique down perfectly, and I'm now guaranteeing a success rate of ninety-five percent. How are things going at your end?" Li the Cat asked.

"Four more barbarian kings have expressed strong interest; two of them are certain customers," the grand warden said briskly. "The real market would be Rome, of course, but sea routes are very risky and every caravan runs the risk of capture by aspiring princes, who might send the stuff back to China as *tribute.* Can you imagine?"

Li the Cat shuddered. "Don't even think about such things," he said. "Any change in the basic sales tale?"

The grand warden shrugged. "Why change it? We have to explain how we got the merchandise, and the story of bandits capturing caravans and then discovering the cargo was intended for the emperor can't really be improved upon. My recent marriage into a bandit clan provides authenticity, and it's easy to explain that my illustrious father-in-law can't dispose of his loot inside the boundaries of civilization, and has to turn to me for outside markets. Let's not gild something that's glowing."

That was when matters changed dramatically. The warden had taken out a large map and they were starting to discuss routes and new markets when a high and shrill, but rather pretty sound rang through the room. It was like the rapid tinkling of a small silver bell, and instantly both men were on their feet. The warden ran to the west wall and pulled aside a calligraphy scroll stretched on a bamboo frame, and behind it was the door of a safe. Then his back covered the view and I couldn't tell how he opened it, but when he turned again I had to suppress a loud exclamation. In his hands was an ancient cage, precisely like the other two, and the sound seemed to come from it. The warden trotted back to the table and set the cage down. Then I could see a tiny flickering light glowing in the center, pulsing to the bell sound, but the warden's shoulder blocked my view and I couldn't see what he was doing as he reached out to the front of the cage. The ringing of the bell stopped abruptly. The little glowing light expanded until it filled the cage, and then my eyes nearly popped from their sockets. Human features were forming inside the bars, and they resolved themselves into the face of a senior mandarin I had seen at the funeral of Ma Tuan Lin! Master Li's fingers were digging into my shoulder like knives, and wrinkles had screwed up so tightly around his eyes I wondered how he could see. Then the mouth of the mandarin opened, and we heard his voice as though he were right there in the room.

"Esteemed colleagues, an incredible development has taken place! Incredible!" he said so excitedly he was spraying spittle, and he made a visible effort to calm down. "All our hopes and dreams, the ultimate goals we have aspired to but despaired of attaining, may be in our grasp! I would never be believed should I explain it myself, and I am honored, I am awed, I am exalted to bring you the message from the source. Further introduction would be gross impertinence."

His image wavered and dissolved like a cloud breaking apart, and then the pieces began to re-form, and I smothered a yelp as an unmistakable face filled the cage. It was the Celestial Master.

"So you're the colleagues of this creature, eh?" the saint said softly. His face flushed and his voice raised to a roar. "You doltish donkeys! You emasculated earwigs! You idiotic apes whose sole talent is to make dinners of your own defecation! Stick the turd-stained tips of your fingers into your ears and dig out the dung beetles, because I am about to demonstrate the error of your half-witted ways!"

The grand warden was transfixed, but unfortunately Li the Cat was not. He was clawing at the warden's arm and pointing urgently at the door, and the warden grasped the simple fact that palaces breed eavesdroppers the way granaries breed rats, and he picked up the cage and ran with the eunuch to the south wall. They opened a small door and dove through, and the Celestial Master's furious roars abruptly stopped when the door slammed shut.

Master Li supplied corrosive words of his own as he bolted from behind the screen and ran to the door. It wouldn't budge, and when I bent down and peered through a tiny crack I could see that lock picks wouldn't be of any use. There was a heavy bar rammed through slots on the other side, and the only thing that would help would be a battering ram.

"We have to hear what the Celestial Master is up to," Master Li said grimly. "He's been too long away from the grimy affairs of the world, and he doesn't really understand how dangerous it is to try to trick men who stand to suffer the Thousand Cuts if they're caught. Ox, go back out the window."

He jumped up on my back and I vaulted out over the balcony and down the wall until we reached the level of the formal reception hall, which was really like a throne room with the grand warden's high gilded chair raised on a small dais that extended from the central tower. I haven't mentioned that the castle was constructed in the style called Pine Tree, with a stone tower in the center supporting floor beams that arched like branches to the outer walls.

"Ox, the passage they took seemed to lead in toward the tower, and almost all Pine Tree palaces use the tower for secret conference rooms, as well as the central source of light and air," the sage said.

He had me climb inside and race to the dais and pull tapestries aside on the wall behind the warden's chair. I found what he expected behind the third tapestry: a small lacquered door that opened to reveal a staircase winding up inside the circular walls. I took the steps two at a time, trusting that the Celestial Master would still be roaring loud enough to drown out the sound of sandals clattering over stone, but when we reached the level of the warden's office we found not one secret room, but two, and to reach the second we had to pass through the first. I sensed disaster the moment Master Li slipped down from my back and opened a gold-embossed door. He pointed ahead at a second gold-embossed door across from us and whispered, "If my orientation is right, they should be in there." I thought I could hear a faint voice that might belong to the Celestial Master, but I was more interested in the territory we would have to cross to reach it.

We had stepped upon an ermine carpet about four inches thick. The walls of the room were covered with velvet, and the centerpiece was an immense bed draped in satin, and all over the place were flattering portraits of the same creature. They were portraits of the Snake, and I was not in a mood to compliment the warden on his cleverness at placing both conference room and catamite within easy reach of his office. I gulped noisily and tried to pretend I was invisible as I tiptoed over that carpet behind Master Li, but it didn't do me any good.

I stepped past a dragon screen and was instantly hit by a flying tree trunk, or something that felt like it. I think I may have still been sailing through the air when the Snake picked up Master Li and neatly stuffed him down inside an immense malachite urn. The velvet on the wall cushioned the crash as I hit it, and I picked myself up from ermine and dove toward a reptile who was making happy hissing sounds. Since I was being kind enough to lead with my head he kicked my chin from his left sandal to his right sandal and back to the left again, rather like playing with a child's bouncing ball, and as I hit the carpet I saw a strange rictus tug at his face. The Snake was smiling at good little Number Ten Ox who had come to entertain him by dying very slowly. The chop of the side of his hand was almost friendly, not hard enough to snap my neck in half. I managed to roll over and kick feebly, and it was clearer than ever that the Snake was playing with me when he let me regain my feet.

Behind him a wrinkled old hand had lifted from the mouth of the urn, holding a throwing knife. Master Li could move his arm only a few inches, so a throw was out of the question, but he could try to give it to me. The problem was getting past the Snake to reach it. All I could do was charge and pray, and I almost managed to lift him and spin him around. Unfortunately I was making him angry, and he hissed at me and stopped playing. The Snake's arms whipped up inside mine and broke my grip effortlessly, and then it was his turn. He wrapped me in a constrictor's embrace, squeezing with power that would turn my bones to jelly, and while I still had breath I gasped, "Throw! Throw!"

I'd hoped for a distraction, and I got it. Master Li flipped the knife as well as he could, and it made one slow revolution in the air before it reached the Snake's back. It must have felt like the bite of an ant. He glanced behind him and saw the extended hand, and he was not pleased. Hissing rather loudly, he tried to get his balance to aim a full-force kick and see which would break into more pieces, the urn or the old man, and in the process he lessened pressure on me. I jerked back with everything I had and broke free, and then I grabbed his waist and almost snapped my spine as I lifted. His feet were clear of the carpet. I only had enough strength for one desperate move, and all I could do was try to bring his spine down on the sharp edge of a large marble table. I gave it all I had, but it wasn't enough. I knew I'd missed the moment I started the downward toss, and his back missed the edge and landed on the smooth flat surface. His cold reptilian eyes were staring straight at me, and there was no force left in my arm as I tried to chop his neck. The eyes didn't even bother to blink. My legs were numb, and I helplessly held to him as I began sliding backward, and the eyes moved with me, cold, hard, without any emotion whatsoever, and then I fell to the floor and the Snake fell beside me.

He was lying on his side with his motionless reptile eyes still fixed on mine, and I finally realized I was staring at a minor miracle. Master Li's knife had stuck to him by no more than a fold of cloth and a tiny pinch of flesh, flopping harmlessly back and forth, but somehow it had flopped into exactly the right position as he descended to the tabletop. It had been driven into his back right up to the top of the handle, directly into his heart, and the Snake was stone-cold dead.

11

Master Li's eyes were incredulous as I peered down into the urn. "You're alive?"

"Sir," I said, "does any deity owe us a favor? If not, we'll have to go into bankruptcy buying incense for the pantheon."

I got him out without smashing the urn and he was able to hobble around quite well after I massaged his legs. He looked at the body of the Snake and shook his head wonderingly when I told what had happened, and then he pointed out a nasty aspect I hadn't got around to considering.

"There's no way this wound in the back can be made to look like an accident," he said. "We're faced with unpleasant complications no matter what, but the first step is a necessity. We have to make the corpse disappear."

I opened my mouth one or two times to make suggestions and then closed it again. The grand warden was going to pull apart the castle stone by stone, if need be, dig up every inch of dirt, drain the moat, and send divers down the wells, and when Master Li said we had to make the Snake disappear he meant *disappear*.

"Step one is to get him out of this revolting love nest, and that, at least, is easy," the old man said decisively.

I made two trips back down the stairs and then down the outer wall to the garden, one carrying Master Li and the other carrying the Snake. The corpse fit into a large wheelbarrow (an invention I have explained to barbarians in a previous memoir) and some burlap from manure sacks covered it. Then Master Li sprawled comfortably on top and I wheeled him out and past the guards while he hiccuped and waved his wine flask and sang bawdy songs, and the captain of the guards did no more than bow. After a battle like the one the old shaman had put on to save the grand warden's wife he was supposed to get stinking drunk, and nobody dreamed of interfering. I wheeled him to the puppeteer's wagon and left the wheelbarrow outside with the covered corpse still in it, certain that nobody was going to get close to the old man's conveyance. Nothing is more dangerous than a drunken shaman. Yen Shih greeted us inside, which had very little space despite the size of the wagon because every inch was filled with puppeteering gear.

"We have a problem," said Master Li.

Yen Shih raised an eyebrow.

"There's a corpse in that wheelbarrow," said Master Li.

Yen Shih raised the other eyebrow.

"The corpse is that of the snakelike creature who damn near killed Ox, and we have to assume the grand warden will search every drop of water and mote of dust until he finds the son of a serpent," said Master Li.

Yen Shih nodded.

"I have precisely two ideas at the moment," Master Li said. "The first is to disguise the corpse as one of your larger mannequins."

Yen Shih pointed out at the moon and made revolving motions, indicating time passing, and then held his nose, indicating a bad smell.

"The second is to find some way to explain how a tiger managed to get past the moat and walls and eat the bastard," said Master Li.

Yen Shih shrugged his shoulders and spread his hands apart
—how?

"We shall think," Master Li said, and his wrinkles contracted
while Yen Shih gazed up at the canvas roof and hummed. Then
he stopped humming.

"Tomorrow," the puppeteer said slowly, "the Grand Warden
of Goose Gate has scheduled a great feast in honor of his wife's
recovery."

"At which a tiger will eat the Snake?" said Master Li.

"At which the Grand Warden of Goose Gate will eat the
Snake," said Yen Shih.

I thought that was weak humor, but Master Li didn't. In fact,
he was regarding the puppeteer with vast admiration.

"My friend, you're a genius!" he cried.

"But he isn't being serious," I said. Then I looked at Yen Shih,
and back to Master Li, and back to Yen Shih. "Are you?" I asked
weakly.

I don't want to describe what happened next but I have no
choice if I am to provide honest accounts of the cases of Master
Li, so I will include a detail that will make me look even more
foolish than usual. Throughout the next horrible hours my mind
insisted upon clinging to a totally irrelevant image. An image I
had acquired in the very first scene with which I began this
narrative, and I haven't the slightest idea why it popped back up
to lodge like a barnacle on my brain, but there it was. I kept
seeing a despicable barbarian with a face of stone and eyes like
icicles, squatting in squalor and scratching for lice in a place
called the Sabine Hills, dipping his brush in viper venom to send
his idiotic criticism all the way to China.

"All right, Flaccus," I said silently as I wheeled a huge load of
fresh vegetables to the castle kitchens, "what would you have
me do? Pretend there isn't a corpse beneath the turnips, because
corpses are excessively melodramatic? Bah, friend Flaccus! Bah!
Bah! Bah!"

A great castle always has a small separate kitchen for the

preparation of ceremonial dishes to be offered to ghosts or gods, and it was to be expected that a shaman would wish to offer to the gods who had aided him and invite his esteemed host to share the feast. Master Li had no difficulty commandeering the place, and in a few minutes he and Yen Shih had the corpse stretched out on the kitchen table and were cutting the clothes away. To tell the truth, I still didn't truly believe this was happening.

"Ox, would you see if they have any pigs' feet jelly?" the puppeteer asked. He turned to Master Li. "It seems to me that the thighs might best be marinated in a broth of pigs' feet mixed with honey and the lees of wine, and then baked inside a crust formed of the marinade thickened with peanut paste."

"A connoisseur!" said Master Li.

"Gllgghh!" I said.

"Ox, while you're at it, see if they have any pickled jellyfish skins!" Master Li called after me as I lurched into the larder. "I've discovered they go marvelously with bears' paws," he continued to Yen Shih. "Bears' paws taste to me like sixty percent glue, so jellyfish skins might be a good accompaniment to glutinous parts, like the soles of this bastard's feet, and perhaps the spermatic cords."

"Gllgghh!" I said.

One of the shelves yielded the pigs' feet, and in a cabinet I found a jar of jellyfish skins. When I started back toward the table Master Li was preparing to remove the top of the corpse's head with a saw, and Yen Shih was measuring fibula and tibia for ax strokes.

"You see, Flaccus, there is more to this world than the uncivilized can possibly imagine," I silently said. "For example—"

Whack! Whack! Whack!

"Gllgghh!"

"Yen Shih, shall we do the brains in a traditional turnip sauce, or would you prefer oyster broth?" Master Li shouted over the sound of the puppeteer's ax.

"You know, I rather favor poaching brains in coconut milk, if Ox can find any," Yen Shih said thoughtfully.

"Brilliant!" Master Li said admiringly. "Ox, see if they have any coconuts, and do you know why our erudite friend made the suggestion? Once upon a time, so the story goes, the great king of Nam Viet was stabbed by assassins, and he realized he was dying, so he pulled off his head and stuck it on a tree as his final gift to the people. The head turned into the coconut, and because the king was drunk at the time the fluid inside it is the most easily fermentable stuff on earth."

Riiiiip! Riiiiip!

"Gllgghh!" I said.

"I shall again seek your invaluable advice before possibly ruining something," said Master Li. "Shall we keep the tongue whole, possibly baked inside a crust of walnut paste, or should we slice and sauté it with butter and garlic?"

"I'm a butter-and-garlic man" the puppeteer said. "Why don't we save the walnut paste for broiling the bastard's balls?"

"Splendid," said Master Li.

"Gllgghh!" I said.

Whack! Riiiip! Whack! Riiiip!

"Ox, would you extract the marrow from these?"

"Gllgghh-gllgghh-gllgghh!" I said.

"Don't bother, I'll do it. How about a casserole of toes and ears?"

"Maybe with breast meat added," Master Li said. "Stewed slowly with bean curd, fagara, red peppers, and a lot of mushrooms added at the end."

"Sounds marvelous," said Yen Shih. "We have time to make a few sausages, don't we?"

"Oh, certainly. Here, let's see what his intestines look like."

"Gllgghh!" I said.

"Ox, look for some of that mustard from the south that goes so well with sausages!" Yen Shih called out. "I once knew a fellow named Meng Kuan who claimed he bought mustard of Tan and took it home and forgot about it," he said to Master Li. "The stuff began to grow, and it sprouted a torso, a head, a tail, and four legs, and Meng Kuan swears it bit him and galloped out the door and he never saw it again."

"What was he drinking?"

"Paint remover, I assume. Speaking of which, is there some way we can disguise the features, yet leave it intact, and serve the grand warden crisp fried face of boyfriend?"

"Gllgghh!" I said.

I staggered back with mustard and a coconut. "You see, Flaccus," I silently said, "there are times when gentlemen must engage in activities which they normally—"

"Will you look at this fellow's kidneys and pancreas!"

"Gorgeous! And the liver!

"Eggplant! Ox, we must have eggplant, tomatoes, onions, green peppers, and at least two kinds of squash!"

I dumped bones into cauldrons and boiled them for the broth, and then I pulverized them into a coarse gray powder that I mixed with meal and molasses to make tiny balls, and leaned from the far window and tossed the balls into the moat and watched fish snap at them. The Snake's clothing went up in flames. His unburnable possessions were melted beyond recognition before joining the bone balls, and drifted down through the water to the accompaniment of piscine burps and belches. Not a trace of the creature remained, except for the succession of splendid dishes that were carried to the grand warden's table the following evening at the banquet. I lacked the social status to receive an invitation, of course, and so did Yen Shih, but Master Li and Yu Lan were guests of honor, and it was a great comfort for me to know that Yu Lan never ate meat. Master Li could eat anything, including "Twelve-Treasure Five-Taste Herb-Honeyed Unicorn," which was served to the grand warden as the dish of distinction. (Yen Shih and Master Li had boiled the Snake's buttocks in an infusion of hibiscus petals, and I had to admit it gave them a lovely shade of blushing pink.) As I said, I didn't attend, but I did hear satisfied comments from departing guests, including the assessment of two very exalted prelates.

"A bit rich for my taste, but quite well done," said the High Priest of Yen-men, and his Confucian counterpart put the seal on it.

"Singularly succulent comestibles."

"Gllgghh," I said.

12

Master Li pleaded exhaustion, as did Yu Lan, and both excused themselves before the banquet ended in boring speeches. Yu Lan slipped away and put on boy's clothes for quick movement and blackened her face and hands with soot. She was preparing to help her father, and Master Li and I were perched on a small parapet on the castle wall looking down at the courtyard and the grand warden's chair in front of Yen Shih's wagon. The grand warden had not been able to pay proper attention to his food, Master Li told me, since he kept getting reports from search parties scouring the castle for the Snake, and it shouldn't be long before he'd get anxious enough to lead a party himself. That, said the sage, would give us our chance.

"Ox, we must get our hands on the warden's cage," Master Li said urgently. "Those incredible things can apparently project images and sounds across half of China, perhaps even farther, and if we can figure out how they work we may be able to contact the Celestial Master in time to prevent him from getting his throat cut."

"Would they dare?" I said in a shocked voice.

"From the excited words of the mandarin whose face first appeared, it's almost certain that the Celestial Master is playing some sort of game to lead them into indiscretion, but I doubt that he grasps the danger," he said grimly. "Mandarins in danger of losing money will do anything, and in this case they're also threatened with losing their hides."

I thought of people like Li the Cat and his servants Hog and Hyena and Jackal closing like rabid rats around the saintly old gentleman, and I shivered.

"Venerable Sir, have you ever heard of anything like those amazing cages?" I asked.

He chewed his scraggly beard thoughtfully.

"Not exactly," he said. "Su O in his *Tu Yang Tsa Pien* describes the Mirror of the Immortals he saw in the country of Lin. He said it was a crystal used by physicians, and when a patient stood in front of it he became transparent, so the physician could examine the internal organs or find cracks in bones. Su O is not the most reliable of witnesses, of course, but in this case his story has been confirmed by a reputable source, the *Hsi Ching Tsa Chi*, which repeats the description with the additional information that the crystal is four feet wide and five feet nine inches tall. Su O also asserts there are smaller portable versions called Discerning Pearls, and that's as close to the cages as I can get. It seems to me that the operating principle of the one shouldn't be much different from that of the other, although I could be totally wrong."

I said we were looking down at the courtyard and Yen Shih's wagon, in front of which the banqueters were gathered, but I haven't yet described the wagon in detail. It was huge, and one whole side could be lowered to form a stage with sliding extensions to make it even larger. The canvas top also extended, and a loft ran from one end of the stage to the other. There Yen Shih practiced a craft that approached magic. The loft was a maze of wires and strings and gears and wheels and pulleys and pendulums, and the puppeteer leaped and bounded across bamboo rafters with the agility of a cat as one hand spun this and pulled that, and the other hand manipulated a tangle of wires so fine they were nearly invisible, and below on the stage the lead puppet soared in the leaps and whirls of the Dragon Dance while an entire chorus of puppets pirouetted in the background. (It is literally true that a deranged duke once had Yen Shih arrested for devising a puppet so lifelike it seduced Lady Wu, and only the intercession of the duke's mother prevented a great scandal.) A battery of bamboo tubes led down to various parts of the stage, through which the puppeteer projected the voices of the characters. In complicated plays Yu Lan would help out from below, hidden behind a screen, providing female and children's voices and manipulating scenery. Backdrops were painted on canvas panels that could be revolved to give four different views, and Yu Lan could do wonderful things with lanterns.

Master Li told me quite seriously that Yen Shih was the greatest puppeteer he had ever seen, and possibly the greatest who ever lived. I mention this in a fit of self-pity. This was the climax of the evening, and Yen Shih was to perform his masterpiece, and I was going to miss it.

A clash of cymbals brought a great cheer from the audience, and the curtains of the brightly lit stage pulled apart to reveal a famous set: the combined house and yamen of Magistrate Po on the left and the town brothel, Mother Hsien's House of Joy, on the right. An even louder cheer greeted the first two puppets, Fu-mo (straight man) and Fu-ching (comic), who would warm up the audience before joining the play as major characters. They traditionally swap fast lines that satirize local dignitaries and lampoon current scandals, uttering howls of mock outrage at each sally and bashing each other over the head with pig bladders. Much of the dialogue that drifted up to us meant nothing to me, but roars of laughter from the audience indicated that Yen Shih had done his homework. Then Fu-mo and Fu-ching began establishing their own characters, bemoaning the fact that suspicious householders were resorting to locks and barred doors and fierce guard dogs, and gamekeepers were making poaching a dangerous occupation, and there were practically no purses to pick, and it had been a month since an easily fleeced simpleton had come to town. While this was going on I was trying to put a spell on the grand warden.

"Stay, stay," I said silently. "Watch all of it before you start searching."

Yu Lan was strumming the pi-pa chords, and tears filled my eyes when I heard the first lines of the most famous song in the civilized world, sung in a peasant accent so pure it practically reeked of mud and manure.

> *"I be a farmer, and damn proud of it,*
> *For soft city slickers I don't give a shit.*
> *Don't want to hear no opera star a-squawkin' through a role,*
> *When I can listen to the toads back at my water hole!"*

The voice was followed by the singer, and I actually began to cry when I saw the puppet. It was a rustic so close to the simple soil that he was barely one step up from a water buffalo. Every in-flection, every slap of a sandal, every scratch at hair lice, every coarse gesture was so perfect that for a moment I could have sworn I was back in my beloved village, and homesickness swept over me like heavy surf. He carried the pig he was taking to market, and Fu-mo and Fu-ching were so stunned by this gift of the gods that they toppled over backward.

The incredibly complex plot of *Hayseed Hong* deals with the peasant's efforts to regain his pig from the two crooks, and in the process Yen Shih would use every puppet he had. I was settling back happily to watch when Master Li jabbed my ribs.

"Let's go," he said.

The grand warden, curse him, had left his chair and collected his bodyguards and was striding toward us, and I could do noth-ing but bend over so Master Li could climb on my back, and then I had to move around the corner of the parapet and lose sight of the greatest of all puppet plays performed by the greatest of puppeteers. Life can be very unfair.

The grand warden and his search party pounded down corridors and through rooms and closets while we followed their progress on the balconies outside. The damn place had more chambers than an anthill and it was slow going, but we had to be absolutely sure that we would be undisturbed when we went for the cage. The maddening thing from my point of view was that we kept crossing balconies with views of the wagon below. I would see scraps of action, as when Fu-mo and Fu-ching bought Hayseed Hong's prize pig with a rare priceless diamond from the frozen north (Hayseed Hong, from the south, had never before seen a piece of ice), and then I had to move, and when I again got a glimpse of the stage the country bumpkin was on his way home and had decided to take out his diamond and admire it.

"Sheeeeeee-ut! The son of a bitch done pissed in my pocket and run away!"

Then I had to move away again, missing the part where the crooks greet the returning peasant with drugged wine and make off with all his clothes, and I just got a glimpse of Hayseed Hong as he toppled through a window into the bedchamber of the wife of Magistrate Po.

"Help! I am assaulted by a naked fiend!"

Magistrate Po, at another window, was admiring the moon in suitably Neo-Confucian fashion.

"Will you be quiet, woman? The superior man does not perceive lewd sounds or indecent spectacles."

Then I was out of sight and sound again, and around another tower, and then back to the glow of stage light.

"I am assaulted by a naked fiend who is not entirely bad-looking!"

"Woman, I must have quiet! The ears of the superior man are undefiled by unpleasant sounds, just as his kidneys and liver are purged of laziness and negligence, falsehood and depravity."

The grand warden had vanished, and I had to crawl through a window and tiptoe down hallways until we found him again. Then I had to race back and dive out to another balcony before his men could see us.

"I am assaulted by a naked fiend who is not entirely bad-looking and who appears to be hung like a horse!"

"Silence, woman! The superior man listens only to the correct chants, accompanied by flute and zither, so that the splendor of his complete virtue shall make the four seasons revolve in harmony and establish the right order of all things."

That was when one of those accidents that cause people to tie rocks around their necks and jump into wells occurred. The grand warden had disappeared again, and again I climbed through a window after him. When we spotted him he was just leading his men into the reception room, and Master Li grunted happily when he saw him open the door behind his thronelike chair and lead his men up the stairs. Now all we had to do was climb up outside his private quarters and wait for him to come in through the door that led from the central tower. Once he left we'd know he was through searching the areas we wanted. Master Li would have time to get that safe open, and if the cage wasn't there we'd be almost sure to find it in the conference room in the tower. I climbed out a side window to a small parapet divided by a large clay drainpipe, and eased around the drainpipe and started toward another window, and I just managed to jump back into dark shadows beside the pipe when a soldier stuck his head out and leaned his elbows on the sill. He wasn't looking in my direction, but I couldn't move an inch so long as he stayed there.

"Of all the goddamn luck," he growled.

"Why complain? It's the kind of luck we always have, damn it to hell," a second voice snarled, and another soldier stuck his head out beside the first.

"You'd think that once, just once, we'd get guard duty on the good side," the first one said. "Can you imagine? Here we are looking at the moon, and what are the guys on duty on the other side looking at? *Hayseed Hong*, that's what, and we can't even hear it."

"So what? We'll hear *about* it, won't we? Over and over, everybody saying it was the greatest goddamn thing ever." The second soldier spat disgustedly, and then reached into his tunic. "Here. We deserve it."

I groaned inwardly. He had a goatskin wine flask in his hand, and it was a fair-size one, and if they decided to keep on leaning on that windowsill in the moonlight . . .

They did, and there we stayed, and it seemed as though hours passed. The moon was moving in the wrong direction, and the shadow from the drainpipe was getting narrower and narrower, and when I looked down I found I couldn't get my sandals out of a small streak of pearl-white light. A few more minutes and Master Li was going to be faced with a very hard decision, because the only sure way to deal with the soldiers if they saw us would be to kill them. Fortunately he didn't have to do anything drastic. Relief made his voice tremble when they finally pitched the flask away and walked back through the room to the corridor.

"Let's go," he whispered. "If the safe has a simple lock we may still have time."

I hurried as fast as I could, and when I got back around to the south side a gale of laughter nearly knocked me off the wall. Looking down, I could see the wagon clearly, and the stage, and I realized we'd arrived toward the end of the first half of the play. *Hayseed Hong* is quite long and is broken into two parts with an intermission to allow the puppeteer to rest. The end of part one may well be the most famous scene in theater, and there isn't one line of dialogue even though it takes up a third of the first half.

The scene has shifted to Mother Hsien's House of Joy, where Fu-mo and Fu-ching have taken the stolen pig. Magistrate Po, who has run out of Confucian clichés long enough to grasp that something is going on with his wife, has arrived to search for her. She is pursuing Hayseed Hong, who is pursuing his pig, and the action takes place in a long corridor lined with doors on both sides.

Magistrate Po bends and peers through a keyhole. He recoils in horror, forearm across brow, other hand outflung, and as he does so another door opens behind him and Fu-mo and Fu-ching dash out carrying the pig. They race across the corridor and dive through the opposite door, and Magistrate Po bends to the next keyhole. From the room the crooks just left comes Hayseed Hong, pursued by the magistrate's wife, followed by a customer who happens to be a pious bonze and is accompanied by a lovely young lady known as the Little Lost Chicken. Nobody has any clothes on, and the last two stand staring in the corridor with eyes like saucers while Hayseed and the lady dive through the opposite door. Magistrate Po recoils from his keyhole, forearm covering shocked eyes, and behind him a door opens and out they come, the crooks, the pig, Hayseed, and the magistrate's wife, followed by a pious Tao-shih and a young lady expeditiously named P'o-shen ("To Be Deflowered") who have no clothes on and whose eyes are like saucers. Customers and ladies remain in the hall while the magistrate bends to keyholes, and doors open and close, and people race back and forth, and gradually the corridor of Mother Hsien's House of Joy fills with every pompous, preaching, self-righteous type of gentleman in the empire, all of whom have no clothes on (except for identifying caps or hats), and all of whom will eventually join the chase for Hayseed Hong's pig.

I wanted to describe that scene with a bit of detail in order to explain the noise that hit us on the wall, bouncing back and forth from towers so we got echoes as well: laughter mixed with howls of recognition, and jeers and catcalls. It wasn't until I had climbed almost to the level of the grand warden's quarters that we could hear a different sort of sound, and even then it took a while to realize the screams weren't screams of laughter. Master Li sharply squeezed my shoulder, and I grabbed a pair of balusters and hauled us up so we could peer over the balcony through the tall window into the room where we had eavesdropped on Li the Cat. Just as I did so the grand warden came running right at us, but he didn't see us. His eyes were glazed with shock and terror, and he was screaming his head off, and I gulped hard when I saw what was following him.

Second of the sketches of demon-deities the Celestial Master had shown us had been *Chu-K'uang,* "mad dog," which had been depicted as a dog with no head, and here it was. The grand warden turned at the last moment and raced back into the room, and as the stalking beast turned to follow I got a close look. The head hadn't been cut off. Hair grew smoothly over a strong thick neck that ended in nothing. It was as though it had been born with no head, yet I was clearly hearing barking. How could it bark with no head?

For that matter, how could it bite and chew and rip and rend with no head? When I raised up a bit higher I could see farther into the room, and I was looking at the remains of the grand warden's bodyguards, who looked as though a tiger had ripped them to pieces. Blood was everywhere, lakes of it, and most of the dead men seemed to have had their throats ripped out. The barking was louder. The headless creature wasn't chasing the grand warden, I suddenly realized, it was *herding* the grand warden, and it backed him against long thick curtains at another window, and the curtains pulled apart. I stared at a disembodied dog head, huge, mouth gaping, teeth dripping red, and then the head lunged and the teeth snapped together and the Grand Warden of Goose Gate departed the red dust of earth, very messily.

Something else was in the room. A dark shape was standing at the far window. It stepped into moonlight as it reached the sill, and it turned and looked right at us. Once more we were gazing at a creature that was half man and half ape, grotesque but unquestionably real, with a silver-gray forehead and bright blue cheeks and a crimson nose and a yellow chin. In its hand was the cage Master Li so badly wanted, and with one smooth movement it was over the windowsill and down the wall and gone.

A bright flash blinded me. My eyes slowly cleared, and I

gazed around and there was no dog's body, and there was no dog's head, and howls of laughter were lifting to the sky where a great white crane was slowly flying away across the face of the moon.

13

Master Li had me haul him up over the balustrade and then he slipped down from my back and walked into the room, avoiding the blood as much as possible.

"Sir, the cage is already gone!" I said urgently. It felt strange to shout when I wanted to whisper, but the laughter from the courtyard below made whispering useless. "I can't possibly catch that creature! It goes down walls as fast as I can run on a flat field, and how can I fly up and catch a crane?"

"Ox, stop driveling," he snapped. "I know the cage is gone, but we're damn well going to get something out of this!"

He looked this way and that, standing on a dry patch of floor that remained like a narrow island in a sea of thick gooey red, and then he turned and pointed.

"Get those curtains. Spread them across the floor to the conference table so we won't leave sandal prints."

"Yes, sir."

I did as I was told, and the old man walked over a path of green damask dragons that looked quite pretty with the crimson background, silver moonbeams, and golden candlelight. At the low jade-patterned table he searched beneath the end where the tea brazier stood, examining every inch of the thick fur rug, and then he picked up some tiny things and grunted in satisfaction.

"When the bell sound announced a message coming from the cage, the grand warden and Li the Cat jumped like rabbits," he said. "I was almost sure the warden dropped something, and he did. Praise the gods for sloppy cleaning maids."

He had some shavings from that cake of tea and one of the uncompressed leaves, and he put them in a compartment of his money belt. His wrinkles were squeezing so tightly around his eyes that they resembled the pattern on the ball of one's thumb seen through the lens of a Fire Pearl, and as usual he was considering problems I wouldn't even see until it was too late to do anything about them.

"Murder is not easily dismissed if the victim is Grand Warden of Goose Gate," he said, thinking aloud. "Li the Cat won't be a problem. The slayings are grotesque and the cage is gone. He knows very well that two other mandarin accomplices have been impossibly murdered and robbed of cages, and his first instinct should be to get the hell out and hurry home and see that nothing weird is taking place with his own cage, or with the other members of the plot. The problem will be the senior members of the grand warden's staff, who must prove they're faithful and efficient if they hope for future appointment. They'll launch an investigation that will hold us here three months, and if we escape before the bodies are found they'll charge us with murder and send the whole army in pursuit."

The wrinkles squeezed tighter, and then relaxed as he came to a decision. He pointed and said, "It will have to be a tiger after all. Get that, and keep your sandals out of the blood."

The walls were partially covered with animal skins. One of them was from a large tiger, complete with head and paws, and the old man had me take it down and neatly cut off the paws, and then hang it back up so the mutilation was as unobtrusive as possible.

"Nobody looks closely at such things. The upper classes say,

'Ah, a tiger skin,' and leave it at that, and for every servant who says, 'Didn't that thing have paws?' there'll be two who'll say, 'You're crazy,'" Master Li said confidently.

He spread curtains until he had a path to the little door that led to the central tower, and he breathed a long sigh of relief to find the door unbarred on the inside and easily opened with a lock pick.

"Ox, dip those paws in blood and give us the clear tracks of a homicidal feline," he ordered. "Make it look as though the tiger ripped the curtains down while chasing men around the room, and plant prints over them. Don't forget bloody prints on the corpses, and work your way backward to this door. I'll return as fast as possible."

So I did as I was told, all the while wondering how on earth he planned to get away with it. Tigers don't swim moats and climb sheer stone walls and make their way through crowded courtyards and palaces, but I knew better than to say it was impossible. If Master Li thought it could be done, it could be done. I was able to cheer myself up with that thought, but I wouldn't then have believed how easy it was going to be and what an extraordinary turn of luck would come with it.

I was just admiring my handiwork when the little door to the central tower opened and there stood Master Li, as I expected, and someone else I most certainly did not expect. The old man had brought the bandit chief's daughter. She had not been considered well enough to attend a play that might last more than three hours, and her eyes widened as she saw the carnage. Then she hissed and reached into her robe and whipped out a very efficient-looking dagger, and the next thing I knew the point was pressed to my throat.

"Playmates should not be presumptuous," she snarled. "I granted you a few minutes in bed, not a claim to be warden of Yen-men!"

"Lady, great lady, Ox is strong but not *this* strong," Master Li said soothingly. "A monster who happens to be a friend of ours lost his temper, not Ox, and we thought it might be a good idea to blame it on a tiger. Pretty paw prints, aren't they?"

The point left my throat, but not very far. The widow's eyes were warily fixed on Master Li.

"It seemed to me, my lady, that a tiger would be useful in more ways than one," Master Li continued. "While treating you I have seen your amulet. You were born in the Year of the Tiger, and the gods are not necessarily subtle when they choose to make their will clear. Very possibly they wish you to wed another and breed heroes."

His voice was half shamanistic, half sage adviser, and for some reason the background of hysterical laughter from outside made the words seem weightier, not lighter.

"Now that you're all out of husbands," he said, "you'll be required to choose either pious Confucian widowhood or priestly dispensation and a second marriage like the first: a business alliance to advance your father's fortunes. There's nothing wrong with that, of course, if the bride is in a position to pick and choose among prospective grooms. Essential to that happy circumstance will be our clean and unchallenged departure."

I knew he had won when she put the dagger away, but I most certainly didn't expect her next words.

"I had not expected murder, but I will admit I saw the monster. When it climbed down the wall it came close by my window." Then she tossed the armload of bamboo on the fire, to coin a phrase. "The moonlight struck the garish face, which is, of course, unmistakable. It is dangerous for you to be a friend of Envy, but not, I think, dishonorable."

I might have said something foolish, but Master Li was close enough to kick me in the ankle.

"Ah, you know him!" he said with pleased surprise. "So few do. Except, of course, for the owners of the cages."

She ignored the baited hook and shook her head negatively. "I did not say I knew him. I have seen the ancient painting in my father's country, and had the verses read to me, that's all.

Now I must know more of what you have in mind," she said firmly.

So Master Li told her, and then I made gooey red tiger prints down the tower stairs and to various places including a passage known only to the young widow and a few senior ministers, and I suppose the story is now known in villages from here to the Sabine Hills: how a beautiful princess was married against her will and carried off to a loathsome country, and how a magical tiger opened the secret escape passage that led from the bridegroom's castle (the doors were later found wide open, with bloody paw prints leading out) and massacred the unworthy fellow and all his men, and how the princess awakened to find upon her pillow one half of a marriage contract ripped in a peculiar pattern, with a bloodstained tiger paw on it, and how a great shaman read the yarrow leaves and explained that the princess when a child had been affianced to the Tiger Spirit by the ghost of her grandfather, and how her brief widowhood was ended with the appearance of a prince (whose mighty chest could not be seen because of all the medals) who had been born clutching a piece of parchment ripped in a peculiar pattern, and lo! it was half of a marriage contract stained by a tiger's paw . . .

It doesn't matter that the lady hasn't actually chosen the lucky fellow yet (at least I haven't heard of it), because not even her father dares cross tiger spirits. She has all the time she wishes to closely examine candidates. I hope she enjoys herself, and I think village storytellers, who are free to edit where historians are not, are wise to leave out the tadpoles.

We had no trouble. The grieving widow took charge of the whole works, bellowing orders right and left, and Neo-Confucians who were outraged at the presumption of a lowly female received white wooden calling cards marked with red tiger paws, and protests ceased. Yen Shih's wagon rolled freely across the drawbridge the following afternoon, with me on the seat beside the puppeteer. Master Li and Yu Lan followed on mules, laden with gifts, and soon we were back in the land of the bandit chief, following his daughter's directions.

The bright sunlight seemed to be swallowed by a long slitlike mouth as we climbed down a narrow ravine. Cicadas were demonstrating why they're called "scissors grinders," and lizards with eyes of coral and agate and turquoise practiced push-ups as they watched Yu Lan study the area's *feng-shui* ("wind and water"). She was clearly disturbed by the totemistic arrangements of two piles of huge rocks.

"From your description the creature called Envy is strongly masculine, but this place is overpowering in yin influences, not yang," she said in a puzzled voice. "Instead of being proud and priapic the totems are humble and bent, and seem to have been planned that way, but why would a shrine to an ape man suggest crawling on one's knees in a female environment?"

Master Li rechecked the map the grand warden's wife had given him.

"This is the place. Unquestionably," he said. "Yen Shih?"

The puppeteer smiled and flicked a hand in an eloquent gesture of passing the cup. "My daughter is the expert, and I can offer only an instinctive reaction." The gesture ended with the forefinger lifted toward the totems. "That doesn't strike me as being strictly symbolic or strictly representational, but something in between. Like primitive writing, for example."

Master Li grinned. "My friend, I'm beginning to think our minds move in lockstep," he said. "I'm guessing it's a pictograph: specifically, the pictograph of a mourner with bowed head kneeling beside a corpse, representing a word in the earliest Shang dynasty writing known to exist. The word is 'death.' Yu Lan?"

"Yes, it could be," she said. "Many goddesses are linked to the Land of Shadows, which would account for female emphasis in the geomancy. Still, that says nothing about a man with the face of a painted ape."

What I wanted to know was whether or not the death influence was aimed at us, but I managed to keep my mouth shut. We fanned out and began to search for the landmarks we had been given, mindful of the fact that the grand warden's widow hadn't been here for ten years and floods and rockslides could have altered things dramatically. She had been sure about a stretch of cliff marked with a white scar, however, and when I hacked through huge thistles I found myself staring right at it. The livid streak where shale had fallen from reddish rock was supposed to point almost straight to the entrance, and I yelled to the others and got a bigger stick and began beating a path through reeds. Inside ten minutes we found the small round opening in the side of the ravine, just as it had been described, and Yen Shih and I prepared to light the torches we'd brought. Then we discovered we didn't need them.

About fifteen feet inside the little cave was a natural chimney leading up to sunlight. The place was illuminated like a corridor in a gallery, with wall carvings on both sides. Perhaps a third of the carvings were pictures, but the other two thirds were pictographs, and Master Li was enchanted.

"It's an early form of the Book of Odes!" he said delightedly. "Very close to the shamanistic sections called Nine Songs, but it tells a tale with a far different emphasis than anything found in later versions."

As the sage translated the old script a tale began to unfold that was very real in parts. This was the voice of a girl seduced by a god:

"His spirit came like a dense cloud descending,
Lit by a voice of blazing radiance:
'Beauty is destined to find its mate,
For who so fair should be without lovers?'
He came thus with sweet words, with no words he left,

Flying aloft, riding pure vapor, leaving below
A soiled skirt abandoned in billowing folds.
'Speedily, Lord, will I go with you!
Let me follow over K'ung-sang Mountain!
Let me see the teeming people of the Nine Lands!'
But my lord is riding the whirlwind, with cloud banners fly-
   ing.
'I will wash your limbs in the Pool of Heaven!
I will dry your hair on the bank of Sunlight!
I will gather sweet flowers to weave wreaths for the one I
   love!'
Wildly I shout my song to the wind
And stand where I am, slowly twisting a spray of cassia."

The pictorial carvings had not fared so well as the crisply incised
old script. Time had done its work, but enough remained to
show the children born to the sad singer. If children they could
be called, because they were the demon-deities described by the
Celestial Master.

   I caught my breath and instinctively stepped backward as I
saw a little old man hurling fire, a murderous dancing master,
and a disembodied dog head. But the subject of the verses wasn't
eight monstrous children but the ninth one, the boy born human, whose only godlike attribute was his beauty. Master Li's
eyes were sparkling as the verses followed the boy's growth and
triumphs until as a young man he had become companion to a
king. No hero could stand against the brave cavalier, no woman
could resist him. He rode one day upon K'un-lun Mountain,
where a great goddess was said to dwell, and this is his voice:

   "Bamboo fragrance fills this lonely place;
      Long-haired grass weeps dew.
      Tall trees form a winding tunnel
      To curtain the sun with red roses
      Whose thorns catch at clouds.

Drunken reeds dance in the pool's mirror,
Sporting with sky shadows;
Dragon's eggs bubble and break upon the water—
Or is it fish spitting pearls?—
And in the depths the Lady lies on her sea-green pillow.
'Lady, don your coat of fig leaves and rabbit-floss girdle,
Climb to your kingdom in the folds of rocky peaks,
Come with rainbows for hair combs and eyes bright with
    laughter,
Resentful with idleness, seeking a dream—
O Lady of Lakes, Mistress of Mountains, seek me!' "

The cavalier has never been refused and he isn't now. Idle,
bored, looking for amusement, a being who might send wise
men racing for holes to hide in answers the presumptuous mortal:

In a carriage of lily-magnolia, banner of woven cassia,
Cloak of rock orchids, sash of asarums
Trimmed with three-blossomed iris,
She drives tawny leopards, leads great striped lynxes—
Thunder rolls and rumbles! Lightning splits the sky!
"I shall build a soft mountain bower
For a pretty boy, peach-flushed with pride.
With walls of iris, and purple stone the chamber,
Flowering pepper shall make the hall,
With beams of cassia, wild plum rafters, lily-tree lintel,
A room of lotus thatched with white flag,
And melilotus to make a screen.
Chrysanthemums strewn to make the floor sweet,
Sweet pollia, deer parsley,
Autumn orchids with leaves of green and purple stems,
And a thousand flowers shall fill the courtyard."

The cavalier becomes a favorite, as he has always been a favorite wherever he's been, and finally the goddess allows him to use her chariot to bring the Peaches of Immortality for a banquet. Driving the team of plunging dragons on the homeward journey, he passes Jupiter, around which spins the never-ceasing belt of skulls that measure Time.

> Pearls of the moon seed the cavalier's headdress,
> His tunic of rainbows brightens the sky;
> Cape woven from comets, a belt of lost stars,
> Shining bright in his scabbard is a shaft of the sun.
> "He dies who dares not!" he cries to the time-star,
> And his sword strikes a skull. "All rot who won't rise!"
> The cavalier eats of the Peach of the Goddess,
> And wins life as eternal as Heaven, or Hell.

The cavalier has been blinded by his envy of immortality, and when nature shudders in horror he sees a dance of delight. He has been deafened, and when the *chiao-ming* bird screeches its warning he hears paeans of joy. He has been maddened, and would take his whip to any mere star that might stand in his path as he calls to the dragons to race faster.

> Alone on the peak of her kingdom
> Stands the Lady of Lakes and Mountains.
> Billowing clouds kneel before her,
> Gray and lowering,
> Smothering silver moonbeams
> While the Lady summons thunder
> To rumble a path for her feet.
> Tiger eyes lift to a streak in the sky;
> Tiger teeth bare, tiger claws scrape,
> Tiger screams reach out to jade dragons
> Bucking in traces, leaping and rearing,
> Tiger laughter greets a small figure

132

Turning over and over, through starlight and moonbeams,
Falling through sky to the mud of the earth.

The cavalier lands unhurt in a bog and makes his way down a path that takes him to one of the Lady's shrines. There he finds the fruits of his life with a goddess. In two boxes he finds two babies and two amulets with names on them. The boy is a twisted, shrunken, miserable little thing, and his amulet reads *Huai-I*, "Malice." The girl is beautiful but her eyes are frightening, and her amulet reads *Feng-lo*, "Madness." In a third box the cavalier finds a mirror and a third amulet, which reads *Chi-tu*, "Envy." When he looks in the mirror he sees that the goddess has indeed given a handsome cavalier the face of Envy. He snatches up Malice and Madness and runs wildly into the woods, and his story abruptly ends with a very peculiar verse.

> Blue raccoons are weeping blood
> As shivering foxes die,
> Owls that live a thousand years
> Are laughing wildly.
> A white dog barking at the moon
> Is the corpses' chanticleer;
> Upon its grave a gray ghost sings
> The Song of a Cavalier.

We stepped back from the last inscription and looked at each other.

"Great Buddha, that sounded like a demented nursery rhyme," Yen Shih said.

"Either that or Li Ho with a horrible hangover," said Master Li.

He had insisted upon translating every word of text before continuing to the artifact the bandit chief's daughter had told us about. Now we squeezed through a narrow gap and turned sharply left to another chamber lit by a shaft of sunlight, and the usually imperturbable Yu Lan gasped, and I yelped.

We were looking at our burglar, painted upon a wall uncounted centuries ago, and still clear in most details. Around the ape man's neck was the amulet "Envy," and in his arms were the terrible children Malice and Madness. The head was bowed, and in a moment I learned why this place was sacred to yin and not yang. Master Li took my torch and lit it and swung it around to the black shadowed area opposite the transformed cavalier, and my liver turned to ice. Nobody moved or spoke. We were looking at a painting twice as large as that of Envy, and I have seen few things more frightening in my life.

"Envy had to be the most daring cavalier in history," Master Li said in an awed tone of voice. "This is Hsi Wang Mu, the great and terrible Lady-Queen of the West, as she was in her glory before we Chinese tried to domesticate her and ease her safely into the pantheon. No wonder the death totems stand outside. The lady is Patron of Pestilence, and her servants are the Ravens of Destruction."

Yu Lan was already on her knees performing the obeisances and kowtows, and Master Li joined her, and Yen Shih and I weren't far behind. We arose in silence, chilled by the image that looked back at us from the wall. The goddess was beautiful except for the fact that tiger teeth protruded from her mouth, and her hands ended in tiger claws, and her lower body reflected the water origin of all goddesses by ending in something like a dragon's tail, huge and scaly and shining and coiling. Her eyes had no knowledge of time, and no knowledge of weakness, and no knowledge of pity, and I thought I might almost be close to understanding the famous line by the great poet Master Li had mentioned, Li Ho: "If Heaven had feelings, Heaven too would grow old."

Master Li broke the spell by turning back to the transformed cavalier.

"Either he's still wandering around after three thousand

years or Ox and I have seen the greatest impersonator in the world," he said. "One wonders what's happened to his charming children, and what he's trying to accomplish."

Yen Shih's eyes were burning as he looked at the painting. Burning with bitterness? I couldn't tell, but in his position I might be. Here was a once handsome cavalier given the face of a painted ape, and Yen Shih himself had surely been handsome before smallpox made him grotesque, and the Patron of Pestilence had mutilated both. Just as I was thinking that, the puppeteer reminded me he was an aristocrat, and aristocrats don't waste time with self-pity. A sudden sunrise smile brought beauty to a landscape of pockmarks.

"I can't speak for anyone else, but I find this delightful!" he said cheerfully. "Whenever I feel sorry for myself I can think of this happy fellow, and when nasty brats like Malice or Madness creep toward me I can put an arm around Yu Lan." His smile faded. "Speaking of which, this cannot be easy for her," he said softly. "As priestess of Wu she is servant to the Lady-Queen, and all the lady's servants live in terror of their mistress."

I hadn't realized that Yu Lan hadn't risen with the rest of us. She was still on her knees before the goddess, white-faced and still, and the puppeteer gently lifted his daughter and put an arm around her, and led her back out of the cave and into the sunlight.

14

Heat waves were twisting and distorting things, making it hard to get my bearings. I saw a lake beside our cottage and I knew it couldn't be real, and I squeezed my eyes tightly closed and opened them again, and the lake was gone but the cottage seemed to be floating three feet up in the air, shimmering and dissolving at the bottom.

"What are we going to do, Number Ten Ox?" said my mother.

My father was silent as usual, speaking through the tired slump of his body. I tried to remember: do about what? Something was wrong, I knew that, just as I knew that both my parents had been dead for years, but what was wrong?

My father had one of the cages in his hand. Then I realized it wasn't an ancient cage but a modern one, a simple bamboo birdcage, and it was filled with swallows, and he was standing on the bank of the river that runs past my village. Now I knew what was wrong. I looked up at the sky and saw there were no clouds, and I stepped up beside my father and looked down at the river.

The river was dry. I was staring at hard cracked earth and dying weeds and a few lizards, so how could my father offer swallows and pray for rain? Every year swallows turn into oysters and back again (the exact date is listed in the Imperial Almanac), and oysters are the favorite food of *lung* dragons, but the dragons who control water had either fled or tunneled deep underground, and I knew without asking that the wells had run dry.

"What are we going to do, Number Ten Ox?" my mother said again.

Behind me someone was weeping softly, and I turned and saw Auntie Hua holding an armload of paper boats. I knew it must be the fifth day of the fifth moon, Dragon Boat day, when real boats race and paper boats called *chu yi* carry away the pestilence that comes with hot weather, but if there was no water how could the boats sail? Uncle Nung stood beside the old lady, twisting his hands together, his face taut with fear, and I thought I heard the bells from the monastery on the hill sounding the alarm, so I began to run toward them. Heat waves lifted around me like a dense cloud. The sound was changing, growing higher and shriller; not from the mouths of bells, but from the mouths of excited children.

The heat waves blew away and I was looking at something that hadn't dried up, a patch of green grass upon which children played. There were seven children with linked hands dancing in a circle around an eighth child, and all eight were extraordinarily ugly: squat stunted bodies that supported grotesquely large heads; features badly out of proportion. Someone was accompanying on a lute as they sang a nonsense game song, high and shrill.

"*Goat, goat, jump the wall,*
Grab some grass to feed your mother;
If she's not in field or stall,
Feed it to your hungry brothers:
One . . . two . . . three . . . four . . . five . . . six . . . seven
 . . . eight!"

At the count of eight the child in the center jerked up a handful of grass and charged, low and mean, and I decided it was a variation of Hog on a Hill, which is not for the timid. The children forming the wall seemed to be limited to kicking, butting, and smothering with massed bodies, but the goat was free to use hands and teeth and anything else he could think of, and it was a grand melee. Eventually the goat broke through and the other children raced away, shrieking with laughter. When the goat gave chase I assumed the child he caught would become the next goat, but I lost interest in them when I saw the musician who had accompanied their song.

Yu Lan was carrying one of the ancient cages, strumming the bars like strings, and a bright flash made me stop and blink, and when my eyes cleared the beautiful shamanka lifted her right hand and touched her left eyebrow, her right eyebrow, and the tip of her nose—one flowing movement—and then nodded to me, and I realized I was to mimic her. I made the same ritualistic gesture. Yu Lan smiled, her hand lifted, and she opened the clenched fingers as though showing me a treasure: a tiny metal object something like a pitchfork, but it had only two prongs.

I found myself walking up to her, very close. Slowly she lifted the little thing to her lips and blew between the tines and a cool breeze reached out to me. Lovely soft mist closed around both of us, a tiny drizzle pattered down, rainbows formed, the scent of wet grass and earth and flowers was strong enough to walk on. The generating yin influences were so powerful that I had no choice but to reach out to Yu Lan, gently wrap my arms around her, whisper her name; the puppeteer's daughter stood very still, and then lifted her lips to mine.

"This is horribly humiliating," I said.

"Oh, I don't know," Master Li said. "You have an extra pair of trousers and there's much to be said for wet dreams. Most men meet a far better class of women that way, and the financial savings are immense. Besides, you have such *good* dreams. Are you positive you've never heard that children's song before?"

"Yes, sir," I said. "I've heard songs like it all my life, but not that one."

"Your ear is a good one," he said matter-of-factly. "Most people inventing fight songs for children use words about fighting. Real rhymes don't mention the subject at all, and stick to things like goats, grass, mothers, and brothers. Were you aware of the fact that those children looked amazingly like the statues of aboriginal gods you saw on Hortensia Island, outside the Yu?"

I hadn't been aware of it, but now I realized he was right, although I couldn't see why my sleeping mind would turn contorted statues into cavorting children.

"It's scarcely a mystery why your dream began with drought, but something I can't quite put my finger on intrigues me," he said. "Let me know if you go courting in dreamland again."

What he meant about my dreams beginning with drought was that we were traveling through one. Everywhere we looked we saw peasants deepening wells and trying to save every drop from drying streams. Not a cloud touched the sky, and the heat was oppressive, and bonzes and Tao-shihs worked day and night at rain prayers and charms. When Yu Lan was summoned at night it was almost always to work a rain ceremony. We heard from travelers that conditions were similar where they came from, and if anything it got drier and hotter the closer we came to Peking.

Along the way Master Li acquired alchemist's drugs and equipment and a bale of horrible cheap tea and began experimenting with techniques that might turn contemptible *ta-cha* into *choo-cha* perfect enough to please an emperor, and one night when we'd pitched camp he cried, "Gather around, my children, and I will show thee a miracle!"

Yen Shih placed a grate over the cooking fire as Master Li directed, and Yu Lan got out the largest frying pan. The tea leaves Master Li piled on a table were really awful, large and coarse and ragged, and the smell was equally unappetizing. Master Li heated the pan, tossed tea leaves in it, and added small amounts of yellow powder.

"Tamarind," he said. "It's from the fruit of a large tree with astringent seeds rich in tartaric acid and potash, and it costs a fortune. However, only minuscule amounts are necessary. The name is Arabic and means 'Indian date,' which is odd because the tree is neither Arabic nor Indian, and must be imported all the way from Egypt."

He had Yu Lan toss the leaves and tamarind powder in the hot pan while he poured stuff from two jars into a mortar.

"Prussiate of iron and sulphate of lime," he said. "See the prussiate change color?"

The blue was turning lighter as he blended the elements with a pestle, with subtle hints of green and purple. Meanwhile, the leaves in Yu Lan's pan were blending with tamarind and changing from ugly black to lovely yellowish orange. When the blue color was very pale Master Li dumped his mixture into the pan and took over from Yu Lan, stirring and shaking vigorously, and something very dramatic began to happen.

"I'll be damned!" Yen Shih exclaimed.

Those miserable leaves were turning green, just like real hyson. What's more, the smell that rose from the pan was beginning to be delicious, and then I stared at the most amazing thing of all. Real before-the-rains, the finest early-spring tea leaves, are very delicate and must be carefully rolled and twisted by hand, and these leaves were doing that by themselves! The coarse shapes became graceful as the leaves rolled and tightened, the frayed edges vanished, and we were looking at perfect tea of the highest possible quality. Fit for an emperor, which was precisely the point.

"In appearance and smell it's perfect Tribute Tea," Master Li said happily. "Actually the only flaw is that it's too perfect: uniformly bluish green, whereas the real thing would have faint yellowish imperfections. For purposes of transport it would be molded into little cakes and stamped with the imperial seal, like the stuff the mandarins are selling to gullible barbarians, and they can turn it out by the ton. I would estimate the profit margin at ten thousand percent. What a lovely racket!"

The taste was another matter. We boiled a pot of water and tried it and promptly spat it out. It was awful, and Master Li said the mandarins had to be adding a certain percentage of decent tea to make it drinkable.

The steam from my saucer swirled upward, distorting images, and I thought Yen Shih was glaring angrily at me, but I blew steam until his ravaged face was clear and all he was doing was grimacing at the tea taste. Yu Lan began putting things away: silent, graceful, distant as a drifting cloud, secretly smiling.

Heat waves were twisting my village as though it were made from soft wax, and laughter was rising on all sides—harsh laughter, hard laughter, forced laughter—and I looked through a gap between cottages and saw the abbot of our monastery gazing toward something. His eyes were pitying and his face was sad. I ran forward until I could see the central lane, and there was my mother laughing and my father trying to. Everybody was trying to. A wedding procession was just ahead, and my heart sank to my sandals. "Laughing at the Dog" is the last resort in time of drought. If sending swallows to water dragons and putting the statues of our Place Gods out in the hot sun doesn't work the only thing left is to fit out a bridal procession complete with flower-decorated cart and gongs and bells and drums, except the bride is a dog. A bitch dressed in a girl's wedding dress, and everybody points and laughs and makes a lot of noise, and maybe that will cause the Little Boy of the Clouds to look down at the silly sight and laugh until he cries, and his tears are rain.

I walked forward toward my parents but the heat waves were back again, swirling like clouds, and I couldn't see anything clearly. The laughter was getting shriller and higher. I saw something moving in a circle, and then I realized I wasn't looking at dancers around a wedding cart, and it wasn't laughter I was listening to.

> *"Goat, goat, jump the wall,*
> *Grab some grass to feed your mother;*
> *If she's not in field or stall,*
> *Feed it to your hungry brothers:*
> *One . . . two . . . three . . . four . . . five . . . six . . . seven*
> *. . . eight!"*

I came through heat waves in time to see the goat break free and run after the other children. The lute that had accompanied them still played. I turned toward the sound and walked through more heat waves. A sudden flashing light blinded me, and when my eyes cleared I saw Yu Lan standing with a cage in her hand. She lifted the other hand in the ritual gesture and I imitated her: left eyebrow, right eyebrow, tip of nose. The shamanka's fingers opened and I saw another little two-pronged pitchfork. This time she didn't raise it to her lips. She looked somberly at me and turned and walked toward the low stone wall around a well, and then she pointed to a huge bucket attached to a windlass. Her gestures made it clear that I must take both of us down inside the well.

The bucket was just big enough. I released the rope and lowered us slowly down into darkness. The windlass was creaking loudly, but the rope was thick and strong. I could see a pattern carved on the walls: frogs circling around and around, head to tail. A terrible odor was lifting from below. It was the reek of rotting flesh, and something down there was growling like muted thunder. I tried to tell Yu Lan we must go back, but she pointed firmly downward.

I kept lowering the bucket. Yu Lan was looking hard at the walls, straining to see in the faint light from above. Now I could hear a bubbling sound below us, and the air was so hot we might have been in an oven, and again a low murderous growl reached up to us. The stench was almost unbearable.

Yu Lan touched my shoulder and pointed. I saw a large dark circle on the wall, but I couldn't reach it. I began rocking, swinging the bucket, hauling back and forth on the rope. We swung in wider and wider arcs. My hands were covered with sweat and I was terrified that the rope might slip through them and send us tumbling down to whatever was waiting below. I held on, though, rocking farther and farther, and finally my left hand could reach out to the circle. It was a hole in the wall. The third time I swung to it I caught a projecting rock, and I was able to haul us right to the edge. Yu Lan lithely swung up and into a narrow tunnel, and I followed her after tying the bucket to the rock.

The shamanka led the way toward a soft glowing light. It was a chamber that had a floor of moss like a thick soft carpet, and holes high up in the ceiling that let sunlight in. The puppeteer's daughter smiled at me and lifted her hand to her lips. She blew between the two prongs of the tiny pitchfork and the healing and generating power of yin filled the chamber, mist and pattering raindrops and rainbows, and Yu Lan stepped into the circle of my arms.

"Peculiarly lascivious," Master Li said, lingering lovingly on "lascivious." "The fact that sex is women's business is recognized in the yin metaphor we use for it, 'clouds and rain,' which accounts for the mist and rainbows, but then you wake up—and clean up—and do you really have to turn the color of a ripe tomato and get your tongue entangled in baling twine every time Yu Lan walks past?"

"I can't help it," I said miserably. "I know it's ridiculous but I can't help it."

"How about jumping like a frightened rabbit every time her father looks your way?"

"Put yourself in my position!" I yelped.

"How can I? I haven't played the cloud-rain game since I was ninety."

The sage sauntered off to collect his wine jar, whistling "In Youth Did Beauties Seek My Bed, but an Old Man Is a Bedful of Bones," and I gathered up an armload of rushes to use for towels and rolled over and went back to sleep.

The terrible drought had showed no signs of slackening by the time we reached Peking. The city was stifling in heat and choking in the acrid red brick dust it's famous for, and in addition the sky was thick with Yellow Wind, meaning clouds of fine yellow sand blowing in from Mongolian deserts. Usually the sandstorms are over by the fourth moon, but when Yen Shih's wagon rolled through the gates on the evening of the second day of the fifth moon the wheels scraped furrows through a hard grainy yellow blanket, and the wind against the canvas was making hissing sounds like cats warming up for a fight.

Master Li arranged for Yen Shih to meet us the following morning on Hortensia Island, and then the puppeteer and his daughter turned the wagon toward their house. I rented a palanquin and proceeded with the sage to the house of the Celestial Master, and we arrived just as drums announced the closing of the gates to the Forbidden City, which was sparkling like a jeweled crown in the light of sunset. We were admitted at once, but at the door to the saint's study our way was blocked by an old woman who had served the Celestial Master for years.

"He is not well today," she said. Her face was worried and tired. "He has great energy, but something is wrong, and I must beg you to come back tomorrow. He usually gets better after he sleeps."

The study door was partially ajar and I could hear the Celestial Master inside talking to somebody, using archaic formal language almost like a priestly chant, and from what little I knew about him that wasn't his style at all.

"If it continues to feel ill," the Celestial Master was intoning, grandly and resonantly, "anoint it with clarified fat of the leg of a snow leopard. Give it drink from eggshells of the throstle thrush filled with juice of the custard apple, in which are three pinches of shredded rhinoceros horn. Apply piebald leeches, and if it still succumbs remember that no creature is immortal and you too must die."

The door opened. I had a brief glimpse of the saint standing beside his desk, eyes closed, hands out as in a blessing, and then the door closed behind a young servant girl who was carrying a small dog on a silken pillow. The dog was clearly sick, panting weakly, and the girl was so concerned with it she didn't even see us. She had a plain, simpleminded sort of face, and I would have bet anything she made her own slippers: a pattern of pink chipmunks hopping through yellow flowers.

"Does your master get like that often?" Master Li asked the old woman.

"No, Venerable Sir. Only now and then, but then he rests and he's his old self again."

"We'll call again tomorrow," Master Li said, and he turned and led the way back outside.

Riding back in the palanquin was like swimming through a sea of fantastic colors—sandstorms are glorious when it comes to sunsets—and Master Li's face was changing from gold to vermilion to purple to pink, while deep furrows of worry made black jagged lines across the palette.

"I fear for my dear old teacher," he said. "Let's not forget that he somehow tricked a mandarin who had one of the cages, and used the thing to give a tongue-lashing to the others. Those fellows are dangerous. If his mind wandered off on a side trip when he was dealing with them we could all be in bad trouble, and we'd best get the bastards behind bars as fast as possible."

"Sir, don't you have enough already?" I asked. "We know

about the cave, and now you know how they're counterfeiting Tribute Tea."

"We also know that the top man is Li the Cat, and he has enough power to make a cave beneath Coal Hill disappear," Master Li said grimly. "He can hold up an investigation for six months, during which time every single witness against him, including us, will drop dead from mysterious diseases. No, our next step must be to identify the remaining mandarins of the conspiracy, find the weak link, and force him to testify against the others."

He flung his hands apart and gazed up toward the stars.

"But, damn it, the mandarins' affairs aren't *important*," he said in a frustrated tone of voice. "It's those cages, and the creatures that seem to be associated with them, and a burglar that may or may not be a cavalier transformed into Envy. If only the Celestial Master could regain full mental control! Nobody knows more about the gods and demons of three thousand years ago, and he'd get to the bottom of it if anyone could."

We'd reached Heaven's Bridge at the junction of the Street of Eyes and the Alley of Flies, and Master Li had the palanquin bearers let us out at the Wineshop of One-Eyed Wong. He hired a few slinky people to trace the whereabouts of Ho Chang-yu, the mandarin whose image had appeared in the cage before that of the Celestial Master, and in two hours we learned that the mandarin had journeyed to the imperial palace in Ch'ang-an and wasn't due back for a day or two. After eating dinner we made our way to the shack in the alley, and this time Grandmother Ming didn't greet us with screams about big monkeys. Both of us slept soundly, but I would have preferred to sleep fitfully, dreaming of Yu Lan.

15

J ust after dawn on the third day of the fifth moon, when the Yellow Wind had temporarily ceased and the sky was clear pale blue, fingers of sunlight reached across the water of North Lake and crawled across the stern of our rowboat as we splashed toward Hortensia Island, and I was astonished to see that already the first heat waves were wriggling like transparent lizards on top of the looming crag that housed the Yu. It was going to be another scorcher, but as I tied to the dock my heart lifted. Yen Shih was already there, and he had torches with him as Master Li had requested.

"It seemed to me that you'd been cheated," Master Li said cheerfully to the puppeteer. "Ox and I witnessed all the excitement at the grand warden's palace while you were stuck with a stageful of puppets, so with any luck you'll get some action today."

"How delightful," Yen Shih said, and it sounded as though he meant it.

"I should have thought of this before," the old man said ruefully. "We need a list of the mandarins and other eminent gentlemen connected to the tea ring, and I also need every bit of information I can find about the peculiar cages Ox and I have described. The key may be the man who apparently found the cages, the late Ma Tuan Lin."

We were making our way down the path toward the place where that gentleman met his end, and Master Li pointed in the direction of the pavilion.

"Ox and I discovered all that was of interest in his island retreat, and I've had his house and office searched, as well as his country estate. I thought we'd reached a blank wall, but now I'm not so sure. Ever hear of Ma before this mess?"

"The honor was never mine," Yen Shih said.

"You were lucky," said Master Li. "To know Ma was to invite ulcers. He was one of those scholars blessed with a marvelous memory, one talent—in his case, a gift for languages—and absolutely no brains or judgment whatsoever. His linguistic skills brought him into the Interior Ministry as an expert on our minority populations, and it is no exaggeration to say that Ma Tuan Lin soon became a living legend."

Master Li seemed to feel a peculiar admiration for the late mandarin, whose career had been amazingly consistent.

"His first post was administrator to the Hu Peh. He arrived during a flu epidemic, during which time that remarkably hygienic tribe fashioned and wore gauze masks," Master Li said. "His official report stated that his subjects were like human beings except they had nothing but blank spaces between nose and chin; their mouths, he surmised, being placed on top of their heads. He was rewarded by promotion to the land of the Kuang Tung, and it was their ghastly luck that he arrived as they were celebrating their Creation Myth. The official report stated that they would require neither arable fields nor fishing rights, since they existed by eating mud."

"Sounds like a delightful fellow," Yen Shih said wryly.

"He got better," said Master Li. "Ma Tuan Lin was promoted to oversee the Chiao, which led to the massacre of uncounted bewildered grandmothers when he accepted as literal truth a tale designed to make youngsters behave, and reported that the old ladies of the tribe turned into bats at night and flew around devouring the brains of Chinese children. They promoted him to Hainan, and he arrived on the island during a full moon, and one can imagine what moonlight did to Ma Tuan Lin. His official report stated that the girls were actually mermaids who wept pearls instead of tears, so legions of unsavory gentlemen set sail for Hainan to grab girls and make them cry, and I don't want to go into the disgusting details."

Master Li had come in sight of the pavilion, and he stopped and waved his hand at it.

"My point is that Ma's fellow conspirators would scarcely trust a man like that with important documents. My guess is that he was still useful to them, so rather than slit his throat they made sure that he worked on anything connected to the scheme —and that includes the cages—in a place *they* supervised. His pavilion was right beside the tunnel, giving him ready access to the cave beneath Coal Hill, and that, I'm willing to bet, is where they gave him an office and had somebody search him for sensitive papers before he left."

"So we're going back into the cave, to find and search Ma Tuan Lin's office?" Yen Shih asked.

"Precisely."

The puppeteer didn't say anything, but those little lights were dancing deep inside his eyes. I helped him reopen a hole in the weeds covering the tunnel entrance, and we stopped just inside and lit our torches. So far as I could see the tunnel hadn't been used since the last time we'd been there, and the evidence was fairly good because white dust still covered the ground in the area where something had been chipped from the wall, and we saw no fresh sandal prints. We descended to the path beneath the lake. All I heard was the ominous drip-drop of water trickling from the roof, and the rapid thudding of my heart. The path began to rise toward Coal Hill. As we got close to the cave I heard a sound that resolved itself into laughter, and it was the laughter of men who had triumphed over the problems men are heir to by reverting to bestiality. I can't describe it. Either one knows that sound or one doesn't. We extinguished our torches. As we got closer the laughter got louder, and when we peered into the cavern we saw ten men at a table eating a breakfast of roast meat. Dog bones littered the floor at their feet, and dog grease dripped down their jowls, and they roared with mirth as they swapped one stale dirty story after another. The three leaders were all too familiar: Hog, Hyena, and Jackal, who had brutally murdered the little clerk, and I took note of the fact that all the men wore daggers, and there were three crossbows propped against the table beside the leaders.

They were too occupied with greasy dog meat and greasier jokes to notice much else. Master Li promptly slipped into the cave and began crawling between stacks of packing cases, and Yen Shih and I followed him to the back wall. He changed position several times, scanning the ceiling and angles of the walls to judge the acoustics, and then he whispered to us to gather pebbles and take positions where we could throw them through deep shadows back through the tunnel entrance. At his signal the puppeteer and I pitched pebbles, and the rattling sound made the men jerk their heads up and turn their eyes toward the tunnel.

Master Li had his hands cupped around his mouth. He's tried to teach me how to do it many times, but I have no talent for such things, even though I realize ninety percent of it is getting the listener's attention focused on the place the sound is supposed to come from. The effect was really remarkable. A high quavering voice seemed to drift from the blackness of the tunnel, a voice I remembered well.

"*Give . . . me . . . back . . . my . . . eeeeears,*" wailed the ghostly voice of the murdered clerk.

The thugs sat frozen, dog legs and haunches half crunched between their teeth. Hyena spat meat onto the table and turned to Hog.

"That was Cricket, sure as you're born," he whispered.

One of the other thugs jumped to his feet, spilling a wine jar and knocking a platter to the floor.

"Cricket? Cricket? But you said you'd killed the miserable little bastard!" he squealed.

"Give . . . me . . . back . . . my . . . noooooose."

Jackal stood up, white-faced, clutching his dagger.

"That's Cricket's ghost," he said flatly. "The little insect's come back to haunt us."

The other thugs were standing now, looking at each other for support. Only Hog remained seated as before, at the head of the table, gnawing on a bone.

"Ghost? Your mama raised you better than that," he sneered. "Don't you know a dead person's got to stay in Hell three years before he can return in ghost form?"

"Then what the hell was that!" Jackal shouted.

"Give . . . me . . . back . . . my . . . eeeeeeeeyes."

"That's Cricket. His *hun* soul got lost," Hyena whispered. "Can't you hear? It's searching for its body, except we cut those parts away."

"Why couldn't you have strangled the bastard!" one of the thugs shouted.

"Hun soul, hun soul," Hog sneered. He made a show of dignity as he slowly got to his feet and picked up his crossbow. "Listen, you ignorant turds, the hun soul lives in the liver and we didn't touch Cricket's liver. I chopped out the bastard's *lungs,* not liver, and it's the *lower* soul that lives in the lungs, and if you think I'm scared of the *po* soul of an insect like Cricket—"

"Give . . . me . . . back . . . my . . . luuuuuuuungs."

Hyena and Jackal were slinking away, but Hog halted them and rallied the troops.

"Alive or dead, Cricket don't have the guts of a sparrow!" he yelled. "Come on, boys, let's give that turd something to moan about!"

He charged to the tunnel entrance, scooping up a torch from a bracket on the wall, and after a moment of indecision Hyena and Jackal and the other thugs followed the leader, whooping and cursing to keep their spirits up, whacking the air with daggers. They disappeared down the tunnel shouting, "Show yourself, you coward!" and "I'll chase your worm-eaten soul halfway to Tibet!" The snap-whang of a crossbow suggested that imagination was providing images to shoot at, and Master Li grunted with satisfaction as he trotted out and started across the cave to the door in the back wall.

"I'll be surprised if they don't keep going until they reach the island, and then they should spend an hour or two hacking holes in underbrush," he said contentedly.

The alchemy laboratory seemed unchanged, but Master Li wasn't interested in it now. He continued back to another door at the rear, and when he opened it we were looking at a long corridor with little alcoves for offices on both sides.

"Ox, Yen Shih, I knew Ma Tuan Lin and how he worked, so I'll do the searching," Master Li said. "Go back to the main cavern and keep watch—not that I expect our friends to return before I'm done."

He was right and wrong at the same time. The puppeteer and I were standing in the center of the room looking at packing cases ten or fifteen minutes later, secure in the knowledge that we'd get plenty of warning from the thugs' voices and footsteps and torchlight, when a sharp clicking sound was followed by the tread of feet, and before we had time to hide a whole new pack of thugs marched out from a doorway we hadn't seen, concealed in a corner behind cases, and stopped in their tracks and stared at us. They were every bit as nasty as the others, and the leader flushed with anger mixed with blood lust and opened his mouth to yell to his men, and then he gurgled and clutched at his throat and slumped to the floor.

Yen Shih had whipped up a crossbow left leaning against the table, cocked, aimed, and fired so quickly that I hadn't had time to move. There weren't any more bolts for the bow, so the puppeteer hurled it at another thug and grabbed his torch in one hand and his knife in the other. By then I'd snatched my own torch to use as a club, and then the thugs were on us.

I'm better with a club than a weapon that requires skill, and I bashed and battered quite effectively, but we were outnumbered and I would surely have been killed if it hadn't been for Yen Shih. The puppeteer was a graceful whirlwind as he hacked a path of death through the center of the pack, and then neatly kicked over a stack of packing cases to block pursuit. A case split open and a thousand small hard cakes of fake Tribute Tea spilled across the floor, and thugs slipped and slid as the puppeteer turned and smashed back through them like the Transcendent Pig on a killing spree, and survivors who howled in fear and jumped away were jumping right into my range. I managed to hurl my torch and drop a man who was about to stab Yen Shih in the back, and his knife flashed through the air to the throat of the man who had his spear poised at my chest, and then it was all over. I couldn't believe we'd done it, but there lay the bodies, and none of them moved.

The puppeteer regarded the mess thoughtfully. "We may be in a bit of trouble when we try to hide the bodies and clean up," he said.

"Forget it," a voice replied, and I turned to see Master Li shake his head rather admiringly as he surveyed the carnage. "The important thing is that I've found Ma's papers. We'd raise more questions than we'd answer by hiding bodies, so we'll leave them as is. Or almost."

He swiftly went through pockets and purses and money belts until he had a stack of silver coins, which he poured upon the table, and a pack of cheap marked cards, which he scattered over the coins and down on the floor. My club went into the bloody hand of one corpse. Yen Shih's lay beside another, and the crossbow was squeezed beneath the body of a third.

"A trained investigator would find ten things wrong with this pretty picture in ten minutes, but they aren't likely to call in trained investigators," the old man said confidently. "The relief guards showed up, found a table with wine and dog meat and decided to take advantage of it, started gambling, somebody got too cute with his cards, and for once in their lives the dolts didn't miss when they started swinging. Nothing is missing, so why not accept the easiest explanation?"

I wasn't about to argue with him, but we still had to get out of there. The tunnel was out of the question. Master Li was standing at the door the relief guards had used, and he obviously didn't like it.

"This has to lead up to the basement of a mansion on Coal Hill belonging to one of the mandarins, and it would take magic to get out through the basement and the mansion without being stopped," he said thoughtfully.

"Over here!" Yen Shih called.

The puppeteer had seen what we hadn't. The remnants of an earthslide could still be seen on the floor beside the west wall, and a patch of light that wasn't artificial was filtering down through a gap that led up to the ceiling. Yen Shih and I widened the gap enough to see that the earthslide had opened a chimney leading up to a patch of blue, and with Master Li on my back I was able to worm my way up to what seemed a very odd closet made from twisted old wood. Light was pouring in through a gap wide enough for Master Li, and then I pretended I was nine years old and forced my clumsy body through, and Yen Shih climbed up and joined us. We had come out on familiar terrain. It was the Lin family cemetery on top of Coal Hill, not far from the grave the vampire ghoul had inhabited, and the "closet" turned out to be the interior of a hollow tree.

"So! The ch'ih-mei happened to use this tree as a resting place during its night stalks, and the earthslide dumped it down to the cave, from which it was accidentally carted with the dirt to Hortensia Island," Master Li said happily. He hates loose ends. "No doubt the mandarins decided not to fill in the chimney that had been formed because it could easily be turned into a rather neat emergency exit."

That tree would never be disturbed by gardeners, and I shuddered as I looked at it: twisted, crouching, powerful, malevolent —as sick and dangerous as the dread dead trees on the Hill of Kites and Crows, and it would remain untouched until a wind finally blew it over.

16

As duly appointed investigator of anything concerning the death of Ma Tuan Lin, Master Li had every right to be at the cemetery where the monster had lived. He sauntered down the hill quite openly and as he did so he reached into his robe and took out a stack of papers. They were rubbings he had taken from the late mandarin's desk in the cave, and they were so superb that Master Li was willing to bet Ma had destroyed the frieze on the tunnel wall so no one else could share his treasure. Not even Ma was so stupid he couldn't figure out how the cages were used in communication.

Even I could see it. To begin with, we were once again looking at the same hooded figures that had been carved on the walls of the Yu, the Eight Skilled Gentlemen. These were the sharpest impressions yet, and one detail was visible that hadn't been before. Each cage they carried contained an object like a writing brush, with the handle sticking up through a hole in the center of the junction of bars at the top, and one sequence was practically a lesson for the slow-witted. (1) One of the gentlemen lifted the brush from his cage. (2) He was shown touching the brush to symbols of the five elements depicted upon the bars. (3) His image appeared inside the cage. (4) Wavy lines symbolized crossing water and distance. (5) A second gentleman was depicted looking at a duplicate image of the first one in his own cage.

"Even Pea-head Chou in my village could understand this!" I exclaimed.

"Pay attention," Master Li said sharply. "Ma's discovery of cage communication led him to conclude he'd found what really mattered, and perhaps he had, but that's as far as he went, and any scholar worthy of the name would realize he had in his hands the only known record of an event still honored in bastard form today, the Dragon Boat Race of the fifth day of the fifth moon." He grimaced violently and shook his head as though trying to rattle meanings from molasses. "Meaning the day after tomorrow," he said. "Supposedly the race honors the great statesman and poet Ch'u Yuan, who drowned himself as a protest against corrupt government, but in fact the race was being run a thousand years before Ch'u was born—if not two thousand. The frieze Ma found and destroyed was clearly a pictorial account of the original event that inspired the race of the dragon boats, although it would take the Celestial Master in his best days to wring the full truth from it."

Seldom have I seen the old man so frustrated. As his right forefinger danced over the rubbings he quickly and surely interpreted ancient symbols and placed them in the context of a story, yet his hand chops and roars of profanity testified to lessons he might have learned at the Celestial Master's knee uncounted years ago; lessons that the saint might not now be able to repeat. He started with something other than pictographs, however. One rubbing was of ancient writing at the very beginning of the frieze, and the old man pointed to the brief inscription.

"The story is clearly a solstice myth, based to some extent upon historical events, and this written title was added by a scholar or priest perhaps a thousand years after the actual carving." He turned and winked at Yen Shih. "A bit gaudy, but rather prettily descriptive, don't you think?"

The puppeteer glanced up sharply. Knowledge of ancient scripts was the province of the privileged, and never before had Master Li directly alluded to Yen Shih's upper-class origins. Then the puppeteer shrugged, and translated the symbols for my benefit.

" 'Sky-flame Death Birds Ghost Boat Rain Race,' and the only language other than Chinese given to fashioning poetic lines from strings of unmodified nouns," Yen Shih continued in a marvelous imitation of a pompous scholar's lecture voice, "is barbaric Latin."

Master Li took over, and this is the sketchy outline of the solstice story he was able to decipher from ancient symbols and images.

Long ago, before writing had evolved to record events, invading barbarians who were to become the Chinese battled aboriginal settlers of the Central Kingdom for earthly supremacy, and at the same time a battle was waged in Heaven between gods of the old people and those of the new. Somehow the earthly combatants managed to infuriate both celestial sides. As a result the gods who normally controlled the physical operation of earth rode off to Heavenly battlefields and left men to manage as best they could, and in no time the world was in chaos. It was clear that men must establish harmonious accord with the powers of nature if they were to survive, and to this end the warring kings finally united and humbly petitioned the greatest of wizards and shamans, *Pa Neng Chih Shih*, to come from the corners of civilization and take charge.

"The Eight Skilled Gentlemen began by ordering the kings to build something," Master Li said. "See the large square? That means 'earth' or 'of the earth.' It has a squiggle carved inside to indicate it's hollow—a cave, for example—and these little lines sticking through the top—"

"Pipes!" I exclaimed. "They had the kings build them the musical instrument of the Yu!"

"I sincerely hope so, since it's a lovely idea," Master Li said in a gentle voice. "They also commissioned two marvelous boats, one yang and one ying, and to seal a pact—this isn't clear to me, but it seems to have been a covenant to bind men and nature in harmonious accord—the Eight Skilled Gentlemen ran the most spectacular boat race in history."

With the most deadly stakes, it seemed. Somehow the Yu was used to form a path of magical water to race on, and the air above the boats was filled with flames, indicating the sky was so hot it was catching fire, as in the days before Archer Yi shot down nine of the ten suns. Obviously the yang influence was grotesquely strong, and when nature is unbalanced disease moves in, and the terrible Ravens of Pestilence wheeled above the boats. Water boiled beneath the Eight Skilled Gentlemen, waves threatened to capsize them, hideous monsters reached out from the banks and sea serpents threatened from below. The yang boat was shown moving ahead, and the death birds of disease swooped down—

"And just when it gets really exciting we lose the thread," Master Li said disgustedly.

The stone hadn't escaped time's ravages where the last panels were. It had worn so that ink from the rubbing gathered in little puddles, smearing and distorting, and in some sections there was nothing but a ridge here and a gouge there to suggest what might have been carved. Then, at the very end, the soft worn area gave way to firmer stone and the frieze became visible again.

"Yin has won after all," Master Li said. "See the slanting lines? Rain is falling, the generating force and symbol of renewal, and the boat has reached some sort of dock crowded with kuei, ghosts. What's happening isn't clear. The flames of the sky have been extinguished and the death birds of disease are fleeing, so one must assume that ghosts have joined forces with the Eight Skilled Gentlemen and tilted the balance. After all, the unknown commentator called the crafts 'ghost boats.' If only the Celestial Master can regain his wits for a few hours!" the old man cried passionately. "He's capable of tying this to the demon-deities connected with the cages, and maybe even to their brother Envy, and above all he might be able to tell us why portions of a solstice tale three thousand years old are popping up today, and why certain monsters aren't myths, and, in short, what in hell is going on."

"Good luck," said the puppeteer.

Yen Shih was delighted with the "interesting morning," as he phrased it, and placed himself at Master Li's service day or night, but for the moment he excused himself to attend to some work at home. He was being tactful. Master Li's next stop would be to give a full report to the Celestial Master, and there might be details he wouldn't want the puppeteer to know about, so Yen Shih simply bowed out before anyone got embarrassed. Master Li insisted upon hiring a palanquin for the puppeteer, and we took another one, and not long afterward we entered the Forbidden City and went straight to the Celestial Master's office. He wasn't in, but he had left a note for Master Li in a sealed pouch, and Master Li took it back to the palanquin and opened it as we started back toward the Meridian Gate.

Kao,

I'm tired and stupid and senile. I confronted a mandarin who had to know about that cave in Coal Hill. I got him to produce his cage and explain they're for communication. Then I used it to do some shouting, but then my mind stopped functioning. All I could think of was to hit the bastard over the head with the thing. I'll have to leave more constructive approaches to you. I've tracked a cage to Yang Ch'i. He keeps it in a case in that damned greenhouse of his, and you can handle the guards if anyone can. I'll send word when my brains are up to something tougher than pre-chewed baby food.

Chang

"How do I look?"

"Sir . . . Sir . . ."

"Ox, not over my robe!"

"Sorry," I managed to say between retches.

Civilized readers will be familiar with Ink Wang's famous portrait of Master Li, and I was there when Wang painted it. After examining the sage's face from all angles the artist pitched his brushes into a corner, unbound his long lank hair, dipped it into the inkpots, and jumped around swinging his head in front of the silk as he sprayed ink all over the place. The end result was a pattern of incredibly complex interwoven lines. Ink Wang then sketched a head-shaped outline, blacked out everything outside the perimeter, painted in a pair of bright eyes, and there was Master Li, so lifelike I almost expected him to walk from the surface and call for wine. Ink Wang said it was the only way he could reproduce the landscape of wrinkles that constitutes the sage's face, and the reason I mention it is to suggest something of the effect when the wrinkles were filled with green phosphorescent Cantonese clay. (Neo-Confucians who have been left behind are invited to think: incredibly old man, bony, labyrinthian wrinkles packed with clay that glows in the dark.)

I was driving a blue-hooded upper-class donkey cart beneath a bright moon that was occasionally obscured by sand clouds. The Yellow Wind hissed against the canvas, and the metal torch brackets lining the elegant lane on Coal Hill seemed to be passing sand-scrape sounds from one to another like one long vibrating lute string. We came to a halt and the guards at the gate of mandarin Yang Ch'i's mansion crowded around demanding passwords or engraved invitations, and the silken curtains parted and the head of a six-month-old corpse slid out, inch by inch.

"Good evening," said Master Li.

The guards were no longer present, although high-pitched notes remained for some time, rending the air, and we proceeded placidly up the drive. At the courtyard another row of guards stood ready for promotion, keen and alert.

"Excuse me. We have been summoned to collect a gentleman, and which one of you is . . ." I fumbled for a list.

Hands pushed the front handle of a coffin through the blue curtains, followed by the head and face of Master Li.

"Good evening."

Since there seemed to be nobody in the courtyard we left the cart and proceeded to the mansion, where a butler automatically accepted Master Li's cape, turned to receive the white wooden calling card, and toppled over backward like a board, bouncing up and down three times with a distinct whang-whang-whang sound. Servants, guards, and various flunkies appeared at every doorway and staircase.

"Hello, the house!" I cried desperately. "My beloved great-great-grandfather has contracted some silly little ailment that ignorant medicasters call vehemently virulent, and we merely seek—"

"Good evening," said Master Li.

Since nobody seemed to be around to receive us we proceeded through the inner courtyards to a central tower, and entered a huge room beneath a great vaulted dome that consisted almost entirely of windows. The heat outside had been bad enough; here it was awful. What's more, it was as humid as a southern rain forest, and Master Li explained that Yang Ch'i was an avid horticulturist who specialized in exotic tropical flowers. Beneath the floor was a great vat of water kept constantly bubbling by charcoal fires. Vents released steam through a thousand tiny apertures, and moisture coalesced into droplets that splashed down from the ceiling with tiny pit-pat sounds. The room smelled of manure and decay, but most of all it reeked of the gross pulpy stalks of immense orchids: stickily sweet, rotting inside.

"Yang also prides himself on his knowledge of primitive artifacts, and in that respect his pride is justified," Master Li said. "He's one of the few who truly respect the craftsmanship of aborigines, and that's why the Celestial Master said he kept his cage in a case. Yang Ch'i couldn't possibly keep such a thing hidden away; it would be the jewel of his collection."

The avenues between plants were lined with display cases containing everything from a costly jeweled hair comb to a child's doll carved from cheap teak, and I may have learned something when I noticed that moonlight made materials irrelevant, and if craftsmanship was the criterion the doll was the more valuable. The avenues converged at the center of the dome where a single case stood on a circular patch of floor. Here steam was taking the place of heat waves; outlines blurred, and everything seen from the corners of my eyes seemed to be floating up and down as on billows of the sea. The moon was directly above the dome. As I walked forward I watched it change color and shape seen through differing patches of glass: now round and golden as a fabled peach from Samarkand, now elongated and yellow as a squash—a crab must see the moon like that, I thought, peering up through water as it scuttled over sand and seaweed.

The glass alone must have cost a crown prince's ransom. Never had I seen so much in one place, and never of such quality.

We reached the center display and gazed down at the case and there it was, an ancient cage like the ones we had seen before. Master Li frowned. "Damn. No brush," he said, and indeed there wasn't a brush like the one shown in the rubbing. It was like the one we'd picked up outside Ma Tuan Lin's pavilion, but this time I noticed the hole at the top through which a brush handle could protrude. I reached forward, but Master Li stopped me.

"Careful."

He examined everything about the floor, the stand, the display case, the ceiling, and only when he was sure there was no visible trap or alarm mechanism did he reach out and carefully lift the glass cover. Steam billowed around us, hissing, blocking my vision, and when it cleared I saw Master Li nod. I reached out and picked up the cage and pulled it back, and Master Li gently replaced the lid.

"Let's take a look at it," he said.

In a far corner was a workbench where a bright lantern glowed, giving clearer illumination than moonlight, and we started toward it. My throat tickled badly and I coughed, and then the old man coughed. The sound seemed to linger inside the dome, moving slowly through the moist air. At the lantern Master Li examined the top of the cage and took note of the symbols of the elements on the bars, symbols the Skilled Gentleman had touched with the brush in the rubbings, and then he turned the cage over and looked at the bottom. He became very still.

"Ox," he said quietly after a long pause, "do you see this tiny little cross scratched on the rim?"

"Yes, sir," I said.

"I put it there."

"Sir?"

"I put it there, Ox, from force of habit, as an identifying mark on a piece of physical evidence. This is the same cage that we found on the island, and that the ape man stole from the shack," Master Li said.

I stared blankly at him. Nothing made sense to me, and I was about to ask stupid questions when a flute began to play. The sound was quite shocking in the thick dripping stillness of the greenhouse, and I jumped a foot. In an instant Master Li's throwing knife was in his hand, and I turned toward the sound and began stalking it, bent low behind great pungent flowers. The music was strange and discordant, almost mindlessly rhythmic, like the monotonous sounds of shamanistic drummers putting an audience in a trance, and it was difficult to pin down: now to the left of me, now to the right. I seemed to be moving with unreal slowness, and as I wormed my way through pulpy orchids beneath the changing moon I began to get the profound impression that I was underwater, like that crab I'd imagined, pushing a path between algae and the limp dangling limbs of drowned men.

I stopped and stared, with my heart trying to get out past my tongue. I'd reached a gap in huge leaves and I was looking at a bright patch of moonlight shining on a stool upon which a small figure sat cross-legged. It was a child. A beautiful child playing a flute, but something was wrong with it, and I heard in my head the faint voice of the Celestial Master.

"The first demon-deity is *Fang-liang*," the saint had said. "It resembles a three-year-old child with red eyes, long ears, and beautiful hair, and it kills by forcing its victims to strangle themselves."

I realized that the tickling sensation inside my throat had been growing stronger, and I tried to cough but all I did was choke, and I whirled and looked back. Master Li had dropped his knife and was staggering in a little circle with his hands clasped around his throat, strangling himself.

I tried to go back to him, and then thought better of it and tried to charge the child with the flute, but all I did was trip and fall. I couldn't breathe. The itching inside my throat was unbearable and I tried to reach it, clasping my neck tightly with my hands. My vision was dimming and I could barely see that Master Li had gone mad and was trying to climb what looked like a tiny tree rising above orchids, shinnying up like a young boy, and then I couldn't see that far. I rolled over on my back, clawing helplessly at my throat.

The flute music had stopped. The moon was blocked out. The child was bending over me, looking down. A happy smile was on the innocent face, and the eyes were indeed red, and the earlobes nearly reached the shoulders. Beautiful hair glistened in moonlight, and a pretty little tongue slid out and licked pretty little lips. Then, suddenly, a dark form hit the child like a hurricane and sent it flying away, and hands grabbed my head and pried my mouth open, and burning acid began to scorch a hole through the obstruction in my throat. Air suddenly entered my lungs. I breathed and gasped and choked and sat up, and in a few more seconds I realized it wasn't acid in my mouth but lime juice, and the dark shape was Master Li.

"Get him, Ox!"

The weird child had been entangled in plants, but now it was free and it had grabbed the cage and was scrambling toward the door. I couldn't possibly catch it—my legs tried to move and gave up—but a small, heavy, earth-packed flowerpot lay close to my hand. I grabbed it and threw as hard as I could, and then regretted it.

"I wanted to hit the legs," I panted.

"You did well to hit anything at all," the old man said comfortingly.

He wasn't going to need to perform an autopsy to determine what happened when that pot landed squarely in the back of the child's small head. We could hear the bones crush from where we were, and before the body hit the floor we knew that Master Li wasn't going to be able to question the creature. I got shakily to my feet and we walked up and looked down. The wig of beautiful hair had been knocked five feet, and one of the fake earlobes had come loose. Red eyes gazed blindly up at us.

"Some kind of ointment to give an effect like pinkeye," Master Li said matter-of-factly. "I recognize him. One of the dwarfs who entertain eunuchs in the Forbidden City, and I rather think I've seen him in the company of Li the Cat."

He picked up the fallen cage and bounced it up and down in his hand.

"Somebody's gone to a hell of a lot of trouble," he said. "When we lifted the cage from the case a concealed spring released a cloud of stuff that looked like the steam in the room. It wasn't. It was a powder derived from *yuan ha*. Barbarians call it Lilac Daphne, and it's related to laurel and the mezereon herbs. It contains an immensely powerful irritant that can inflame the larynx to the point where airflow is cut off, and since a victim instinctively tries to get at the constriction he appears to be strangling himself. One antidote is citric acid, and it was a lucky thing that a lime tree was growing among the orchids."

The sage glared at the tiny corpse.

"But why such a ridiculously complicated murder plot?" he asked rhetorically. "There were a thousand surer ways to kill us, and all this did was tell us that Li the Cat has a spy in the Celestial Master's household. Somebody managed to read that note and set a trap before we arrived, and we'd better make sure they haven't harmed the Celestial Master himself."

"Yes, sir," I said, and I automatically bent over and he hopped up on my back, and I set out at a gallop.

17

We paused only long enough for Master Li to remove the clay from his face and make himself presentable. Then I turned the donkey cart into the entrance of the Celestial Master's house, and my heart sank when I saw the outer courtyard crammed with soldiers from the Black Watch, which is the militia guarding the important eunuchs of the Forbidden City. Clearly something was wrong and Master Li didn't waste time. He simply climbed out and marched toward the door yelling orders right and left as though he'd arrived to take charge, and we strode inside like conquering generals.

As we reached the inner court a body was being carried out on a litter. One foot protruded from beneath a cloak. It was enough to tell me that the body was not that of the Celestial Master, but of a woman, and then I realized who she was. On the foot was a silly little embroidered slipper with a pattern of chipmunks hopping through flowers, and I recalled the young maid who had been carrying a sick dog on a silken pillow. Master Li held up a hand and stopped the procession.

"The Celestial Master?"

"Not here, sir. He's been away and doesn't know about this yet."

An oily eunuch had come out and seen Master Li, and he trotted forward as the old man lifted the cloak and looked at the body. Master Li's back blocked my view, and I saw him stiffen, and then he gently replaced the cloak. His eyes lifted to the eunuch, who seemed to be the official in charge.

"The blood isn't fresh. When did this happen?" Master Li asked in a calm, unemotional voice.

The eunuch licked his lips nervously. An old woman shoved her way through the soldiers, and I remembered her as the one who had turned us away the last time. Her eyes were red and her voice was hoarse.

"She was murdered yesterday," she said. "We thought she had gone to her family, and we only found her body a few hours ago, but the men who killed her came yesterday. I know. I admitted them myself. They had a note from the Celestial Master allowing them to enter."

"Adoptive daughter, can you read?" Master Li asked gently.

"No, Venerable Sir, but the Celestial Master always draws a little bird on messages sent to the house, and I saw the bird," the old lady said. "They called poor Little Numskull out to the garden, but then I was busy and forgot them. Just now we found Numskull's body in the boat shed down by the lake."

"Could you identify the men if you saw them again?" Master Li asked.

"Yes!" the old lady said vehemently. "How can I ever forget? The leader looked just like a hog, and the two men with him were like a hyena and a jackal."

I felt sick to my stomach as I remembered those creatures back at the cave, first murdering the clerk and then laughing at dirty stories while dog grease ran down their jowls. Master Li had pointed out there had to be a spy in the Celestial Master's household, and had the little maid called Numskull discovered the spy, and was this her reward? Master Li was looking thoughtfully at the eunuch.

"The Celestial Master's house and office are under imperial

jurisdiction. Do you have proper authority to investigate the murder?"

The eunuch was suddenly self-assured and oozing honey. "This worthless one has indeed been so honored," he said, bowing to the ground, and he presented a scroll with imperial seals all over it.

Master Li glanced at the document and handed it back. Foxes would investigate the death of a hen, but what could he do about it? "Very well. Carry on," he said crisply, and he swiveled on his heels and I followed him back outside to the donkey cart.

"Sir, was it very bad?" I asked as I drove away.

"The killing? She was sliced to pieces," the sage said gruffly.

"Bastards!"

"If you mean Hog and Hyena and Jackal I agree, but they didn't kill the girl," Master Li said.

"What?" I yelped.

"They may have taken her, and they may have held her, but they didn't kill her. Those animals would have hacked and chopped like amateur butchers, and the man who killed Numskull was a master of the art."

"Do you mean we have to deal with an insane surgeon on top of everything else?" I said weakly.

"Not at all," the sage said. "We have to deal with a very competent fellow whose craftsmanship in slaughter is as unmistakable as fine calligraphy, but first we're going to pay a call on a puppeteer. Ox, don't forget that the spy in the Celestial Master's household might have learned that Yen Shih and his daughter have been helping us, and helping us could be an unhealthy occupation."

Yen Shih did well in his trade and his house was large and comfortable, although on the wrong side of the Goldfish Ponds southeast of Heaven's Bridge. Nobody was in the courtyard, and my heart began to hurt when nobody answered the door, but then I heard the sound of a hammer in back, and cheerful whistling. We found Yen Shih at his wagon beside the stable, whacking away at a mechanism for a new puppet by the light of a lantern.

"Yu Lan's off again on shamanka business and I couldn't sleep," he said after greeting us. "She'll be gone all night. Anything interesting come up?"

Master Li tersely explained what had transpired, and Yen Shih appeared to hang on every word. I've mentioned that his horribly disfigured face couldn't register normal emotions, but his eyes and body could be eloquent. He was furious when Master Li told about the peculiar murder plot, and his rage was barely contained when he heard of the fate of little Numskull.

"You say those three animals didn't kill her," the puppeteer said quietly enough, but his hands were shaking with the urge to strangle somebody. "Who did?"

"We're going to talk to him about it now, if you'd care to come along," Master Li said. "There's something else I want to do while I'm there, so it will take a little time."

"I have all night," Yen Shih said grimly, and he hopped up on the cart seat beside me.

Half an hour later Master Li and Yen Shih and I were admitted to a gloomy room in a gloomier tower that squatted at the end of the Wailing Wall behind the chopping block at the Vegetable Market. Devil's Hand was red-faced and sweating and drunk, and he spilled wine over the big wooden table he sat at as he shoved a jar toward Master Li.

"Hell of a time we live in, Kao," he growled. "The whole world has gone mad. Monsters pop up to ruin my swing, and the swords won't forgive me for missing, and people hand me horrible orders to carry out, and I have to— Listen! Listen to them! They've been like this ever since that vampire ghoul wrecked the record!"

He meant listen to the swords, and my blood was running cold as I heard the hard mocking jangling sound of clashing steel. The Chief Executioner of Peking is entrusted with the four greatest swords the world has ever known: First Lord through

Fourth Lord, children of the incestuous union between the male sword Gan-jiang and his sister sword Mo-ye, who had been forged from the liver and kidneys of the marvelous metal-eating hare of K'un-lun Mountain. When not in use the swords hang by velvet cords attached to their handles in a small tower room with a window overlooking the chopping block, and on windy nights people who pass the Wailing Wall can hear the four bright blades sing of sanguinary triumphs. They were singing now, mockingly, and the executioner buried his head in his hands.

"Make them stop, Kao, can't you? Tell them it wasn't my fault I missed. I didn't mean to disgrace them," Devil's Hand sniffled.

"Certainly," Master Li said. "You've forgotten that royalty must be addressed in writing; only those of equal rank can speak directly to princes. Ox, remember your manners and ask permission to read this appeal, and I'm sure the swords will forgive our friend."

He scribbled a note and handed it to me and I trotted up the stairs to the tiny tower room where the great swords hung on their pegs. I unfolded the note.

"Close the goddamn window."

The glittering blades made small screeching sounds as they rubbed the stone wall behind me. I shuddered as I looked out and down to the chopping block, and then I shut the window—which was slightly ajar—and fastened the catch and the swords stopped complaining.

"Well, is Devil's Hand forgiven?" Master Li asked as I trotted back down.

"Yes, sir. They say the circumstances of his error were extreme, and they will protest no more," I said.

"Thank Buddha," the executioner whispered. He swallowed a pint of alcohol and opened another jar. "That's only one demon off my back, Kao. There are others," he said gloomily.

"Yes. Like that silly little serving girl. That was a Slow-Slash sentence?" Master Li asked.

"What a world, Kao, what a world," Devil's Hand muttered. "Slow-Slash is no joke, and on top of that I had to put up with those three animals as witnesses. The bastards snickered and joked as though they were at a fair, but I rammed it to them anyway. After the first few seconds that poor girl didn't feel a thing, and they never knew the difference."

Yen Shih had been silent and motionless. Now he looked up quickly. "You used the bladder?" he asked.

"Damn right," the executioner said.

"Good man," said Master Li. "Explain it to Ox, who has question marks in his eyes."

"I'll do better than that." Devil's Hand lurched to his feet and fumbled in a drawer and pulled out something like a pig bladder with peculiar knots tied in it. He slipped it beneath his left arm. His right hand flickered, and as if by magic a long slim blade had appeared in it. Then with another flick the blade was gone. "An executioner distracts the witnesses for half a second and the victim's sufferings are all over," he said in a solemn lecture voice slurred by alcohol. "The witnesses don't know the difference, because the executioner has the Squealbaby under his arm, and he makes another long slow slash . . ."

Even Master Li and the puppeteer jumped, and they knew what was coming. I almost hit the ceiling as a hideous horrible scream smashed against my eardrums, and then another one.

"Short rapid squeezes for a man, long slow ones for a woman," Devil's Hand said. "I'll tell you a secret. I've used the Squealbaby on every Slow-Slash for the past ten years, and that's whether the family's bribed me or not."

"You do beautiful work whether it's blades, bladders, or both," Master Li said. "I'm certainly not complaining, but I would like to take a look at the execution order, if you don't mind."

"Mind? Why should I mind? It's like I said, Kao, the world has gone mad. Everybody's crazy, and this proves it if nothing else will."

He fumbled in another drawer and tossed Master Li an official document, and the sage held it close to the light for a long moment. Then he folded it and handed it back.

"My friend, I'm about to add to your opinion of the world's sanity," Master Li said. "I want to confer with an eminent gentleman, and on the way over I even bothered to compose a document making it official. You can add this to your collection of lunacies."

He took a piece of paper from his robe and passed it over, and Devil's Hand stared at it as he might view a cobra.

"You can't be serious!"

"Ah, but I am."

"Kao, you might just as well invite the Black Plague to tea! Or take a swim in boiling oil! I'm a killer, Kao. That's my job and I'm good at it, but I turn faint and pale when *this* creature—"

"Would you mind?" Master Li interrupted, adding a slight official intonation to his voice.

Devil's Hand turned and lurched out the door, and I could hear him muttering "Crazy! Whole damn world!" as he stamped away down a hall. Master Li turned to the puppeteer.

"Yen Shih, I think it might be a good idea for you to try to trace your daughter's whereabouts and stay with her," he said quietly. "I don't quite know what to make of it, but one thing is sure: this affair is entering a rather nasty phase."

The puppeteer raised an eyebrow.

"The execution order for that little maid specified Slow-Slash," Master Li said. "I know the signature well, and it was authentic. The order was issued by the Celestial Master."

I stared at him, stunned and uncomprehending. Yen Shih stood as if frozen in place. Then he took a deep breath and spread his hands wide apart. "The executioner had it right. The whole world's gone mad," he said, and he turned and walked rapidly out the door, and as his footsteps faded away I could hear his soft baritone voice fading with them, singing to the sand-scoured sky.

"Blue raccoons are weeping blood
As shivering foxes die,
Owls that live a thousand years
Are laughing wildly.
A white dog barking at the moon
Is the corpses' chanticleer;
Upon its grave a gray ghost sings
The Song of a Cavalier."

I walked to the table and picked up one of the jars and swallowed some of the raw alcohol that Devil's Hand and Master Li called wine, and after I stopped coughing I felt a little better, although not much. The executioner was returning, and by the sound of it he was dragging a prisoner in chains.

"You're ten times as crazy as the rest of the world, Kao!" Devil's Hand shouted.

"Why? For seeking the company of a splendid fellow who's as cute as a little lamb and twice as gentle?" Master Li said sweetly.

The executioner and his prisoner came through the door, and I reeled. The soft squat body, the froglike posture, the saliva spraying from fat flabby lips . . .

"Three times as gentle," said Sixth Degree Hosteler Tu.

18

Every historian is faced with a chapter in which he cannot win. If he includes the relevant material he will send his readers screaming into the night, and if he doesn't include it he isn't writing history. Thus scholars wrestling with the wars of the Three Kingdoms must grit their teeth and include learned commentaries on the Seven Sacrileges of Tsao Tsao, and I must confront the task of transcribing the words of a horrible hosteler. It was difficult for those first hearing him not to conclude that his speech was simply another weapon in an overstocked arsenal, but no, it simply reflected his second obsession, his first being murder.

"Ox," Master Li once told me, "never forget that Sixth Degree Hosteler Tu is half aborigine. Our forefathers stole the fertile fields from his people and chased them into rocky mountains where there was almost no food. Then mineral deposits were discovered, so we chased the survivors into malarial marshes where there was even less food. Hunger became the heritage of aborigines, their birthright, and in a psychological sense Sixth Degree Hosteler Tu was born *starving.*"

Today as the hosteler comes closer and closer to deification, even minor editing of his pronouncements is considered to be heresy. If I leave out one adjective I may be ripped to pieces by the howling mob, but I plead special circumstances. When I saw his ghastly face in the executioner's office everything went fuzzy, and for some time I heard nothing but a loud buzzing sound in my ears, and when the buzzing died down the interview was already underway.

"... oh yes, oh yes, oh yes, the Yu was built by the Eight Skilled Gentlemen to make music that turned into water, 'Water of the Setting Sun' my old grandmother called it, although the name is probably as misleading as 'Three Fish Lamb Soup,' which contains no fish. It also contains no lamb. The characters for 'lamb' and 'fish' when written together mean 'delicious,' so the name is actually 'Three Delicious Soup,' and it is made from chicken breasts, abalone, ham, bamboo shoots, snow peas, sesame seed oil, chicken stock, and rice wine. I like to serve it followed by Su Tung-po's carp, which is extremely simple, as befits a creation of genius. You just wash the carp in cold water and stuff it with hearts of cabbage and rub it with salt, and then—"

"Hostler Tu," Master Li interjected, "the Eight Skilled Gentlemen carried—"

"—pan-fry it with onions, and when it's half cooked you add a few slices of ginger, and finally some bits of orange peel and a little turnip sauce. Su Tung-po also invented Poor Man's Salad, which goes wonderfully well with the carp: *sung* cabbage, rape-turnip, wild daikon, and shepherd's purse. Add a bit of—"

"Hosteler Tu—"

"—rice and some boiling water and you can turn it into soup, but you must be careful about the water. The great Chia Ming wrote in his *Essential Knowledge for Eating and Drinking* that the water for Poor Man's Soup must be from snow or frost, which had to be swept into the pot with a chicken feather. To use a duck or goose feather was to invite stomach cramps, which he also said could be caused by cooking pork, eels, or mud loaches over a fire made from mulberry wood, and Chia Ming grew quite upset over the subject of spinach."

"Hosteler Tu! The Eight Skilled Gentlemen carried cages that they sometimes used for communication, but I think they contained something else that was guarded by eight demon-deities. Do your people say anything about that?" Master Li asked.

"Oh yes, oh yes, oh yes, cages—oh my, yes. The cages held the keys."

"Keys to what?"

"Keys to the music that turned into water, of course, and the guardians were said to be very strange and almost as dangerous as spinach, which Chia Ming said is an alien substance imported from Nepal, a very unpleasant country inhabited by perfidious men, and its character is cold and slippery and eating it weakens the feet and causes stomach chills, and if young dogs or cats eat spinach it will cause their legs to bend so they can't walk. In that case the dogs can at least be used for *k'eng hsien,* the canine stew Confucius loved so much he put the recipe in the Book of Rites, but I don't know what one can do with bent-leg cats."

"Hosteler—"

"Unless the cats happen to be nursing mothers. I've read that the boy emperor Ching Tsung was devoted to 'Clear Wind Rice,' which was made with rice, dragon's brains, dragon eyeball powder, and cat's milk, but to tell the truth I think 'cat' is a misprint—besides, that could be a dangerous dish if the cat was white, because white cats climb up on roofs and eat moonbeams, and eating moonbeams can cause people to go mad. Of course, cats are consumed along with everything else in the south, where they even eat giant water b—"

"Hosteler Tu!" Master Li shouted. "The eight demon-deities who guarded the keys in the cages had a brother, born human, who became a great cavalier. Do your people know anything about him?"

"Brother? I didn't know they had a brother who was human. They were very strange, and a brother would probably be like the giant water bugs they eat in the south. They say they taste like lobster but in fact they taste like soft overripe cheese, and they serve them with dried salted earthworms that don't taste of anything except salt. In southern Hupeh they eat the fried flesh of white-flower pit vipers, and stewed marmots, and in Lingnan the delicacy is baby rats. 'Honey peepers' they call them, because the little things are first stuffed with honey and then released upon banquet tables and they crawl around going 'peep-peep-peep' and diners pick them up by the tails and pop them into their mouths and eat them raw. The better houses tint the creatures with vegetable dyes to harmonize with the service: emerald baby rats peep-peeping around purple porcelain bowls, for example, from which come faint hiccups."

"Hosteler Tu—"

"The hiccups are made by soft-shell crabs floating in rice wine flavored with rock salt, black Szechuan peppercorns, and anise, and the crabs are far too drunk to mind when diners scoop them from the bowls and eat them raw. Like the rats. On the opposite end of the scale are elephants, of course, and the elephant feet of the south are among the great delicacies of the world, providing one steers clear of the bile. Elephants store their bile in their feet and it moves from foot to foot with the changing of the seasons, and a bileless foot is stuffed with dates and baked in a sweet-sour mixture of vinegar and honey. The only thing they won't eat in the south is—"

"Sixth Degree Hosteler Tu!" roared Master Li. "How about a creature that's half man and half ape, and has a silver-gray forehead, blue cheeks, a crimson nose, a yellow chin, and is sometimes called Envy?"

"Envy, oh yes, oh yes. Envy caused it, of course. Somehow he got the gods to turn their backs on earth, and he had the sun ready to set the sky on fire, and he had the birds of pestilence ready to strike, because of the solstice, you see. If the solstice didn't take place and the sun got hotter and hotter—but that was where the Eight Skilled Gentlemen took over, and when they

BARRY·HUGHART

finished with Envy he was as harmless as a lamb, which is what they won't eat in the south. I think it's a misunderstanding involving lamb *liver*, which can be poisonous if eaten with pork. Just as common ginger can be poisonous if eaten with either hare or horse meat, not that horse meat needs help to be poisonous. Emperor Ching swore that horse kidneys were deadly, and Emperor Wu-ti told Luan Ta, the court necromancer, that Ta's predecessor had expired from eating horse liver. Still, a horse's heart when dried and powdered and added to wine will restore memory, and sleeping with a horse skull for a pillow will cure insomnia—"

"Hosteler—"

"—and another use for horses leads us back to lamb. In barbarian Rome lambs grow from the earth like turnips, and when they're ready to sprout the farmers build a fence around them to keep out predators. The baby lambs are still tied to the earth by their umbilical cords and to cut them is dangerous, so the farmers get horses and have them run around and around the fence."

"Hosteler—"

"The lambs get alarmed and break the umbilical cords themselves and wander off in search of grass and water, and when I get a lamb I like to save pieces of shank meat for 'Eight Exquisite Lion Head,' which doesn't contain any lion, of course: lamb, lichees, mussels, pork, sausage, ham, shrimp, and sea cucumbers. The name is ridiculous because 'lion head' in culinary terms is simply a large sausage, and I think the error was on the part of a tipsy scribe who heard *shi-zi,* 'lion,' when a chef really said *li-zi,* 'lichee,' as in the case of the fish stew called—"

"Hosteler Tu!" screamed Master Li.

And now I must confess I blanked everything out. I saw the hosteler's horrible mouth opening and closing, but all I heard was a chirping sound like a small cricket inside my skull, and I don't think I was alone. The Chief Executioner of Peking was sitting at his desk with a silly smile on his face and glazed eyes,

180

apparently listening to birdies chirp in the woods, and he was not pleased when Master Li finally dragged him from his reverie.

Master Li had learned nothing else of value. He huddled with Devil's Hand and discussed something I didn't overhear, eliciting more cries of "You're crazy!" and "The world has gone mad!" and finally we prepared to leave. Devil's Hand dragged the prisoner away in a rattle of chains, and there was something oddly pathetic in the hosteler's last words to Master Li.

"Wait! It's very important! I wanted to tell you that the best lotus roots are those from Nanking ponds! Get the red horned nuts from Ta-pan Bridge! Jujubes should be from Yao-fang Gate and cherries from Ling-ku Temple! You must try the sea horses of Kwantung served with Lan-ling wine flavored with saffron, and pork glazed with honey and cooked with cedar wood in the style of—"

The iron door slammed behind them, and that, I prayed, was the last I would ever see or hear of Sixth Degree Hosteler Tu.

19

The fourth day of the fifth moon began with a bang of firecrackers. A great many bangs, as a matter of fact. It was the Feast of Poisonous Insects that warms things up for the great Dragon Boat Race of the double fifth, and usually it's a merry affair, but not this time. The heat wave hadn't broken and rain still hadn't fallen, and everybody knows that when there is no fluctuation in weather for an extended period of time an unhealthy atmosphere is created in which sickness spreads like swarms of locusts, and great plagues begin their incubation cycles, and horrible omens tend to appear: flesh and frogs falling from Heaven, for example, or hens turning into roosters.

Children enjoyed themselves, of course. They'd been laboriously embroidering tigers on their slippers for months, and their mothers dressed them in black-and-yellow-striped tiger tunics, and they shrieked with delight as they hopped around the streets stamping imaginary scorpions and centipedes and spiders, or battled clowns dressed as toads and snakes and lizards with long leaves of *ch'ang-p'u* grass, shaped like the blades of swords. The parents dutifully set off firecrackers and daubed everybody's ears and noses with streaks of sulphur as a precaution against poisonous bites, but their eyes were worried and their faces were drawn as they watched heat waves again lift from the streets. The temples were crowded with grandparents praying to Kuan-yin, Goddess of Mercy.

Tempers were rubbed raw. A bloody battle erupted at the Dynastic Gate when a herd of sheep with red-painted tails, meaning they were being led to sacrifice at the Altar of Heaven, somehow got entangled with camels on their way to the caravan loading area at the other end of the city, and nobody could go anywhere for two hours. The Mongol herders were forced by custom to wear heavy sheepskin robes caked with grease, and the Turkish camel drivers were bound to their thick grimy robes and huge felt-lined boots, and everybody was melting, furious at the world, and spoiling for a fight. I mention the incident because Master Li and I got trapped in the middle of it when we set out early that morning for the Celestial Master's house, and we had to abandon the palanquin and hack our way through the mobs and eventually hire another one, and when we finally reached the house we were told by a soldier guarding the gate that the saint had indeed returned, late at night, but had already left for the Forbidden City.

I didn't know what to think, and Master Li had withdrawn into his own thoughts the moment we left the executioner's office the previous night, and he was still uncommunicative.

We entered the Forbidden City without incident, and instead of going straight to the Celestial Master's office the sage made a stop at the Bureau of Import. When he came back out a short time later the look on his face suggested that at least one thought sequence had paid off.

"Ox," he said as he climbed back into the palanquin, "I should have done this earlier, but things kept happening to distract me. Do you remember the drugs I used to turn cheap bohea into Tribute Tea?"

I turned red. "No, sir," I said.

"Prussiate of iron, sulphate of lime, and powder from the fruit of the tamarind tree," he said patiently. "That last item is rare. Very little is imported, and one must be licensed to buy it. One legacy of late unlamented Legalism is the requirement that companies requesting such licenses must list the names of all corporate officers. Secrecy can still be maintained because such lists are filed by the company name. An investigator has to have the name before he can ask for the file, and some of the names are quite ingenious. Suppose you were one of a group of mandarins involved in a counterfeit tea racket. Suppose you were able to communicate with each other because of old cages, and suppose the use of the cages was explained by a rubbing of an ancient frieze, and suppose you didn't want people asking for your file. What would you call your company?"

He knew very well I couldn't answer that. He let me stew in confusion for a moment, and then he took out a piece of paper upon which a clerk had obligingly copied a list of company officers beneath the corporate name Master Li had specified: *Skyflame Death Birds Ghost Boat Rain Race Tea Company, Ltd.*

"This is the bunch?" I asked admiringly.

"Exactly. Every bastard involved, including Li the Cat and two other eunuchs of ministerial rank," Master Li said. "Now, if only . . ."

He let the sentence die a natural death. He meant "If only the Celestial Master is sane and in one piece and able to help," and worry returned, and he was silent the rest of the way to the Hall of Literary Profundity. There we were told that we had just missed the Celestial Master, who had hobbled out for his morning walk, but we would surely find him on the lawn leading to the Palaces of the Young Princes. Master Li dismissed the palanquin and set out on foot, and both of us stopped in our tracks and let out long sighs when we reached the lawn. Ahead of us, painfully pushing his canes toward Nine Dragon Screen, was the unmistakable form of the Celestial Master, unchanged from the last time we'd seen him.

"I had feared torture," Master Li said quietly.

So had I, since that or insanity was the only explanation I

could think of for the saint's signature on a terrible execution order. Now Master Li had to face the likelihood that for once he'd made an error judging calligraphy, and the signature had been forged, but the prospect didn't seem to bother him. He was almost cheerful as we took a shortcut past the Archery Grounds, but when we came to Nine Dragon Screen there was no Celestial Master.

"Ha! That was a remarkable optical illusion," Master Li said. "I could have sworn he was right here, but look."

He pointed to the left and far ahead, and my eyes bulged as I saw a small distant figure hunched over a pair of canes, inching like an arthritic snail past the Gate of the Bestowal of Awards toward the Gate of Peaceful Old Age.

"Better carry me. Somebody must have given him a lift, and it's too damn hot for my rickety legs."

I took the old man on my back and started off again, but soon we were out of sight of the saint, wending our way through mazes of high hedges. The gardens of the Forbidden City are for aristocrats, not peasants, so every view is planned for eyes riding at ease at palanquin level. Pedestrians can't see much of anything until they reach clear spaces, and when I got to a clear space I stopped so suddenly Master Li almost bounced over my head, and when he was settled again I asked in a tiny voice, "Sir, can there be more than one Celestial Master?"

The ancient saint was so far past the Gate of Peaceful Old Age that he had actually reached the Great Theater, and I would have been hard pressed to cover the distance in the elapsed time even at a trot.

"Let's concentrate on this one," Master Li said in a tight grim voice. "Catch him, Ox."

I took off at a run, taking an angle to come out far ahead of him, and I kept racing through lanes of flowering oleander and pomegranate until I panted to a halt at the Well of the Pearl Concubine. I turned and looked back where the saint should be. There was no slow shuffling figure, and I saw nothing to my right. Ahead of me was the outer wall of the Forbidden City, so the only direction remaining was left, and I turned and almost toppled over. Far, far away, between the Hall of Imperial Peace and the Pavilion of Ten Thousand Springs, a tiny stooped figure was straining to move a pair of canes ahead of his shuffling feet.

Master Li was very still on my back. Then his hands squeezed my shoulders. "Let's try something," he said quietly. "Turn away and cut between the Palaces of Tranquil Earth and Sympathetic Harmony, as though we're giving up and making for West Flowery Gate."

I did as I was told, and in a few seconds I was again running through mazes of shrubs and trees, and after about four minutes Master Li told me to stop, double back, and take the first opening to the left. I climbed a small hill and got down on my stomach and wormed through low shrubs, and Master Li reached past my ears and parted a pair of leafy branches. We were looking out across the long velvet lawn in front of the Palace of Established Happiness, and my liver turned ice cold.

The Celestial Master was racing across the lawn like a panther, stooped low, leaping gracefully over obstacles. His simple Tao-shih robe billowed behind him like a kite, and he was running so fast the robe's ten ribbons and cloud-embroidered sash were pop-pop-popping in the air like the blurred wings of racing pigeons. He leaped over a huge stone I would have had to climb, hanging suspended in air, legs spread like a dancer's, and pushed down with his canes to give his body an extra forward vault as he hit the ground. The saint sped on until he reached the Hall of the Nurture of the Mind. Had we continued on the path we had taken we would now be coming out of the shrubbery in view of the hall, and of the Celestial Master, and suddenly he stopped, and tentatively extended his canes, and an aged, frail, crippled gentleman was painfully pushing himself across the grass.

"Sir . . . Sir . . . Sir . . ."

"Why the note of surprise? We haven't witnessed a miracle since a disembodied dog head chewed the grand warden, so we were overdue." Master Li said in a high hard voice. "Ox, back to the Hall of Literary Profundity, and hurry."

At the hall he had me go around the side and through a maze of little gardens, and then he pried a window open and we climbed through. He picked a lock, made his way through an empty office, had me carry him out the side window and across a balcony, and we climbed through another window into the office of the Celestial Master.

"Remember the little object like a brush used by the Eight Skilled Gentlemen to activate the cages? I assume the Celestial Master had one when he sent his message to the mandarins. Find it," Master Li ordered.

The room was crowded with mementos of more than a century of service and it could have taken us a month to search it all, but now and then the obvious choice pays off. Master Li overturned the jar of writing brushes and pawed through them, and suddenly his hand stopped. Slowly he picked up a brush and held it to the light. It was incredibly old, with a stone handle and a tip made from the tail of a musk deer.

"Same period, same type of craftsmanship, and same feel to it," Master Li muttered.

We went outside again, back in the silent shadowed recesses of the library garden. Nobody was around. Master Li wasn't going to take any chances with the cage we'd almost been killed for in the mandarin's greenhouse. He had it firmly tied to his belt beneath his robe, and he took it out and examined it with speculative eyes.

"We know that it's activated for sending messages by touching the symbols of the five elements with the brush," he said thoughtfully. "What I'm hoping is that it also *retains* messages. If so, one would logically assume the Doctrine of the Five is also involved, such as the five colors, directions, seasons, celestial stems, mountains, planets, virtues, emotions, animals, orifices, tissues, or flavors."

My knowledge of the Five begins and ends with the fact that

the odor and sound connected with the planet Mercury are "putrid" and "groaning," so I kept my mouth shut.

It took some time because there was a maze of symbols engraved on the bars, but finally he decided to try the animals associated with the seasons in backward order, and I jumped a foot into the air when the brush touched the head of a tortoise. A sudden glow of light filled the cage, and then I was looking at the face of a mandarin I didn't know. He was obviously struggling with fear and rage as he tried to keep himself under control.

"Why haven't we killed the old fool?" he demanded. A tic jumped in his left cheek. "I must know, I demand to know, why haven't we killed him? Don't you fools realize that since the Cat dealt with that clerk we have corpses to account for? If we don't slit Li Kao's throat he'll toss us to the dogs!"

Touching the tiger got us another mandarin demanding Master Li's head, and the water buffalo and phoenix produced boring messages about trading routes and sales figures. Then Master Li touched the brush to the dragon, and the face that filled the cage was that of the Celestial Master. From the first scathing words I realized this was the message Master Li sought, the message to Li the Cat and the Grand Warden of Goose Gate we had almost heard, but not quite.

". . . Stick the turd-stained tips of your fingers into your ears and dig out the dung beetles, because I am about to demonstrate the error of your half-witted ways!"

Oh, he flayed them. He turned them inside out. Acid scoured the air as he depicted the idiocy of getting involved in some sort of smuggling racket that could lead to the Thousand Cuts, confiscation of estates, loss of rank and privilege for entire families, and the near certainty that pauperized wives and concubines and children would be led to the auction block and sold as slaves.

"If you idiots have to steal, why not steal something worthwhile?" the saint roared. "In the process you might do good despite yourselves and contribute to the restoration of morality!

Listen to me, my wayward children, and I shall lead you toward the light."

Then he led them toward the light, and I listened with disbelief, and then horror, and then despair to an agonizing degree I have seldom known. The Celestial Master was proposing to revive the ghost scheme of Confucius.

Barbarians must understand that in a civilized country the dead are immensely influential. The living are far too busy with the process of staying alive to pay attention to anything else. Human senses are in actuality "the Six Evils" because sight, hearing, touch, taste, smell, and thought are barriers against the messages of Heaven. Only the dead are free from such shackles, and when the ghost of an ancestor appears in moonlight or in dreams and bears a cryptic message it is the most important event in a family's existence. Sometimes it's a hugely dramatic warning: the Black Stag God is angry and you must flee the valley before influenza strikes, and sure enough ten people who stayed behind die from influenza. Sometimes it's a great-grandmother appearing in a dream to provide the perfect protective milk name for a new baby, and speaking of babies, who doesn't know of the ghost of a child who died at birth suddenly appearing to make an older brother jump back in fright—just before that brother's foot was to land on a poisonous snake? The power of ghosts is awesome, and their pronouncements are unchallengeable.

Confucius knew that, and it inspired a brilliant scheme. He counseled his aristocratic clients to grind the lower classes into the mud once and for all by imposing strict ghost laws. The only ghosts recognized to be valid would be those that had the decency and civility to appear at a properly hallowed shrine in a respectable family temple, and who could afford hallowed shrines in private temples? Aristocrats, of course, and no peasants need apply. Any claim to "ancestral" lines by those without decent family estates would be greeted by lashes of the rod, a second occurrence would mean mutilation, a third would merit death. Any claim to having received a message from a family ghost by one too low to have a "family," in the feudal Confucian sense, would be justification for being sold into slavery.

What made the ghost scheme so glorious was the fact that it was without limits. An aristocrat who coveted fertile land belonging to a commoner merely had to reveal that the ghost of his great-great-great-uncle had appeared to tell him that the land in question actually belonged to the family, and deeds to that effect would be found in the brass box in the cellar. (If need be, the ghost could reappear to explain that the deeds may have been written on paper that hadn't been invented at the time of the supposed transaction, but that merely applied to the earth. The paper had already been invented in *Heaven*, and the gods had graciously presented the great-great-great-uncle with a sample.) Any legal challenge was referred to a feudal court composed of other aristocratic landowners, and as Confucius himself so charmingly put it: "The superior man is like wind, and the common man is like grass. When the wind blows, the grass bends."

In the days of Confucius there was no empire. China was a collection of squabbling feudal states, and the single most important reason for the ghost scheme never being put to full effect once the empire was formed was Taoism. The Tao-shihs battled tooth and nail to protect the rights of the peasantry, but now the Celestial Master, leader of Taoists and the empire's greatest living saint, was proposing that the mandarins put the profits from their illegal operation into judiciously placed bribes, and together with his immense influence and active support the ghost scheme could at last be installed throughout China. In practically no time only aristocrats would be entitled to power, property, and legal protection, with—as the Celestial Master put it— "unimaginable improvement in public morality and civility."

I should mention that throughout this incredible speech the saint showed no signs of senility. Indeed I had never heard him so forceful and coherent, and when he finally ended his proposal and the cage went dark I turned helplessly to Master Li.

"Sir, can he have suffered some sort of a stroke?" I asked.

Rarely have I seen the old man as perturbed as he was then. He was furiously chewing the end of his scraggly beard as he thought, and then he spat it out and said, "I've yet to hear of a stroke that allows an arthritic centenarian to race across lawns like a Tibetan snow leopard. No, Ox, something far more dramatic than a cerebral disorder is going on, and the consequences could be almost beyond imagining."

He had been sitting cross-legged in front of the cage. Now he jumped up and gazed at the searing brassy sky. The Yellow Wind was a huge hand lifted above the horizon; great grasping fingers reaching toward a sun that was blood red and pulsing in haze as it began to set—I hadn't realized so much time had passed—and fine grains were whipping against branches and leaves, hissing, scraping: a giant invisible cat at a scratching post, playfully unsheathing its claws.

"Something as dramatic as a solstice that doesn't take place?" Master Li said softly. "My boy, few disciplines are more dismal than theology, but it may be important to consider the Doctrine of Disaster, which is the Han dynasty's chief contribution to the subject. Both the *I-ching* and the *Huai-nan-tzu* assert that natural disasters are not caused by Heaven, but allowed by Heaven. If men willfully disrupt the natural order of things, the gods will refuse to intervene while nature purges itself of the toxin, usually violently, and if the innocent suffer along with the guilty— well, the only way men learn anything is to have it smashed into their heads with an ax."

He picked up the cage and retied it to his belt and covered it with his flowing robe.

"According to Sixth Degree Hosteler Tu, aborigines believe Envy almost caused a solstice disaster that was prevented by Eight Skilled Gentlemen," he said slowly. "We know damn well that either Envy or an incredibly talented impersonator is still with us and up to something, and the problem with Chinese myths is that in China it's difficult to tell where myth ends and reality begins. The August Personage of Jade will not be pleased to receive a petition to install the ghost scheme from the leader of Taoists, but that in itself shouldn't . . ."

He fell silent, and then he told me to bend over and take him on my back.

"All we can do now is go down that list of involved mandarins and find the weak link. You may have to break a few of the bastard's bones, my boy, but one way or another he's going enable us to toss the rest of them in jail," the sage said grimly. "Back to the city and One-Eyed Wong's, and hurry."

"Yes, sir," I said, and I took off like a racehorse.

20

At the Wineshop of One-Eyed Wong, Master Li recruited some idlers and sent them out to track down each mandarin and eunuch on the list, and then he led the way out the back door to a maze of buildings squeezed together and leaning over each other to form the dead end of the Alley of Flies. Interconnecting passages run every which way, and by the time bailiffs can make their way to somebody's room he's probably in Tibet.

"The Weasel is an aborigine," Master Li said. "I very much doubt he can add much to what we've learned from Hosteler Tu, but I'd like to ask. Do you know where he lives?"

I was delighted to provide something. "Keep turning left," I said. "Believe it or not, you won't wind up back where you started."

We turned left, left, left, left, and would have been back at the end of the alley if there hadn't been a tiny parallel passageway that led up and across and to the right. The Weasel lived on the top floor, but we stopped short when we saw prayers pasted to his door and smelled incense and heard wails of woe. I pushed the door open, and it was obvious that Master Li wasn't going to be able to ask. The Weasel was in a very bad way, rolling over his pallet in delirium while his young wife tried to do what she could. She was overjoyed to see Master Li.

"Save him, Venerable Sir," she begged. "If anyone could save him, it would be you. Everyone else fears contagion and has fled, and I don't know what to do."

Master Li had me hold the Weasel still. He examined the red eyes, and a dry tongue that had a peculiar yellow fuzz coating it, like fur, and he probed small swollen bulges like boils on the man's groin and armpits.

"Did he complain of headache and lethargy?"

"Yes, Venerable Sir."

"Followed by fever, and a peculiar reaction to light?"

"Yes, Venerable Sir! He screamed that light was burning him!"

Master Li straightened up and squared his shoulders. "My dear, I promise nothing," he said gently. "We must hope and pray, and to that end I'll need food, wine, some paper money, twelve red threads, and a White Tiger Great-Killer-Thunder."

I knew it was all up with the Weasel. Master Li resorts to faith healing only when he wants to give the grieving something to do, and now he opened the tiny window that looked out over mazes of rooftops of Peking, and muttered, "One hundred thousand White Tiger Great-Killer-Thunders, and it still may not be enough."

"Sir?" I said.

"Not enough, Ox. Not if Envy has his way." Then he shook himself like a dog shedding water, and added, "Hell, I'm probably imagining things. Let's do what we can."

That meant cutting a tiger shape from a piece of paper and writing on it, "The Unicorn Is Here!" This invokes the auspicious star that neutralizes baneful influences, and I cut the sick man's arm to draw enough blood to stain the tiger red. The Weasel's wife had brought the other things, and the two of us knelt in prayer while Master Li spread his arms above the patient.

"Weasel, having fallen ill on a *jen-hsu* day you have collided in the north with the Divine Killer with Hair Unbound Who

Flies in the Heavens," the old man intoned as a priestly chant. "In the south you have encountered the Vermilion Bird, and in the east you have met the Five Specters, but it is in the west where danger lies, for there you have angered the Tiger who is the End of Autumn, the Edge of Metal, the White of Mourning, and the End of the Great Mystery."

Master Li spread water and incense around and lifted his eyes and arms to the west.

"O Divine White Tiger of the Despoiling Demons of the Five Directions, of the Talismans of Sickness and Ruin of the Year, of the Gate of Mourning and the Funeral Guest and the Spirits of the Dead, of the Celestial Departments and Terrestrial Forests, of the Earth and of Heaven, of the Seventy-two *Hou* and the Eight Trigrams and the Nine Palaces and the Central Palace Thunder, O Great Lord Tiger who enters houses and carries out great massacres, O Tiger who lies in wait beside the road and behind the well, O Tiger who lurks behind the stove and in the hall, O Tiger who stands beside the bed and behind the door of each dwelling, O Tiger who must enter into all fates, O White Tiger, Great White Tiger, your humble servant the Weasel has grossly insulted you, and we bring you his food! We bring you his wine! We bring you his money! We bring you his blood!"

Master Li signaled for the wife to rise and make offerings of food, wine, and money after touching each item to the bloodstained paper tiger.

"O Tiger, eat of the Weasel's food, and take away with his food the Divine Killer of Ascents and Descents and the Beginning and Ending of All Roads! O Tiger, drink of the Weasel's wine, and take away with his wine the Large Dead King and the Small Dead King Who Pull Out the Intestines and Drain the Stomach! O Tiger, take away the Weasel's money as you take away the Divine Killer One Meets as One Moves the Bed and Replaces the Matting, and the Killer Who Drives In Stakes and Puts Up Enclosures! O Tiger, Great White Tiger, eat of the blood upon this talisman of your sacred image, for it is the blood of your offending servant, and if your anger still demands his death, we offer his body in sacrifice."

Master Li pulled straw from the patient's pallet and swiftly twisted it into a man-shaped doll. He touched the doll all over with the bloodstained tiger image.

"You that are nothing but a body of straw have been touched by White Tiger Great-Killer-Thunder, and lo! you have become the body of the Weasel," Master Li chanted.

He signaled, and the Weasel's young wife connected twelve red threads to the straw doll and touched the other ends to her husband's body, and Master Li made hieratic passes as he coaxed the last sickness demons to cross the bridges of the threads from the Weasel into the doll. Then Master Li removed the threads, symbolically cutting each one. He passed the doll three times over the Weasel's stomach and four times over his back, and finally he raised the doll on high and plunged his knife through it.

"Behold, Ye Who Are the Beginning of all Endings and the Ending of all Beginnings, he who has offended you is dead! Great White Tiger, Lord of the Universe, your triumph is now complete!" the sage cried.

The Weasel had been in delirium throughout all this, but the mind is a strange creature. Somehow something got through, and he calmed and breathed much easier, and his fever had almost vanished when we left. Nonetheless, Master Li immediately proceeded to the neighbors to make sure help was ready and waiting when the worst happened. He has great respect for faith healing, but there are limits.

When we wound back through the labyrinth and out into the Alley of Flies the sage stopped at One-Eyed Wong's refuse mound, stinking in the heat. It was sunset. Again the Yellow Wind compensated for lack of clouds to form an incredibly gaudy sky, and rainbow colors played through the seams and wrinkles of the old man's hand as he swatted flies away and reached down and came up with a dead rat, swinging it by the tail. He tossed the thing to me.

"Any visible cause of death?" he asked.

I looked it over. "No, sir," I said.

He tossed a rotten squash away and swung a second dead rat over to me. "And this?"

"Not a mark on it," I said after I examined it.

He tossed more garbage aside and produced three more dead rats, all unmarked so far as I could tell.

"Well, what do we have here?" he asked. "Five consecutive coronaries? Five simultaneous suicides? Five adverse reactions to bee stings at the same time in the same alley?"

He picked up another piece of junk from the pile and looked at it gloomily.

"How about five early victims of a disease that has the capability to spread very rapidly?" he said. "You know, Ox, we tend to sneer at the medical ignorance of our ancestors. Brilliant in other matters, perhaps, but childlike when it came to science. For example, when they finally got around to devising a written word for 'plague' the best they could do was to attach the radical for 'rat' to the character for 'sickness.' Childlike, wasn't it?"

He was still looking at the piece of junk in his hands. It was the remains of a cylindrical parchment shade that fit on a revolving rim around an oil lamp. Eight views of a moving horse were drawn on it, each one having the feet in a different position, and when the heat of the wick made the shade turn round and round the effect of movement was amazing.

"Pacing Horse Lantern," Master Li muttered. "Pacing . . . horse . . . lantern . . ." Whatever was trying to work up through his mind didn't quite make it, and he shrugged and tossed the thing back to the mound. "Oh hell. I was talking about rats, and speaking of the creatures, let's go see what's been learned about our mandarins."

What we learned wasn't good. Every single one that Wong's men had been able to trace had gone to hiding in the most unreachable place in Peking: the barracks of the Black Watch. It's actually inside the walls of the Forbidden City, separated from the sacred confines by another interior wall, through a gate in which the soldiers can charge to the aid of the emperor—or the eunuchs. One reaches the barracks from the Imperial City through a sloping tunnel leading under the moat, and no place is more heavily guarded.

"Li the Cat is gathering his kittens around him," Master Li muttered. "Damn it! Something big is scheduled, and soon, and I don't know quite enough to ask the right questions. Even if I had somebody to ask questions of," he growled. "Still, two mandarins are unaccounted for, and Wong's men are out looking. Better get some rest, Ox. It's going to be a long night."

Yen Shih was dressed in black, with a great lord's winged hat, and a scarlet sash around his waist. His black cloak billowed in the stinging Yellow Wind as he gracefully waved toward a landscape of cracked dry earth baking in heat waves.

"This puppet play, Ox, requires a proper setting," Yen Shih said, and his voice was soft and melancholy. "A setting for shrieking phoenixes, shivering hares, toothless tigers, crying mole crickets, half-starved horses, drooling dragons, blind owls, weeping camels, and old aching turtles endlessly dying in dry wells."

Yen Shih strode forward into the heat waves. I tried to keep up but he was melting in mirages, and I stopped short with a hard stinging pain in my heart when I saw an old cottage standing forsaken on desolate dead cracked ground. It was my cottage, and this was all that remained of my village, and tears blinded me. Something lived, however. I could hear a sound and I tried to run toward it, groping through sweat and illusions woven from hot rising air. Suddenly I stepped through miasma into clear light and green grass and moving figures.

"Goat, goat, jump the wall,
  Grab some grass to feed your mother;
  If she's not in field or stall,
  Feed it to your hungry brothers:
  One . . . two . . . three . . . four . . . five . . . six . . . seven
    . . . eight!"

The laughing children ran over a low hill, and I turned eagerly to Yu Lan. The lovely shamanka strummed the bars of a cage, and my eyes blinked shut when light flashed, and when I opened them she was making the ritual gesture. I touched my eyebrows and my nose, and Yu Lan opened her hand to display another of the tiny two-pronged pitchforks.

As I stepped closer I saw beads of perspiration on her forehead, and I could have sworn there was a look of desperation in her eyes. Yu Lan reached out and took my hand and turned and pulled me rapidly toward the well. Again I lowered us down in the bucket, and again something growled below, and again I smelled the stench of rotting flesh. I swung to the hole and we made it into the little tunnel, but this time Yu Lan didn't stop.

The shamanka took my hand again and began to run. We ran through twisting passages lit by green phosphorescence, and finally we reached a stone shelf and I gazed down into a great cavern. I gasped and jumped back in fear because it was filled with immense coiled serpents, but Yu Lan tugged me forward again and started down stone steps, and then I saw they weren't serpents but coiled pipes of some sort, connecting at junctions to smaller ones, and then smaller and smaller, and finally eight tiny pipes ran into eight small boxes in two groups, four on the left and four on the right.

Yu Lan reached down and opened the lid of one of the boxes. There was a small rack inside. Her eyes lifted to mine, and the two-pronged pitchfork lifted to her lips. She gently blew between the tines and placed the pitchfork on the rack, where it fit perfectly. She closed the lid.

Mist was swirling. Cool refreshing raindrops pattered down, and rainbows were wrapping around us, and I reached out to take the shamanka in my arms. She was smiling at me, her lips parted and her eyes half closed. Then her eyes opened wide and she gasped. Yu Lan jumped backward into the mist, and her voice was filled with pain and loss and fear.

"No! Please, no!"

Something terrible was attacking the shamanka. Mist made it indistinct, but I saw a flash of teeth like fangs in the area of her head, and claws at her waist. A great thick terrible slithering thing was at her legs, and I tried to reach her but I couldn't. I was running blindly into clouds of mist like heat waves, and everything was twisted and distorted. Yu Lan's voice reached me from very far away.

"Ox, the boats! Both boats must race! Both of them! One boat must not race unchallenged!"

Then the voice was gone, and the shamanka was gone, and the mist was gone, and I was lying on a pallet in the Wineshop of One-Eyed Wong beside Master Li, and bright moonlight was pouring through the window, and the Yellow Wind was hissing like a great scratching cat against the roof tiles of Peking. I rolled over and shook the old man's shoulder. He awakened in an instant.

"Sir, I can't explain it, but something is wrong with Yu Lan," I said urgently. "I don't know where she is, but she's in bad trouble, and unless you have a better idea I'd like to get to her father's house as fast as possible."

He looked at me for a moment. Then he hopped up and prepared to climb on my back. "Why not. We aren't getting anywhere here," he snarled.

Yen Shih's house was dark and quiet as we turned through the gates. Master Li slid down from my back and hid behind a post with his throwing knife cocked behind his right ear as I stepped forward in moonlight and hammered on the door. All I heard was echoes.

"Yen Shih!" I shouted. More echoes answered me. "Yu Lan! Hello the house!"

Something stirred and I jumped back and looked up and saw a curious cat looking down at me from a corner of the roof, and then there was a sudden outburst of sounds, wheels rattling, horses' hooves pounding like a bamboo grove exploding in a brush fire, and I had to leap out of the way to avoid being crushed as a black carriage pulled by a team of four horses raced into the courtyard from the stables. Ten horsemen served as out-riders, black-cloaked, hats pulled low, swords glittering in moon-light, and more men clung to the sides and back of the carriage, holding on very professionally with one hand while the other wielded a short spear. In an instant they had come and gone, racing out the gate and down the street, and Master Li stuck a leg out and tripped me as I ran after them.

"Ox! You can't catch them, and you know damn well you can't follow where they're going," he shouted at me, and then he grabbed my arm and held on. "You'd only get killed, and what would that accomplish? All we can do is wait until morning when the gates open to the Forbidden City."

He was right, of course. I had recognized the insignia. Those men were of the Black Watch, and their carriage would soon roll down the tunnel and beneath the moat into the barracks where the mandarins had taken shelter, and to try to sneak in at night would be suicide.

"But, sir . . . sir . . ."

He squeezed my shoulder. He'd seen what I had when wind whipped window curtains aside and moonlight poured in. Four people occupied the carriage. Three, laughing as they rode away with their prize, were Hog and Hyena and Jackal. The fourth was Yu Lan.

"Come. Her father may have been here, and if so he may need our help," Master Li said.

So now we searched for the puppeteer, or his body, but Yen Shih wasn't in the house. Instead we found a sealed missive that had been left in plain sight on a table in the little entrance hall, and it was addressed not to Yen Shih but to Master Li. He opened it. The script was elegant scholar's shorthand, unintelligible to me, and Master Li read it aloud.

"Most esteemed Li-tzu, supreme among scholars, unchallenged among seekers after truth, greetings. This unworthy one begs the honor of your company in order to discuss the future of the young lady who has sought to improve her position by entering our humble household. Should your young assistant and the lady's talented father care to join you they will be more than welcome, and so desirous am I to bask in your glorious light that each hour of darkness will be agony."

The old man raised his eyes. "It's signed by Li the Cat," he said quietly. "Ox, don't get overly concerned about 'each hour of darkness will be agony.' Eunuchs like to play around with elegant threats, and Yu Lan is not only a shamanka, she's one of the best I've ever encountered. She isn't defenseless. Now let's check the stable for her father, and if he isn't there we'll get more men from Wong's to search the city for him."

The stable was dark and deserted. The moon was so brilliant that I realized a sand haze must have partially obscured it before, and the wind was causing a branch to move back and forth. The shadow of the branch moved across the shining canvas of the puppeteer's great wagon, and the image looked amazingly like a maid mopping a floor. Back and forth, back and forth.

"Pacing Horse Lantern," said Master Li, who was standing very still.

Then he ran forward and jumped up into the wagon. I followed, searching for Yen Shih, but Master Li was looking for something else. He had clambered up on the walkway above the stage and was examining the maze of gears and wires and wheels. Puppets dangled below, swinging slowly as the wind reached them, and I realized that the *Hayseed Hong* set was still in place. Suddenly Master Li spun a wheel and set a pendulum swinging, and I stared as a door in the set swung open. Out came two crooks carrying a pig, followed by Hayseed Hong, followed by the magistrate's wife, followed by the occupants of a bed-chamber who had no clothes on and whose eyes were like saucers. Master Li started another pendulum and the magistrate puppet sprang to life, bending to a keyhole, reeling back in horror with a forearm covering his eyes while behind him the mad procession moved in and out of another bedchamber. It was quite eerie to see puppets move to the moan of wind rather than howls of laughter. They continued to move for some time after the sage climbed down, and then once more they dangled limply on wires, slowly swinging to and fro.

Master Li took a deep breath. "Well, Ox, you always knew you'd come to a terrible end if you continued to assist me," he said.

"Yes, sir," I said. I was so miserable with fear for Yu Lan that I really didn't care one way or another, but I went through the motions. "Which terrible end did you have in mind?" I asked.

"That's up to Li the Cat," he replied. "I've just realized we have no choice but to try swan dives into boiling oil, so we're going to accept his kind invitation. The moment the gates to the Forbidden City open we're going to pay him a call, and if you can sleep during the hours until then you'll be immortalized by P'u Sung-ling, Recorder of Things Strange."

21

The morning of the double fifth is traditionally one of the busiest times of the year. Before dawn on the fifth day of the fifth moon the streets of Peking were already crowded with people, and I knew some of them.

Mrs. Wu of the bakery was standing in line at the shop of the Persian alchemist to buy arsenic, sulphur, and cinnabar mixed into an insect repellent lotion, and her next stop would be a public scribe's booth to buy a paper stencil of the written word "king." Then she would hurry home and apply the stencil and lotion to her sleeping children to give each one the 王 mark on his forehead. It resembles the wrinkles on the forehead of a tiger. Even sickness and bad luck run away from tigers, and it's most effective for children early on the fifth day of the fifth moon.

Old P'i-pao-ku, "Leatherbag Bone," was Mrs. Wu's grandmother, and she was waiting at the confectioner's to get hard sugar decorations of the five poisonous insects (centipede, scorpion, lizard, toad, snake) to spread over the top of her *wu tu po po* cake, which she would purposely make as inedible as possible without being actually deadly. Every family member eats a slice on the fifth day of the fifth moon, and sickness demons stare at people capable of eating stuff like that and go elsewhere.

Feng Erh, "Phoenix," was the chandler's concubine, and she was waiting for the first finger of sunlight to reach a patch of grass she had staked out in a park. She would pluck a hundred blades and put them in a jar and walk straight home without looking left, right, or back. Boiling water would be added to the jar to make Hundred Grass Lotion that the whole family would use as a cure-all until the next double fifth.

Ko Sheng-erh never had any luck. His name means "Left Over from a Dog," and he had idiotically gone up on his roof to fix some thatching three days ago, and he was waiting for a down-at-heels shaman to open shop and chant "Grow, grow, grow!" at his head, not that it would do any good, because everyone knows that working on a roof during the fifth moon will cause you to go bald.

T'ien-chi, "Field Chicken," was a God Boy, meaning a male prostitute, who wasn't getting any younger and he was waiting with his best friend, Lan-chu, "Lazy Pig," an ageing courtesan. They had been saving for years, and they were disguised in beggars' rags as they clutched sacks of gold and waited at the door of Szu Kui, "Dead Ghost," a mysterious magus three times arisen from the grave, who would sell them pieces of polished cedar wood, hollowed out and filled on the fifth day of the fifth moon with twenty-four beneficial and eight poisonous ingredients, and if they used the logs as pillows for one hundred consecutive nights the lines on their faces would smooth out, and after four years their youth would be completely restored. The ingredients are a closely guarded secret, but Master Li once told me they included cassia, ginseng, dry ginger, magnolia, broomrape, angelica, plumeless thistle, kikio root, Chinese pepper, japonica, aconite seeds and root, slough grass, and cockscomb.

The Imperial Way was jammed almost from the Phoenix Towers to the Altar of Earth and Grain with the crowd waiting for the Meridian Gate to open and admit them to the Forbidden City: aristocrats in sedan chairs and palanquins and blue-painted carriages; merchants and entrepreneurs in donkey carts with canvas hoods emblazoned with crimson slogans praising the occupants' genius; scholars ostentatiously listening only to little songbirds they carried in bamboo cages at the ends of long poles; petitioners of all sorts who wore artistically ripped rags to prove the hazards of their journeys and waved buffalo horn lanterns to show they had traveled without rest day and night; legions of secretaries, battalions of bureaucrats, armies of clerks. Rumors flew as thickly as the flocks of vultures that circle a peace conference, and leading the list was the news that for the first time in a thousand years there might not be a Dragon Boat Race. There were four principal reasons:

1) Six reliable members of the Tanners' Guild had seen a white bird (white is the color of mourning) fly over North Lake carrying a burning candelabrum, following the exact route the race would take.

2) At the exact same time a huge lizard had appeared at the Bakers' Guild dock and breathed flames over their Dragon Boat, reducing it to cinders.

3) The ghost of Emperor Wen had walked into the great hall of the Salt Monopoly and passed right through the hull of their Dragon Boat while wailing, "Beware the fifth day of the fifth moon!"

4) The Physicians' Guild had issued a statement saying all the above was rank superstition. What wasn't superstition was seventeen fatalities in the past ninety-six hours from a disease that looked suspiciously like a form of plague, and the authorities would be wise to consider canceling any activity that would bring great masses of people into close contact, such as squeezing together on the banks to watch the Dragon Boat Race.

And finally, as a considerable anticlimax, Master Li and I were waiting for the gate to open so we could go in and be killed in a ghastly manner by Li the Cat.

It was not a pleasant period. Pain is bearable because there's a limit to it. The body takes only so much and then goes into shock, but I had plenty of time to think about clever eunuchs and their little games and I didn't think I could take it if he had me sewn up in a sack with the mangled remains of Yu Lan. Master Li, as usual, kept his own counsel. It was quite impossible to tell from his face whether he was agonized or bored, and when the gate did open and our palanquin carried us toward the Palace of Eunuchs he decided to entertain me with a witty travelogue, pointing out things that should certainly be interesting since I wasn't likely to see much else on this earth. I must admit that little stuck, although I do remember the "prettiest and most pathetic prison in the world," the Garden of Dispossessed Favorites, where imperial concubines who lacked the means to properly bribe eunuchs were sent to live lives of celibacy, after having been slandered and removed from favor. Lonely ladies were made to suspire in the shadow of the Tower of Raining Flowers, which is a tall white cylindrical structure capped with a pink dome, from the top of which splashes a river of white oleander blossoms. "The delicacy of the deballed is somewhat overrated," observed Master Li.

I remember nothing else until we came in view of the eunuchs' palace. "Notice, my boy, how eunuchs have cleverly arranged to have their quarters rise a good fifty feet higher than the neighboring Palace of Southern Fragrance, where portraits of the emperors are displayed. Thus, in China, do the gelded squat above the gilded," said the sage, but I was not in the proper mood to provide an appreciative chuckle.

I doubt that an imperial audience could be more impressive. Massed trumpets and a roll of drums announced the opening of great gilded doors, and a gorgeous creature with a golden censer marched in front of us down a dragon carpet between ranks of soldiers who stood at attention in uniforms of red brocade studded with pearls, with gold-sprinkled turbans emblazoned with the emblem of the double phoenix. The walls of the audience chamber were studded with turquoise, tourmaline, amethyst, topaz, malachite, and opal, and more soldiers stood against them: red armor and a yellow banner with a green dragon at the west wall, blue armor and a white banner with a yellow dragon at the east. Li the Cat sat upon a throne facing south, like an emperor, and as on an imperial throne, the back bore the seven-jeweled pattern and the arms were five-clawed. The eunuch himself was dressed quite simply, however, in a red gown embroidered with flowers and stars, and a hat with a single straight plume that designated a Eunuch of the Presence. As befitted one allowed to attend the emperor, his face glowed with Protocol Soap and his breath was sweet with Chicken Tongue Aromatic, meaning cloves. The only jewelry I could see was the crystal vial on a golden chain around his neck that contained his pickled parts. (Castration in China is total emasculation, performed with a special tool like a small sickle, and the unsexed person keeps the organs to be buried with him so he can be made whole again in Hell.) At the approach of Master Li there was a flurry of bowing by lesser dignitaries, and Li the Cat graciously descended from the throne and offered a courteous greeting as to an equal. It was impossible to ignore the charm of the eunuch's smile, accentuated as it was by perfectly placed dimples, but I noticed that the smile didn't lift as far as his eyes. They were completely without expression, and cold as first-moon clams.

"Well, Most Exalted One—congratulations on the recent promotion, incidentally—how goes your scientific inquiry into the strength of square holes?" asked Master Li, who seemed to be employing the badinage of the court.

Square holes meant money, of course, and the eunuch modestly displayed a lack of rings. "Paupers and braggarts are reduced to vomiting clouds and spitting out mist, and since gold still flees my fingers I do the best I can with fog."

"And no man in the empire can better becloud an issue," Master Li said warmly. "I've obviously been misled, since I was informed you'd joined me in investing in the tea business."

"Indeed? And how much had you invested?" the eunuch asked blandly.

"Too much," said Master Li. "In fact, I was just thinking

about trading my shares for an equal equity in the flower business, although one investing in flowers must first inspect them for aphids or beetles. It's shocking to consider how much damaged merchandise is offered for sale."

"Shocking and silly," Li the Cat said sympathetically. "One continually hears of such things, yet it's such a stupid business practice! After all, one can always get a far higher price for flowers whose beauty is intact. The trade you had in mind was without conditions?"

"Providing the goods are undamaged, yes," Master Li said. "I might even toss in a bonus, for the simple reason that I've become fascinated with certain unusual teas and have some ideas about improving the taste."

"Better and better," the eunuch said warmly. "The taste we've been able to get is just one step up from awful."

I didn't know what to think. Clearly the flower they meant was Yu Lan ("Magnolia"), and clearly Li the Cat was saying she was still in one piece, and clearly Master Li was offering to buy her back in exchange for forgetting he knew anything about the tea racket—but would Master Li really do such a thing? Could Li the Cat be trusted to make an honest trade? It was too much for me, and my head was chasing thoughts in circles as the eunuch led the way out a side door and down a flight of steps. He and Master Li seemed to be getting on splendidly as they quite freely discussed the difficulty of making fake Tribute Tea taste better than donkey piss.

"Your profit margin couldn't stand the expense of enough real hyson to make a significant difference?" Master Li asked.

"It was ruinous. You must remember, Li Kao, that we need to make enormous profits and then get out of the business fast. The chances of winding up as *tsang shen yu* are simply too high," the eunuch said matter-of-factly.

That means "bodies buried in fish bellies," and Master Li nodded sympathetically. "What I had in mind was something nowhere near as costly as pure *choo-cha*. Specifically, a blend of light but acidic Yunnan such as Drunken Concubine Wang with semi-fermented oolong like Iron Goddess of Mercy."

"Expensive!" Li the Cat protested.

"Not if used in minute quantities, and I think I see the way to manage it. But you're right, I've chosen the very finest of the types I have in mind, and experiments involving slightly lesser grades would certainly be called for."

They continued to discuss fake tea like partners, considering the virtues of adding Trouser Seat as opposed to Old Man's Eyebrows, or Purple Fur and Hairy Crab combined to equal the same quantity of White-Haired Monkey, and I was actually charmed by the dimpled smile as Li the Cat stopped and turned and said with an apologetic gesture, "Number Ten Ox, would you mind? I'm quite incapable of moving the thing."

He meant a heavy iron door. I had to grunt as I hauled it open, and then we started down a steep flight of stone steps.

"I apologize for the environment, but the builders provided no other quarters for sudden guests," the eunuch said wryly.

He meant the dungeons, and I briefly thought I was getting all too familiar with dank dripping stone walls covered with rotting lichen, clanging metal doors, guards stamping heavy nail-studded boots, weeping sounds from cells, and all the rest of the atmosphere that so frequently embraces those who accompany Master Li. Li the Cat delicately held his nose. I wanted to ask about Yu Lan, but what could I say? Whether or not she was in one piece she would be down here, and we reached the end of the corridor, where two guards flanked an iron door, and at the eunuch's gesture they tugged and panted and finally got the door open. We entered into darkness.

A light flickered, a wick flared up, and we saw the bright points of a circle of spears aimed at us.

"What is the meaning of this?" Master Li asked.

"Li Kao, how is it that a man who has seen so many moons speaks with a mouth still redolent of mother's milk?" the eunuch said contemptuously. "Did you seriously think I would bargain

with an antique? Frankly I am disappointed to find a senile peti-
tioner where I hoped to enjoy a formidable opponent, but I will
at least honor the man you once were."

Yes, first-moon clams, I thought as I watched the eunuch's
eyes in the lamplight. No more emotion than a sea creature
reaching into the food chain. But then I decided I was wrong.

"You have annoyed and inconvenienced me," Li the Cat said
softly. "Not many people can do that, and therefore I shall honor
you with the most remarkable last minutes known to man."

That wasn't clam-cold. A tic momentarily disturbed the perfect dimples, and then the eunuch turned and marched out. The
soldiers closed around us and in seconds we were chained to two
thick wooden posts in the center of a circular cell, and then the
soldiers marched out and slammed the iron door shut, taking the
lamp with them. Pitch-blackness closed around us. I listened to
my heart pound, and then to the slow drip of water from the
rank lichen-covered stone walls.

"I'll be damned," Master Li finally said. His voice was slightly
incredulous. "I didn't dare dream we'd be so lucky. Is this some
sort of trick?"

What could I say? I was trying to get my tongue unwrapped
from my larynx, and that might take days.

"I thought he'd at least string us from the ceiling by our heels,
although there are very good reasons why he wouldn't ruin the
final effect by wrapping the wires around our balls," Master Li
said. "You know, Ox, I've underestimated that creature. I
thought it would take an artist to understand that the best torture would be none, since pain creates its own universe in which
further considerations are impossible. A greater agony depends
upon thought, upon imagination, upon expectation growing wilder and wilder with each drip-drop from dank walls, and then
the hideous reality finally appears and it's far worse than imagination can conceive—ah, that is the stroke of artistry! Yes, I've
badly underestimated Li the Cat, and I hope I don't do it again."

Again? What did he mean by again? If he meant some tenuous Buddhist concept of a later existence as a mosquito I wasn't interested, but I *was* interested in a fate far worse than hanging from the ceiling by my balls. What on earth did the eunuch have planned for us? I had to admit that Master Li had a point about subtlety when I noticed that moving my left thumb three inches to touch the chains binding my wrists took six and a half minutes, according to the count of my pulse, and I seemed to be measuring the drip-drop of water in terms of months.

I won't speculate how long it took. All I know is that I wasn't 306 years old at the time—although I would have taken bets on it—when the silence of our cell was shattered by an incredible scream, and then another, and then a ghastly sequence of shrieks, howls, squishy squealing noises, loathsome sucking popping sounds, a final sequence of screams so horrible I thought my bones would shatter like vibrating porcelain, and then silence. A silence that grew to be as horrible as the screams, and was finally broken by slow, sucking, squishing, slithering noises moving toward our cell door.

The door creaked open. A low, squat, hulking black outline was briefly visible against the dim light from the corridor, and then the door squealed shut. The blackness was as heavy as a shroud of velvet soaked in blood. Slithering sounds were slowly moving toward the stakes we were chained to, and I began to hear something panting moistly. I glimpsed a faint yellow streak that gradually resolved itself into a pair of tiny luminous eyes. A slobbering noise was followed by heavy hard panting, and a hiss of insane excitement, and a spray of spittle: *"—and tell you of the dried oysters of Kwantung! The frogs of Kuei-yang! The summer garlic of south Shensi and the limes of the Yangtze Valley! The clams of the Shantung coast and the sugar crabs of southern Canton and the dried ginger and thorn honey of Chekiang!"* shrieked Sixth Degree Hosteler Tu.

22

My mouth burned as bile and stomach acid surged up around my teeth. A red haze replaced the blackness, and a high buzzing noise filled my ears. Then the happy thought that this must be one of the recurring nightmares in which I was a helpless victim of the hosteler flooded my mind, washing terror away, and I almost laughed with relief as the red haze faded and the buzzing sound died down. I was rewarded with pale luminous yellow eyes moving even closer, and soft fingers like worms crawling over my left cheek, and excited spittle flying like ocean spray.

"The sago cakes of central Honan, and desert thorn honey with almonds from—"

"Sixth Degree Hosteler Tu—"

"But you must know! A record must be left! Finest of all caviars is roe of the Yangtze sturgeon simmered in a decoction of the seeds of the honey locust!"

"Hosteler Tu!" Master Li shouted. "You know very well that you hyperventilate and collapse in gustatory orgasms after you've murdered and mutilated in your inimitable manner, and I've told you a hundred times that it will be the death of you!

Now get hold of yourself before you suffer a stroke, and you might begin by unlocking these damned chains."

I had lost my mind, that was it. Terror had driven me completely insane. So much so that I imagined I was hearing keys click in locks, and the rattle of Master Li's chains falling to the stone floor. Splayed froglike fingers slid over my ankles to the lowest locks, and I stopped breathing.

"Sorry, Ox," Master Li was saying apologetically. "I thought you'd be better off not knowing about this little precaution. You see, before leaving the Celestial Master's house when we learned the poor little maid had been murdered, I asked about the dog."

"S-s-s-sir?"

"The dog, Ox. Remember that the maid had been carrying a sick dog the first time we saw her? Well, the dog died."

"Died?"

The old man sighed in exasperation, and then relented and said in a kindly voice, "Yes, my boy: The . . . dog . . . died. The maid's murderers had been carrying a note supposedly written by the Celestial Master, authorizing their admittance, and that was very much on my mind when I went to Devil's Hand to find out who had ordered such an execution. When the Celestial Master's signature again popped up, I decided I had better plan for the worst."

This, I decided, would probably begin to make sense in a month or two, if I survived that long.

"The eunuchs," Master Li said, "are always after Devil's Hand to find them truly monstrous executioners for their own dungeons, so I arranged for the release of Sixth Degree Hosteler Tu and his transfer to the prison of the Palace of Eunuchs. I assumed he'd have no difficulty taking over as king of the butchers, and apparently I was right."

A series of moist snickers suggested that Hosteler Tu was enjoying himself. "The others were rather jealous, but eventually they saw the effectiveness of my little ways," he said.

"And felt it as well, no doubt," Master Li said. "I assume they were the ones screaming their heads off just now?"

"Oh, I could have done better!" the hosteler protested. I could hear the soft wet smack of his long froglike tongue against his flabby moist lips. "One needs time for such things if art is to be fully honored."

"Hosteler, you're preaching to the converted," Master Li said dryly. "Don't you recall that we were once guests in your very peculiar cellar? Ox, you might as well know the rest of it. Sixth Degree Hosteler Tu is to do his best to aid us in escaping from the eunuchs' dungeons, and then we're to do our best to aid his escape from the authorities. He gets three months to settle where he likes and get back in business, and then we go after him again."

"Oh no. Not again," I faintly whispered.

"But, Ox, it was so exciting!" the hosteler hissed.

Exciting? He thought that ghastly chase had been as entertaining as a horse race or a sled down an icy slope? Suddenly I was free of chains. I felt like a dog released from a tether and I almost bolted and ran into a wall, but then the image of a dog stuck in my mind. A small sick dog on a silken pillow carried by a little maid with silly slippers, and I heard the voice of the Celestial Master chanting archaic words like a priestly chant. "If it continues to feel ill, anoint it with clarified fat of the leg of a snow leopard. Give it drink from eggshells of the throstle thrush filled with juice of the custard apple, in which are three pinches of shredded rhinoceros horn. Apply piebald leeches, and if it still succumbs remember that no creature is immortal and you too must die."

Master Li had checked. The dog had succumbed. "And you too must die," said the Celestial Master. You too must die . . . you too must die . . .

I snapped out of my reverie as the cell door creaked open. Sixth Degree Hosteler Tu was tugging at it, and dim torchlight played over his unpleasant features and those of Master Li, and I trotted out after them into the corridor. Master Li took the great ring of keys from a hook on the wall and began unlocking cell doors, but prisoners didn't stream out. They were all huddled in corners in fetal positions with their hands over their ears, trying to block the screams the junior executioners had made when the hosteler got his hands on them, and I doubted that any would dare to move.

"Hosteler, last night the Black Watch brought in another prisoner. A girl named Yu Lan. Do you know anything about her?" Master Li asked.

"No, I have heard of no girl."

"Anything unusual?"

"Yes," the hosteler said thoughtfully. "A number of prisoners condemned to death have been taken from their cells to some other holding place where they are to be dedicated for a ceremony sometime today."

"Dedicated? You mean like animals for slaughter?" the sage asked.

"I assume so. Rumor has it that the ceremony is to be held in the eunuchs' courtyard at the time of the solstice," said Hosteler Tu.

Master Li was silent for a time. Then he whispered, "Yes, that might do it. The August Personage of Jade is hot-tempered, and if Heaven turns its back . . ." Then he broke from his reveries and snapped, "Hurry. We have to get up to the courtyard where that ceremony is to take place."

Hosteler Tu knew part of the underground labyrinth, and what he didn't know firsthand Master Li could fill in theoretically, from architects' plans seen fifty years ago and never forgotten. Like everything else in the Forbidden City, the Golden River is artificial, and a marvelously effective system allows it to pour prettily over a fall and then travel uphill so it can splash down another. The water boils down through crevices into connecting caverns where huge water wheels lift it level by level to the desired height, and then back up to the surface. We slipped through side passages from the dungeons into caverns that reminded me somewhat of the Sixth Hell. Cursing overseers lashed rows of slaves who powered great horizontal wheels connected to vertical ones, and water splashed incessantly as immense buckets lifted and vanished through crevices in the roof. One good thing was the noise level, which meant we wouldn't be heard as we made our way along a narrow path close to the overseers. The misty spray from the water helped hide us as well, and I was just thinking how lucky we were when one overseer turned to another.

"Did you hear the latest?" he shouted. "The guilds made it official! They've canceled the Dragon Boat Race, and they even canceled their banquets!"

I could have strangled him.

"Tragic, even though the banquet of the Beggars' Guild is totally unimaginative," said Sixth Degree Hosteler Tu. "Eleven courses for beggars of the first and second degrees, seven courses, two jars of wine, and a box of salted meats to take home for third degree beggars, five courses, two jars of wine, and a box of preserved fruits for the fourth degree, and fifth through seventh degree beggars receive three courses, one wine jar, and no home box."

His voice was getting louder and louder as he warmed up, and I tried to clap a hand over his mouth. The trouble was that we had to walk single file and he could easily fend me off unless I wanted to start wrestling and really give us away.

"The Merchants' Guild, on the other hand, is a credit to civilization and cancellation of their banquet is a national tragedy," the hosteler said loudly. "Even the lowest degrees, seventh through fifth, receive birds' nests, pigs' trotters, domestic duck, chicken, and three kinds of pork. Merchants of the fourth and third degrees are entitled to the same plus shark fins, salmon, and fried lamb. These courses are also offered to second and first degree merchants who additionally receive bear paws, deer tails, goose, crabs, and mussels. The merchants of the Mongolian guild, however—"

"Hosteler Tu!" hissed Master Li.

"But you must know!" yelled Sixth Degree Hosteler Tu. *"It must be recorded that guilds are allowed local delicacies, and in Mongolia they add for all degrees slices of mutton dipped in a mixture of raw eggs beaten with chopped ginger and then seared over charcoal fires!"*

That did it. Overseers wheeled around and yelled for soldiers, and an officer and ten men appeared out of nowhere and charged with spears, and after that things got very confusing. We'd backed into a wall that was almost beneath one of the great rising water wheels, and the spray that closed around us was blinding, and the noise of wheel and water blocked out almost everything else. Li the Cat hadn't bothered to have Master Li's throwing knife taken away—after all, we'd been chained to posts—and he was able to fend for himself. I was trying to pick up one soldier and use him as a battering ram against others, but that left most of the work to the hosteler, and I will freely admit that of all the killers I've encountered few could come within leagues of Sixth Degree Hosteler Tu. Those long webbed fingers, those sharp-pointed teeth filling a mouth that could stretch wide enough to swallow a muskmelon, the feet that slipped from sandals to reveal prehensile toes planned for strangling, that soft unresisting body absorbing the hardest blows like a feather pillow, and then falling in folds over a victim and clogging air passages like an obscene shroud of flabby fat. All the while the hosteler giggled, mind you, and his reptilian tongue flicked happily over his lewd lips—still, not even Hosteler Tu could ignore blows from a dagger.

When I finally staggered up from my pile of bodies and looked around I saw Master Li apparently unhurt, but the hosteler had been battling the bulk of them and now he had his arms around the last, the officer, crushing him in a bear hug. The officer was stabbing the hosteler in the back with his dagger, again and again, and then the two of them toppled to the ground beside the water, wrapped in their final bloody embrace. There was a gasp and a sickening snapping sound, and the officer twitched and lay still. Master Li knelt beside the hosteler and examined him.

"I'll be damned. He's still alive."

The hosteler's eyes opened.

"Hosteler Tu, I wanted to ask you something very important," Master Li said, speaking slowly and carefully. "I have reason to believe that Number Ten Ox has been receiving a message, again and again, but the meaning has been disguised because to impart it is taboo."

Me? A taboo message?

"I also have reason to believe that the disguise is formed from slang of the first Dragon Boat Race, slang which your people may still preserve," Master Li said. "The first slang term is 'mother.' "

Hosteler Tu's eyes were partially focused on this world and partially on the next. "Mother? Boat race?" he whispered. "The mother is the same as *t'ou*, the head, meaning the boss of the boat. Mother stands on the high prow and sends commands with long flowing scarves, but what you must understand is that the Merchants' Guild of Canton offers all degrees an additional course of *fo siu u*, 'roast pork fish,' which actually does taste a little like pork but is poisonous if cooked with broccoli."

"Hosteler Tu, the next word is 'grass,' " Master Li said urgently.

"Grass is slang for *k'i*, the scarves used by mother to send commands. They're green with white tips and look like tall grass waving in the wind, and in Shanghai the guild adds herrings called 'little father's eldest sisters,' and—"

" 'Brothers,' Hosteler Tu, the word is 'brothers,' " Master Li said.

"Brothers, yes, oh yes. Eight of them. Four in front of the wall and four behind. Lead oarsmen who set the stroke, and they wear red bandanas and have red ribbons around their oar handles, and in Shanghai they also add a delicious threadfin called 'horse-friend-gentleman-fish,' which is—"

"Hosteler Tu, you just mentioned the 'wall'. What is it?" Master Li asked.

"The wall is the raised platform in the center of a Dragon Boat, where the drummer takes the commands of the mother and transmits them with his beat," the hosteler whispered.

He was sinking fast. Master Li raised his voice to shout directly in the hosteler's ear.

"Hosteler, I assume the ancient *wu hing* system of parallels was in place, so 'field' means east and 'stall' means west, but I must know about the goat!" the sage yelled. "What . . . is . . . the . . . goat?"

I thought Hosteler Tu was dead. Then his eyes opened, and they were perfectly clear, and his voice was firm.

"The *shao*, the steering oarsman of a dragon boat, is always called the goat for two reasons," he said as if lecturing. "First, he butts head with almost the entire stern while wrestling with his oar, and second, he's an outsider who's expected to take the blame if the boat loses. A goat is a professional, a hired oar. No amateur can handle a hunk of wood that stretches forty feet and weighs more than a ton, and no amateur can cook for the guild of Nam Viet, where the additional course is lips of *hsiang-hsiang*, meaning gibbons, seethed in beer made from juice of the areca nut."

His eyes popped wide, staring up at something invisible to the living. A spasm caused him to jerk backward, and then Sixth Degree Hosteler Tu slid down the bank with the dead officer in his arms. They landed in the water and disappeared. Frothy pink bubbles popped to the surface, and a red stain slowly spread and drifted toward the huge lifting buckets of the wheel.

"Farewell, Hosteler," Master Li said softly, and the frothing water answered, "Burp . . . Burp . . . Burp."

23

We met no more soldiers as Master Li directed me toward one of the staircases that led to gardener's sheds, but when I took the old man on my back and climbed up and out beside a swirling pool where water was being dumped from a wheel we both received a shock, this time from nature. I was sure the day had passed and it must be midnight at least, but it was only early afternoon, and what an afternoon! The Yellow Wind had closed around Peking with a vengeance, and whirlwinds danced and darted through the city and sent clouds of debris spinning up into the air to sail this way and that and then drift back down to earth like dirty snowflakes made from ripped canvas, reed matting, splintered bamboo, garbage, and dead rats. Sand lashed our faces. Wind howled like wolves as gusts ripped between rows of elegant palaces, and a giant hissing noise came from lashed leaves and scraped tiles. The water of the Golden River was covered with a frothy cloud of spray from the impact of a billion tiny yellow grains, and the sun behind the haze seemed grossly swollen and as red as blood. Rows of blackbirds sat motionless upon towers and parapets, silhouetted against a burning sky.

"Sky-flame," Master Li muttered in my ear. "What happens

once can happen twice, even including a Death Birds Ghost Boat Rain Race. Ox, the fastest route to the eunuchs' courtyard is the Golden River, so find a raft and a pole and let's go."

I knocked the shearing blade from the end of a long bamboo tree-trimming pole and ripped the large wooden door from a gardener's shed and tossed it down into the water. It made a good enough raft, with enough buoyancy for the two of us, and I pushed off with the pole and caught what current there was. I rammed the pole rhythmically, shoving with long smooth strokes, and we picked up respectable speed. Several times we plunged down over falls that were too decorative to be dangerous, and soon I could see ahead to our destination, and my heart felt squeezed as I realized the huge basilica I was looking at was the barracks of the Black Watch, where Hog and Hyena and Jackal had taken Yu Lan. In front of it was a low wall that also formed the back wall of the eunuchs' courtyard, between their elegant palace and the Palace of Southern Fragrance. All this was slightly downhill from us. The Golden River was taking us to falls that frothed down a low stone cliff that was one of the few natural barriers in the Forbidden City, and formed the front wall of the eunuchs' courtyard. I want to clearly establish the scene as viewed from that little cliff. One looked down into a large circular courtyard paved with marble, in the center of which was a raised stone platform around an ancient well that had once been used for sacrifice during religious rites. A second raised platform stood at the base of the cliff so the waterfall could form a dramatic background, and there dignitaries perched in their pride during great occasions. Left was the Palace of Southern Fragrance, right was the eunuchs' palace, and back was the basilica of the Black Watch.

The closer we got, the more clearly I could see that every window and balcony was packed with people gazing down to the courtyard, which was in turn packed with eunuchs and soldiers. When we were close enough to see the river disappear over the cliff Master Li had me pole to shore and lift the raft out.

We continued on foot, and when we stuck our heads through some reeds beside the waterfall we were looking almost straight down at the dignitaries' platform, where chairs were arrayed like thrones. In the center sat Li the Cat, flanked by the two powerful eunuchs whose names had been on the list of corporate officers. Then on each side were the chairs of the remaining mandarins of the tea conspiracy, and Master Li's fingers tightened on my shoulder as we saw the five ancient cages beside the thrones.

"It's the cages, Ox," Master Li said quietly. "Now our only hope is to reach those cages before Envy gets to them. If I'm right he only needs one more, and that must not be allowed to happen."

Apparently we had arrived at a pause in some sort of ritual. I hadn't realized how abnormally silent the crowd had been until a vast collective sigh greeted the chief figure of the ceremony, who stepped from behind a screen decorated with sacred symbols. It was the Celestial Master. His cape was decorated with skulls, and behind him came a high priest carrying an ancient stone club on a gold-embossed pillow. They slowly mounted the steps to the platform around the old well. There was a long ritual prayer I couldn't hear and probably wouldn't have understood anyway, and then the ranks of soldiers parted to make way for two lesser priests leading a line of chained prisoners. The first prisoner was released from the lead chain. Still manacled, he was hauled up the steps and kicked down on his knees before the Celestial Master.

The high priest raised his arms and voice to Heaven, chanting something or other, and the Celestial Master raised the stone club above his head. I gaped in disbelief as the club swung viciously down and smashed the skull of the prisoner, and then with a powerful contemptuous kick the ancient saint shoved the corpse to the edge of the well, and it toppled down into darkness. A great cheer rang out from the crowd, and the mandarins applauded. I stared at the sage.

"They've been praying to get the attention of Heaven, and the emperor of Heaven is not likely to be pleased," he said in a hard tight voice. "If the August Personage of Jade has a fault it's his hot temper, and we'd better do something fast before the Doctrine of Disaster gets an unfortunate workout." He punched my arm with short rapid strokes. "The cages, Ox. We must get those cages and we can't worry about risk. Let's go."

"Yes, sir," I said.

A second human sacrifice was being hauled to the Celestial Master's ax, which meant nobody was watching the cliff as I carried Master Li down it. I heard the cheer as again the stone ax crushed a human skull, and I began praying for help. Fervently, but not blindly. I had a very clear image in mind. Where was the puppeteer? If Yen Shih would only appear with that dancing daring light in his eyes, swords in each hand flashing faster than the wings of hawkmoths . . .

We reached the shallow pool behind the platform and started slogging forward, and then Master Li let out a tiny yelp and stared up and to the left. I gasped as I saw a figure climbing down the wall of the Palace of Southern Fragrance. It was not the figure I'd been praying for, but it was just as powerful, and it was headed straight toward that platform and those cages. Blue cheeks and crimson nose and yellow chin and silver forehead seemed appropriate to the scene that framed them: whirlwinds tossing dark clouds of debris into the air, hissing Yellow Wind, a swollen blood-red sun, gusts howling around palaces.

"Hurry, Ox! He can't get another cage!" Master Li yelled.

I did my best, leaping forward with the old man on my back, vaulting to the platform. I was still on my knees on the platform's edge, preparing to stand and leap, when the great ape man landed light as a leaf between the thrones. He snapped a mandarin's neck with an easy chop of one hand and scooped up his cage, and for a moment the creature's eyes looked directly at me, and at Master Li, and I almost thought I saw amusement in them. Then with two more leaps Envy was off the platform and racing to the wall. One alert soldier managed to hurl a spear that fell five feet short as the ape man began to climb. I could scarcely run as fast as Envy could scale a wall, and in a few seconds he was gone, carrying the cage.

Unfortunately we were still there. The mandarins were shrieking and pointing at us, and squads of soldiers were racing forward, and we were saved from being turned into pincushions by massed arrows because they would have hit mandarins and eunuchs as well, but it was only a brief reprieve. Li the Cat was howling for blood, and the Black Watch was closing around us, and at that instant something happened that caused every head to turn. I thought I had heard the most horrible screams possible when Hosteler Tu had practiced his art down in the dungeon, but I was wrong. These screams were even worse, and they were coming from the Black Watch's basilica, and my eyes jerked that way along with everyone else's.

Just above the level of the intervening wall was a long balcony in front of apartments on one of the upper floors, and Hyena and Jackal were staggering along it. They were stark naked, and they screamed in unimaginable agony as they tore their hair and rent their flesh. Hog followed, also naked, with a naked girl riding on his back. It was Yu Lan. Hog howled as horribly as the others as he tried to pluck his eyes out, and I realized that the three men were mad. Hopelessly, horribly insane, and the heat waves that rose around them were causing illusions like dreams, and as in a dream I thought I saw glittering fangs in the blurred area of Yu Lan's lovely head, and terrible claws at her waist, and something scaly and coiling near her legs. The mirage made the beautiful shamanka appear to be laughing with delight as she rode a madman's back—but Master Li was pounding me, jerking at my arm, and I felt him jump from my back.

He was diving for the cages. Li the Cat and the soldiers stood transfixed, staring at the balcony while Master Li snatched a cage from beneath a throne and jerked the brush from it. He squinted at the symbols engraved upon the bars, and then touched the figure of a man at an oar with the tip of the brush, twice.

"Goat, goat, jump the wall," he chanted, and the brush touched the symbol of a drum, "grab some grass to feed your mother"—the brush touched a scarf and a head— "if she's not in field or stall"—the brush moved to the blue dragon of the east and the white tiger of the west—"feed it to your hungry brothers"—the brush moved rapidly over a sequence of rowers—"one . . . two . . . three . . . four . . . five . . . six . . . seven . . . eight!"

A bright flash blinded me, and when my eyes cleared I was gaping at *Tuan hu*, a great toadlike creature squatting in the center of the platform. Terrible eyes glared at me, the immense mouth opened.

"Ox!"

Master Li was touching the tip of his right forefinger to his left eyebrow, right eyebrow, and the tip of his nose, and I hastened to repeat the sequence I had dreamed of, and the horrible eyes moved away from us. The mouth gaped, a huge tongue flicked out, and streams of burning acid shot over soldiers and mandarins, scorching through flesh and clothing alike.

"Ox, this is what the cages carry! This is what we need!" Master Li yelled.

A small compartment had opened in the bottom of the cage, and Master Li slid his fingers between the bars and pulled out something else I knew from dreams: a tiny object shaped like a pitchfork, but with only two prongs. He swiftly stuck it in his money belt and dove for another cage, and at that point we were overcome by a rapid sequence of startling events.

Mandarins and soldiers shrieked, acid sprayed the platform, and a roaring, howling, furious saint leaped up between writhing bodies. The Celestial Master was quite out of his mind with fury. He ignored the great demon-deity as he charged Master Li with his stone club, smashing to jelly the head of a mandarin that got in the way. I dove for the Celestial Master's legs just as he tried to decapitate Master Li, and the three of us tumbled over the back edge of the platform and toppled down into the pool beneath the splashing waterfall.

Fortunately my fall had been slowed by water when my head hit a rock beneath the surface. I wasn't quite knocked unconscious, but I had no control of my body until the numbness went away, and I could only watch helplessly as the Celestial Master attacked Master Li. The saint had lost his ax in the fall, but immensely powerful hands had closed around the sage's throat and I knew that Master Li had no chance at all. Incessantly lifting water wheels kept pouring the contents of great buckets into the Golden River, and the water kept pouring and foaming down around us, and something bumped against my legs. It was the body of an officer with a broken back. Then a pair of hands emerged from the spray, reaching around me to grab the hands of the Celestial Master and slowly pry them from Master Li's neck.

"In Singapore the Merchants' Guild offers the remarkably named 'stone-nine dukes,' meaning baby groupers," the clotted gurgling voice of Sixth Degree Hosteler Tu said into my left ear. "It must be recorded that the groupers are steamed in a stew with parrot fish, yellow croakers, and pig-oil butter-cake fish, although certain authorities claim that eating too many stone-nine dukes will cause falling hair, blindness, and bone decay. That, I believe, is a misconception caused by the fact that the written character for the fish is very similar to that for 'apricot,' and apricots, of course, will do all those things if eaten to excess."

Master Li was able to breathe again, and with breath came the ability to free his knife, and he plunged it into the Celestial Master's chest and ripped a great slash. Then he withdrew the blade and repeated the blow, slashing diagonally across the first wound. There was no blood. Not a drop. Then as I gaped in horror I saw two small greenish paws reach out from the cavity and spread ribs apart, and a monkey's head thrust out from the saint's chest. Eyes of hate glared at us. It chattered and spat at

Master Li, and then it climbed from the empty shell that was the Celestial Master and splashed through the water to the cliff, and in an instant it was gone, swinging up and away before I'd fully realized where I'd seen it before: a charming little gift monkey bowing to the Celestial Master and being led into the house by an enchanted old servant.

The sage was kneeling in the pool, cradling the body of his old friend and teacher, weeping. I looked up to see Li the Cat staring from the platform, and then the eunuch turned to beckon soldiers. I dove and grabbed the cage from Master Li and jerked the brush from the hole in the top.

"Goat, goat," I panted, "climb the wall . . . grab some grass to give your mother . . . if she's not in field or stall . . . give it to your hungry brothers . . . one . . . two . . . three . . . four . . . five . . . six . . . seven . . . eight!"

I blinked in the flash and hastened to make the propitiating gesture, and above me Li the Cat and the soldiers screamed in terror and dove for safety. My eyes cleared and I was gazing at the terrible but somehow touching Wei Serpent, with its two human heads and its silly hats and its little purple jacket. It was huge, though, and fangs protruded from the mouths of the heads, and great coils slithered and glistened. A panting sound behind me was followed by the body of Sixth Degree Hosteler Tu, who painfully shoved himself toward the demon-deity with his arms outstretched. The hosteler's eyes were glazed in ecstasy, and his voice rang with reverence.

"O fabled Savory Serpent of Serendip, ye shall be bathed in wine and honey warmed by babies' breath! Ye shall be poached in the truffled milk of nursing sea serpents! Ye shall be basted in broth of pearls dissolved in unicorn tears! Ye shall be worshipped! Ye shall be adored!"

Sixth Degree Hosteler Tu spread his arms as wide as possible and wrapped them around the snake in a loving embrace, and the Wei Serpent's coils closed around the hosteler, and for a moment the two of them were still and rapt. Then a flash blinded me, and when my vision cleared a great white crane was skirting a whirlwind, flying away across the bloated surface of the blood-red sun.*

"Ox!"

I tore my eyes from a flying crane to see Master Li scrambling for another cage. I dropped the cage I was still clutching, squawked like a goose, dove back on top of it, and reached inside and pulled out the little two-pronged pitchfork. Then I leaped for another cage and found myself battling the last two mandarins and Li the Cat. The problem was they had three or four soldiers with them, and I was pinned between two overturned throne-like chairs as I tried to fend them off with a pike I grabbed from a dead soldier.

The toadlike demon-deity was still spitting acid but it took care not to scorch friends, meaning those who made the proper gesture, so at least I had no problem there. As I tried to keep somebody's spear from becoming my second backbone I heard ". . . four . . . five . . . six . . . seven . . . eight!" This time I closed my eyes before the flash did, and I opened them to make the propitiating gesture and see the only female sibling, *Nu Pa*, who seemed to be a low cloud no more than two feet tall. Then endless arms of fog reached out, and out, and out, and immense hands made of swirling marsh mist opened and fingers touched howling soldiers and screeching eunuchs, and horrible black blisters spread over their faces and bodies and they ran around clawing at the spots, and then they fell and went into convulsions and died.

A black blistered eunuch had rolled screaming between the

---

* Sixth Degree Hosteler Tu was never seen again. Three months later the magistrate in charge of digging up bodies in the hosteler's basement discovered the 214 notebooks of recipes, culinary comments, and aesthetic essays that were to form the backbone of the second-greatest cuisine the world has ever known. Within a year a powerful lobby had formed to press for proper recognition, and in record time all charges against a mad innkeeper disappeared from the ledgers. Sixth Degree Hosteler Tu was elevated to the pantheon, where his godly form is that of a prominent star in the Hyades asterism, and in many parts of China he is still worshipped as Tu K'ang, Patron of Chefs and Restaurateurs.

feet of the men surrounding me. That allowed me to snatch the brush from the last of the cages. "Goat, goat, jump the wall, grab some grass to give your mother, if she's not in field or stall, give it to your hungry brothers: one, two, three, four, five, six, seven, eight!" I closed my eyes tightly, gestured, and opened them to see the end of Li the Cat.

Ch'i is one of the strangest of the demon-deities. Its odor is musty, its color is the grayish white of mourning, its sound is a faint sighing moan, and its form is the winding cloth of a corpse. The limp cloth slid over the platform like a snake and reached a pair of legs and began wrapping around them. Li the Cat stopped shrieking at me and looked down. He hacked with his sword and succeeded only in slicing his left thigh. He yelled and dropped the blade and grabbed with both hands. The cloth was unresisting. It fell away if pulled properly, but it began winding once more as soon as it was released. Now the other end was sliding up the eunuch's back, and a curl of gray-white, musty, moaning burial cloth wrapped around his chest, pinning his arms to his sides. The eunuch was screaming, one shriek after another, and his eyes were bulging in horror. The ends were wrapping faster now, climbing his knees, waist, chest, shoulders, and then they wound around Li the Cat's neck and up over his chin. The crystal vial containing the parts he'd had severed to advance his position in life was shoved up in front of his face, and the cloth wound around and around, and his screams stopped and his horrified eyes disappeared. Only his forehead, glistening with Protocol Soap, and the top of his head remained, and then they too vanished beneath burial cloth. A gray-white cocoon toppled over and wriggled on the platform, and the last I saw of the eunuch he was still wriggling, but slower.

I grabbed the last little pitchfork. Master Li had a running start and he landed high on my back and shouted in my ear, "The well! Get to the well!" I jumped down to the courtyard and vaulted over writhing bodies and jumped back up to the stone platform around the well, and Master Li slid from my back. Acid and marsh pestilence were still seeking victims, and the shrieks were so loud he had to lean close and yell.

"Ox, look down inside the well at the walls and tell me what you see!"

I dropped to my stomach and craned over the edge as far as I could, and my eyes spread even wider than they were already. I got back up and shouted, "The frogs! There's a pattern of frogs around the inside, just like in my dream!"

"We have to go down! Fast!" he yelled.

Unlike my dream, there was no windlass and bucket. I turned and saw that the guards had fled, but the lead chain linking the prisoners had been looped over a post and they couldn't move. The key ring lay upon the marble pavement, so I unlocked the prisoners and let them run for their lives and then I hauled the chains to the well, linked them together, and attached one end to an iron post that might at one time have held a windlass.

It was a lot harder than lowering a bucket, but in one sense it was a great improvement over my dreams. There wasn't any horrible stench of rotting flesh—although there would be when the sacrificial victims began to stink—and there wasn't any frightening growl from below.

"There!"

The light from above was just good enough for us to make out a circular spot on the wall. I started the chain swinging, wider and wider, kicking off from the back wall, and finally my foot found a toehold inside the hole. We made it over the edge into a small low tunnel, and I found a rock to wrap the end of the chain around in case we had to come back. Then we started down a narrow passageway that was partly illuminated by greenish phosphorescence.

A vibration was making small pebbles fall from the stone ceiling. It shook harder and harder, and then air rushed at us and hit like a physical blow. A great sound was forming, turning my bones to jelly, and it resolved itself into a musical note that quite literally hurled me against a wall. Even as I was being battered I recognized it. It was the mysterious sound that had announced the solstice ever since a great musical instrument had been built by Eight Skilled Gentlemen, and quite frankly I had completely forgotten that the solstice was today. I realized with horror that we must be actually *inside* the Yu. This tunnel was one of the pipes, and the sound so far had been merely warming up, a throat clearing, and what would happen if the full sound reached us when we were trapped in a tiny tunnel?

"It's Envy! He's installed the first yang key!" Master Li shouted. "Hurry, Ox, hurry!"

So I hurried with the old man on my back, even though I had no idea what lay in front. If a pit opened in the path we were dead. All I could do was run ahead as fast as I could, almost blindly, and when the second blast of sound came it spun me around like a top.

"There will be two more! Hurry! Hurry!" Master Li yelled.

The next two musical notes were worse because we were closer to the source, but my fear that my eardrums would burst was unfounded. I had been racing downhill, but now the path leveled. The phosphorescence grew brighter, which was a blessing because I was able to see and stop in time, and I panted to a halt at the edge of a cliff overlooking a cavern and there they were: great coiling shapes that weren't serpents but pipes, connecting to smaller pipes and still smaller ones. I found steps and ran down, and at last we reached eight tiny pipes leading into eight small boxes in two rows, four on each side.

Master Li hopped down. "Left is yang, and all male boxes should be filled," he muttered. He tried to open the lids on the left but they had virtually melded with the grooves. "Yin waits," he said, and he reached to the right and the first lid opened easily.

Inside was a little rack like in my dreams, and I could also see a hole in the bottom leading down through solid rock, probably to the wind-chest below. Master Li had taken out his two little pitchfork things and I gave him my two.

"Some kind of tuning forks, but designed to do something very unusual with sound waves," he said. "One would like to be able to talk to the Eight Skilled Gentlemen and ask a few questions."

He placed the first tuning fork in the rack, where it fit perfectly, and closed the lid, which sealed itself tightly in place. The old man repeated the performance with the remaining three forks and boxes, and then turned and walked rapidly into the shadows. When I trotted up beside him I saw the gates. There were two pairs of immense iron gates side by side. The ones on the left stood open and the ones on the right were closed, and Master Li walked to the closed gates on the female side. A great vibration was beginning, and then the first of the yin notes blasted against us. I held Master Li to keep him from being blown away, and as the sound faded the great gates swung slowly open.

We walked through, and then I stopped in my tracks and stared. We were walking on a path of stone between two wide channels. The channel to the left was filled with water, but what water! It seemed to be made of vibrating translucent air with rainbow colors woven through it, and Master Li exclaimed in delight as he saw it.

"Remember Hosteler Tu, Ox? 'The Yu was built by the Eight Skilled Gentlemen to make music that turned into water.' Well, here it is, and here comes some more."

The channel on the right had been dry, but now the vibrations of the Yu seemed to be coalescing into visible form, and a shining rainbow path of water appeared.

"Hurry."

We ran forward to a second pair of gates, open on the left, closed on the right ("Locks?" I wondered. "Like in a very strange canal?"), and the sound from the second tuning key caused great gates to swing open, and music-water formed on the right to match that on the left. Gates opened twice more, and water formed in front of us, and the fourth and last shining path of water reached ahead to a dock that matched the dock on the left, and there waited two great Dragon Boats, different only in that the yang symbol marked the one on the left and the yin symbol marked the one on the right.

They were each at least a hundred and fifty feet long, but so slim that only a narrow passageway ran between seats for single oarsmen on each side. On the platforms in the center waited drum and clapping boards, and lying on the high prows were the green-and-white scarves used to send commands. Each immense steering oar was forty feet long, and I noticed that the prow of each boat had the traditional dragon-head shape, but with a long tapering horn thrusting straight out from the center of the forehead.

The crews were waiting on the docks, standing at attention, eighty-eight oarsmen per boat, and I could distinguish the red bandanas around the foreheads of the "brothers," the lead oarsmen. I saw other figures I couldn't identify, and then as we came close a gentleman in a simple white robe stepped forward and bowed. In this setting the blue cheeks and crimson nose and silver forehead and yellow chin seemed entirely appropriate, and his voice was clear and resonant.

"Believe it or not, Li Kao, I prayed that you would perform the impossible and come to honor the solstice with me today," said Envy.

Despite the claims of my critics I am not a total idiot. I was not surprised—saddened, yes, even agonized at certain implications—but not at all surprised that the voice of Envy was the voice of a puppeteer.

24

Master Li regarded Yen Shih with ironic eyes, and bowed with almost equal grace.

"And I am honored to greet the most talented as well as most dangerous of cavaliers," he said. "It was inexcusable of me not to have seen the face behind the mask from the very first, or nearly."

Envy shrugged. "Inexcusable? Surely human nature is excuse enough." He lifted a piece of the disguise he had discarded and pressed it to the left side of his face, like malleable flesh-colored clay, and again I saw the terrible ravages of smallpox. "No one looks closely at deformity," he said gently.

"It was a brave disguise for a cavalier to choose," Master Li said with ungrudging respect. "It was also brave to travel the world as a puppeteer whose formal social status would be as low as that of a prostitute or an actor. You could have chosen to be the empire's greatest fencing master, or the most accomplished of imperial advisers. But then, cavaliers are naturally drawn to crafts involving the pulling of strings, and I speak with the authority of having been one of the puppets," Master Li said with another bow.

"For a time, Li Kao, for a time," Envy said. He flicked a wrist in a casual gesture of dismissing a trifle I couldn't imitate with a thousand years of practice, and the sunrise smile I had seen illuminate a landscape of pockmarks now lit the grotesquely painted face a goddess had given him. "You would have needed supernatural powers to guess at the beginning who I was and what I was after, and when I consider the array of marvels and monsters coming at you from all sides I am awestruck that you could untangle it at all, much less get here in time. An extraordinary performance, and you will forgive me if I begin to wonder who is the manipulator and who is the mannequin."

Yen Shih stepped toward Master Li, and smiled when I jumped protectively to the old man's side.

"Don't worry, Ox. If murder were on my mind I would have killed both of you the moment Master Li found the remaining mandarins, which meant he had found the remaining cages that my peculiar siblings still occupied as guardians. Master Li has earned the right to challenge, and I would be a poor cavalier if I did not accept the challenge eagerly. We shall race, he and I," he said. "The boats await as they awaited three thousand years ago, as do the crews, and it is time to meet them."

The figures we walked toward were indistinct in mist that floated low over the twin channels of water and in the smoke from rows of torches. As we grew closer I began to realize that it wasn't only mist and smoke that blurred the forms and features of the crews. They themselves were like wax dolls placed too close to a stove, partially melted, twisted and squashed down as had been the ancient statues of dying deities around the upper cavern of the Yu. They still carried an aura of awesome strength but they smelled of abandoned tombs, desiccated and dusty, crumbling with age, and I wondered how much longer they could keep their vigil beside antique Dragon Boats.

Sixteen stepped forward and bowed, eight from each boat, the ones wearing the red bandanas of lead oarsmen.

"Allow me to introduce those who will set the stroke for the yang boat," said Envy. "These eight on my left are the four Roving Lights, *Yu-kuang*, and the four Junior Brothers of the Wasteland, *Yeh-chung*, who are wrongfully accused in innumerable ancient accounts of spreading pestilence. They do no such thing. All they do is row, and if pestilence follows their victories it is no concern of theirs."

The eight oarsmen bowed again and stepped back into the ranks. Envy waved toward eight figures on the right, who lifted their heads one after another.

"Your lead strokes, *Pa-ling*, 'Eight Ghostly Powers,' and very great oarsmen of yin are they," said Envy, who was using the intonation of a chant. "From left to right they are First Doer, Lungs and Stomach, Ancestral Intelligence, Rising and Soaring, Seizer of All, Sharpener and Amputator, Husky Lusty One, and, finally, Extreme and Extraordinary One, who has been accorded the honor of a brief description in *Classic of Mountains and Seas.* 'On Shensi mountain dwells a creature that has the shape of a bull, the bristles of a porcupine, and the sound of a howling dog. It eats people.' "

The oarsmen bowed and stepped back into the ranks. Four other creatures, two from each boat, stepped forward.

"The wielders of drum and clapping board, who receive the commands of the scarves and transmit them through their instruments to the rest of the crews," said Envy. "Beating for yang: Male Elder on the left and Elder Extraordinary One on the right. Beating for yin: Bounding and Rushing on the left and Gliding Sliding One on the right."

The four bowed and stepped back. A slim slight figure stepped forward, and my heart did strange things. For a long moment I was sure it was Yu Lan, but then I realized the girl had a slightly blurred face, like all the others, and her eyes were deep and cold and frightening, and where she walked a puddle formed. The awesome man-ape that was Envy, and who I still loved as Yen Shih, turned to me.

"Number Ten Ox, pay the closest attention," he said quietly. "In the ancient *White Marsh Diagrams* is a charmingly innocent entry: 'The essence of old wells takes the form of a beautiful girl called Kuan, and it likes to sit on rocks and blow a flute, and if you call it by name it will go away.' This is indeed Kuan, Essence of Old Wells, and you must know two things. The first is that her strength has never been measured and probably can't be, because wells draw power from earth and water alike. The second is that she has been my faithful companion during my exile on earth. As such she shall use her great strength at the steering oar of the yang boat, and you, as companion of Master Li, shall steer the yin boat, and the role of the one they call goat is a hard and dangerous one. Do you understand me?"

"Yes, sir," I whispered.

Master Li and Envy walked forward together to the yang boat on the left, and as I helped them light the purifying fire on top of the platform in the center I was struck by the wording of their ancient solstice chant: "The sparks of the suns are burning the sky! The fire of the earth is burning the Five Regions! Flames destroy all that is not auspicious!" Then we crossed a gangplank to the yin boat and repeated the purifying ritual. There were other ceremonies and chants I didn't recognize and couldn't understand, and finally Envy returned by himself to the yang boat. The gangplank was pulled in. Master Li was totally relaxed now that the issue was clear-cut, and he regarded his counterpart with speculative eyes.

"As a matter of purely academic interest, am I correct in assuming that the appearance of that vampire ghoul was no more than a weird coincidence?" he asked.

"I sincerely hope so since I prefer not to wander into the morass of metaphysical speculation," Envy replied with equal nonchalance. "I assume the creature fell into a load of earth that was being carried to Hortensia Island, and Ma Tuan Lin accidentally moved the bead on the cage in the proper sequence not long afterward and released the first of my brothers. Monsters worship demon-deities. The ch'ih-mei crawled from the pile and was too late to greet my brother, but at least he found a meal."

"And your original involvement?" Master Li asked.

"I was as ignorant as the ch'ih-mei," said Envy. "I had no idea the cages had survived until I heard the *'Pi-fang!'* cry and saw the crane cross the moon. It was a marvelous moment. If one brother survived, and surely that meant the cage he guarded also survived, why not the others? Once long ago, I had nearly accomplished an extraordinary feat, only to be denied by incredibly persistent shamans, and now if I could get my hands on those cages I might use their own tools to complete the job. But how could I get my hands on the cages?"

"Enter a puppet," Master Li said sourly.

"You were a godsend. The great Master Li tracking down mandarins and cages for me!" Envy exclaimed delightedly, without the slightest trace of sarcasm or irony. "I was sure you would discover the mechanisms that enabled puppets to operate with minimum help from Yu Lan while I myself roamed free, but I was also sure you would discover it too late."

Master Li had walked up to the captain's post on the high prow and was arranging his scarves, and on the left I saw Envy doing the same, and with a lump in my throat that nearly choked me I made my way astern to the raised platform and the long handle of the huge steering oar. It was beautifully balanced. So much so that I could lift it easily from the water with downward pressure from my body, but lowering it gently was far more difficult, and when the boat rocked very slightly as the hawser was cast away I was almost knocked off my feet. Sideways movements of the oar were murder, and I hated to think what would happen with up-and-down movements if the boat hit hard waves.

The twin boats were moving, floating side by side in the two channels, picking up speed even though no rower had touched an oar, and now I could see far enough through the mist to make out a perfectly straight streak of light ahead of us, cutting across our path like the edge of a knife.

"Like a starting line," I thought, and as I thought it I felt a

powerful series of vibrations: one . . . two . . . three . . .
four . . . five . . . six . . . seven . . . eight . . .

The eight tuning forks, yin and yang, were allowing the Yu to
perform a song unheard in three thousand years. Great rumbling
notes—soft for all their force—were blurring the water and the
air as though blending elements together, and then a long, slow,
steady throbbing note seemed to evolve and take over. It was
perfectly steady, quiet but with unimaginable power. This was
the full song of the Yu, weaving music into water that stretched
out from the horizontal line perpendicular to the boats and
blended both channels into a river fit for a race, and Master Li
turned to the puppeteer with wonder in his eyes.

"Can those remarkable men have created a racing path that
also measures the solstice they sought to preserve?" he asked.

"The course is permanently set as though it was the shadow
of a giant gnomon, yes," Envy said. "I haven't the slightest idea
how they managed it, although I once read that a similar phenomenon was produced by a barbarian called Oenopides of
Chios. Needless to say, the gnomon is correct to the precise second of the solstice."

Master Li heaved a melancholy sigh.

"What a pity. The one man in the empire who could have
explained it to us, on his better days, can't be here," he said. "I
can forgive much, but I cannot forgive the fate of the Celestial
Master."

"Li Kao, he was dying! His mind was nearly gone," Envy
protested. "I had to find some way to infuriate Heaven with
mankind. Your discovery of a smuggling and counterfeiting ring
gave me the idea of using aristocratic greed to resurrect the ghost
scheme, but in itself it wouldn't be enough. However, the August
Personage of Jade is hot-tempered, as we all know. I was certain
he would remove his protection from earth before the matter
had been fully investigated if the Celestial Master were to insult
Heaven with human sacrifice in the name of righteousness and
religion, which could be done if Malice took over the Celestial

Master's body. As it turned out, my miserable son almost ruined the whole thing."

For the first time Envy showed strong emotion, and the garish colors of his face received an additional flush of rage.

"That idiot boy and his pathetic plot to kill you in the greenhouse," he said with venom dripping from his voice. "Kill you? You hadn't yet tracked down the remaining mandarins and their cages! And then he had a little maid murdered because she let a dog die, he said, but the real reason was that he wanted to exult in the power that went with the new body he occupied, and murdering someone was the best use of power he could think of. On top of that he had to amuse himself by playing tag with you around half the Forbidden City, and the most persuasive argument for celibacy I know of is my son Malice!"

"Yet that would deny you a daughter," Master Li said quietly. "She is surely compensation enough."

"Yes," Envy said, very softly. "Yes, no man has ever had a lovelier and more dutiful daughter, though few daughters have been born bearing such a curse."

The garish face turned in my direction, and I still think I wasn't wrong to feel honored to receive a nod of his head.

"I would say that my daughter chose a most inopportune time to seek love, if I didn't know that such things are not a matter of choice," he said. "My heart went out to her, poor girl. Fleeing to fragmented passion in the world of dreams—the only medium in which Madness moves more freely than can her mother, and one does not disobey her mother—but even in dreams metamorphosis was sure to seek her out. She wept long and hard, and although she never told what happened I knew she could no longer approach Number Ten Ox in sleep lest her fangs sink into his brain and her claws clasp his heart. Godhood cannot be refused," Envy said, and his grimace and wry tone of voice suggested he was talking not about Yu Lan when he added, "but it need not be sought."

Master Li looked silently at Envy for a long moment.

"You have known grandeur and debasement to degrees far beyond human comprehension, which leads one to wonder what you hope to gain by tricking Heaven into allowing mass destruction on earth. The gods, you know, will simply blame it on Destiny and go about the delightful business of rebuilding," Master Li said. "As for the earthly massacre, would you stoop to the level of the legendary king who summoned all the world's elephants to trample an ant who bit his royal toe?"

Envy looked at him with a faint smile. The shining straight line was much closer now, and the boats were traveling faster, and the lead oars were spitting on their hands and rewrapping their bandanas. Water slapped the boat, and the handle of the steering oar smacked my ribs.

"Li Kao, you already know that I act as I do because I must," Envy said.

His eyes turned to me, and in them was a strange light I couldn't decipher, almost, but not quite, like the moon-glow eyes of Kuan, who stood across from me at the handle of her steering oar, riding easily with the movement of the boat, thinking the slow deep thoughts of wells.

"Number Ten Ox," Envy said quietly, "once there was a great king who gazed down from a tall tower upon a gardener who sang as he worked, and the king cried, 'Ah, to have a life of no cares! If only I could be that gardener.' And the voice of the August Personage of Jade reached out from Heaven and said, 'It shall be so,' and lo, the king was a gardener singing in the sun. In time the sun grew hot and the gardener stopped singing, and a fine dark cloud brought coolness and then drifted away, and it was hot again and much work remained, and the gardener cried, 'Ah, to carry coolness wherever I go and have no cares! If only I could be that cloud.' And the voice of the August Personage reached out from Heaven and said, 'It shall be so,' and lo, the gardener was a cloud drifting across the sky. And the wind blew and the sky grew cold, and the cloud would have liked to go behind the shelter of a hill, but it could only go where the wind took it, and no matter how hard it tried to go this way the wind took it that way, and above the cloud was the bright sun. 'Ah, to fly through wind and be warm and have no cares! If only I could be the sun,' cried the cloud, and the voice of the August Personage of Jade reached out from Heaven and said, 'It shall be so,' and lo, he was the sun. It was very grand to be the sun, and he delighted in the work of sending down rays to warm some things and burn others, but it was like wearing a suit made of fire and he began to bake like bread. Above him the cool stars that were gods were sparkling in safety and serenity and the sun cried, 'Ah, to be divine and free from care! If only I could be a god.' And the voice of the August Personage of Jade reached out from Heaven and said, 'It shall be so,' and lo, he was a god, and he was beginning his third century of combat with the Stone Monkey, which had just transformed itself into a monster a hundred thousand feet tall and was wielding a trident made from the triple peaks of Mount Hua, and when he wasn't dodging blows he could see the peaceful green earth down below him, and the god cried, 'Ah, if only I could be a man who was safe and secure and had no cares!' And the voice of the August Personage of Jade reached out from Heaven and said, 'It shall be so.' And lo, he was a king who was gazing down from a tall tower upon a gardener who sang as he worked."

Envy lifted one shoulder in a slight shrug and turned away, but not before I realized there was no amusement in his parable. The light in his eyes did not carry the clean coldness of deep water, like the eyes of Kuan, but the cruel coldness of hatred, because Envy could never rest, never relax, never enjoy, never gain what he wished and never cease wishing, never satisfy the terrible hunger that wracked his mind and body. He was a great nobleman condemned to envy not only clouds, the sun, and the gods but even mindless gardeners as humble as Number Ten Ox, and for that insult the Number Ten Ox's of the world were going to die.

25

The starting line was very close. Master Li lifted his left hand and the white tip of the green silk scarf snapped back, and the great twisted figure of Bounding and Rushing extended his cloth-wrapped sticks over the taut surface of the huge tympan atop the center platform and began a quiet steady drumroll. Across the rainbow water Male Elder was doing the same in the yang boat. One hundred and seventy-six oars slid out on the four sides of the two boats and hovered above the surface. A dark straight shadow touched the tips of the horns that extended straight out from the dragon-head prows, and slid backward to touch the pilot posts against which the captains braced themselves, and Envy and Master Li flicked out their right scarves. Gliding Sliding One raised his clapping boards and made a sharp crashing noise, as did Elder Extraordinary One across from us, and each team of eighty-eight oars dipped into the water with long, smooth strokes. The boat seemed to jump forward beneath my feet. The clapping boards and drums worked steadily and unhurriedly as they set the beat: crash, rat-tat-tat, crash, rat-tat-tat, crash . . .

Steering oars as big as the ones on racing boats produce a terrible drag once they hit the water, like brakes on wagon wheels, and the steersman spends half his time sailing through the air with his body stretched out over the handle, trying to keep the huge key-shaped blade just above the surface of the water but not touching it. When the scarves signal a turn, or a drift must be corrected, the goat earns his pay. Down, shove, up! The tiniest extension of steering time means that much extra drag. Fractions of a second at the start can add up to an equal number of feet at the end, and the strange supernatural girl across from me was controlling her great oar with a touch of a finger. I was already fighting mine, and I knew there was no chance of matching a well spirit who lived in complete harmony with immortal cavaliers and ancient demigods and water woven from music. I could only do my best and trust in Master Li.

Bounding and Rushing continued the stroke beat with his drum, but Gliding Sliding One was giving a different sound with the clapping boards. At first I couldn't make it out. Then I saw the long flowing end of Master Li's left scarf flick up and down, and at almost the same time the oar bucked up against me, and I realized the clapping boards from now on would transmit warnings and commands. This was no placid pool we were riding on. The clapping boards were describing waves, and we lifted high and swooped down, and as we lifted again the drumbeats on both boats stepped up a notch, and the oar strokes quickened.

I saw the right scarf wave an instant before the clapping boards repeated the command. Wait . . . wait . . . now! I dropped the blade into the water and leaned left: one . . . two . . . three . . . up! Getting it up smoothly wasn't so easy, but I managed with nothing more serious than a bloody nose when the handle kicked me in the face. Wait . . . wait . . . down! Lean right. One . . . two . . . three . . . up! It wasn't pretty, but we'd made a turn and were back on course again. I stared at the great black rock that both boats had veered around, thrusting through rainbow waves. It had sun and moon symbols engraved on it, yang and yin, and I wondered if it had something to do with the gnomon nature of the course, like a measuring mark.

Master Li signaled and the clapping boards repeated the command and the smooth, powerful strokes of the lead oarsmen stretched out a notch: boom, rat-tat-tat, boom, rat-tat-tat, boom, rat-tat-tat. Across from us Envy had given the same command at precisely the same time, and the boats were dead even.

The captain is the most important member, of course. The goat is so far back he can't possibly see the hazards ahead, and the world of rowers begins and ends with their oars, and the drummers' job is to inspire, regulate, and transmit, not to originate. The captain must serve as eyes and brain from his pilot's post in the prow, and one wrong message from a flapping scarf can mean the end of the race. My faith in Master Li is limitless, but I had to admit that his situation was something like mine. Across from him was a cavalier who had dared to love and betray the most powerful and dangerous of all goddesses, and who had once run this very race against Eight Skilled Gentlemen, and who had even driven a team of plunging dragons along a path between the stars—or something almost as dramatic, if one allows for poetic exaggeration. The puppeteer didn't seem to have a care in the world as he easily shifted his body with the movements of the boat, not bothering to brace against his pilot's post.

Boom, rat-tat-tat, boom, rat-tat-tat, boom, rat-tat-tat. Now the boats were fighting the waves, bucking up and down, and I was learning the first reason for the goat's name. On a rough course the steersman must swing his oar to provide the best balance for the boat, using wind drag to correct drift as much as possible without resorting to the much greater water drag of conventional steering. Half the time I was flying through the air, butting everything in sight as I wrestled with that huge heavy thing, and when I looked through the spray to my left I could see Kuan controlling her oar with no more than a shove and a tug. How could she do it? Strength wasn't entirely the answer. Somehow she was anticipating each wave and chop of water, each plunge and bounce of the boat, and was already in position when the instant for correction came. All around us the vibrations of the

Yu music were growing stronger and stronger. The cavern seemed to have disappeared. The sky (was it really a sky?) had grown very dark, and the rainbows woven through the waves were shimmering like fire. I thought I saw banks on both sides, with trees and tangled shrubs, and then I saw people on the right bank and great terrible creatures on the left.

The scarves signaled and the drums quickened and the eight lead oars on each boat picked up the pace. The boats were shooting ahead like skimming arrows, spray flying up as prows smacked short choppy waves. The clapping boards called urgently. Wait . . . wait . . . down, shove, up . . . wait . . . wait . . . down, shove, up! We safely veered around a second jutting solstice-marked stone, but this time I was a fraction too late in lifting. I doubt that anyone else would have noticed the tiny jump ahead that the yang boat took when Kuan managed the turn perfectly, but I did. She was several inches in front of me now, and if those thrusting rocks were gnomon measures there should be four more of them, half a year, and I didn't want to think how far she'd be leading when we passed the last one. Scarves flicked and clapping boards urged and drums picked up the pace, oars flashed faster and faster: boom, rat-tat-tat, boom, rat-tat-tat, but I was having a terrible time concentrating on my oar. On my left I could see a bank where huge horrible creatures roared and fought and killed, and flames and lava poured from volcanoes, and terrible cracks appeared in the earth as the ground heaved and shook. On my right I could see men and women crouched and fearful, dressed in furs, and priests wearing bearskins with four gold eyes sewn on them who raised arms to Heaven and prayed, and a girl was thrust forward and a stone ax lifted, and just as I had seen with the Celestial Master the ax fell and a soul was offered to the gods.

Wait . . . wait . . . down, shove, up . . . wait . . . wait . . . down, shove, up!

The yang boat was leading by a foot now. The jutting rock flashed past, and as it did I saw people staring up in fear at a tiny

pale sun like a fading candle, and they shoved children out from
the shelter of caves and had them run around and play with
special caps on their heads, just as we still did in my village
during the first moon: bright-colored caps shaped like flowers
and grasshoppers, vivid against white snow to catch the eyes of
gods looking down. Fires were put out to save all heat for the
sun. Hard-cooked eggs dyed as bright and cheerful as the flowers
of spring were brought out beneath the dark cold sky, and the
shells were ceremoniously cracked and the round yellow yolks
removed and held up high.

Faster, the scarves and clapping boards signaled, and faster
flashed the oars, and the boats bounced over waves with teeth-
jarring impact, one right after another, and the sterns swung
around as the slim hulls tried to go sideways. I flipped like a rag
doll tied to the handle of the steering oar, trying to use air drag as
much as possible and water drag as little, but still Kuan was
always ahead of me, always anticipating, always balanced and
calm and sure. The yang boat's lead was more than a yard now.

Through sheets of spray I could see blurred images on the
banks. There was a village very much like my own, and with a
pang in my heart I saw the beautiful girls wearing their brightest
clothes being pushed in swings by the young men, higher and
higher, lovely flowers reaching to the sky, and the older women
in equally bright dress holding bright ribbons as they danced like
petals around a stalklike pole. Fathers urged sons to keep the
shuttlecocks in the air longer and longer, and each shuttlecock
was painted bright yellow like the sun. The last ice was ceremoniously cracked, and the graves were swept, and the spirits of
the dead were invited to join the festival of the first bath in the
stream, where wine in buoyant cups floated from hand to hand.

I had lost track of gnomon markers. The Yu vibrations were
tremendously strong, and suddenly I realized how the spirit of
old wells could anticipate every command. Kuan wasn't watching the water, she was listening to the sounds that formed it, and
I discovered that if I stopped thinking and let my body react to

the music of the Yu I was already in place when the scarf and clapping boards reached me. But it was too late. Already the gap had spread to ten feet and it was going to get worse unless Envy gave a bad command. I could only see his back now, far ahead, glimpsed momentarily through spray, and even at that distance he exuded the calm control of a gentleman out for a holiday paddle on a pool.

Master Li was doing the only thing he could, which was to pray. I could see him straight ahead on the high raised prow with his head lifted to the sky, and scattered words drifted back on the wind: "Lady of Mysteries . . . Guide of Lost Souls . . . Blender of the Hot and the Cold, the Wet and the Dry, the Done and the Undone . . ." The right hand lifted and the long scarf flicked out a command. But I had already heard something in the vibrating music, something ahead, and I was ready now: down, shove up, wait . . . wait . . . down, shove, up! I could have wept in frustration. This time Kuan didn't gain on me and we made the turn around the rock in unison, but too late, too late. Still the ten-foot gap remained.

"Lady of Highest Prime . . . Guardian of the Greatest Sacrifice . . . Solace of All That Sickens and Dies . . ."

We had flashed past a rock into searing sunlight that made the sky appear to be on fire. Black-funneled waterspouts lifted from frothy rainbow waves, and I saw a dragon rear up through the surface, one of the terrible ones, a *kiao lung* as opposed to the beneficial water dragons. Horrible creatures had claimed the left bank. On the right bank an unrelenting Yellow Wind was ripping cottages apart, and sand covered everything, and all the crops were burned and withered.

"Lady Who Grieves . . . Lady Who Comforts . . . Lady Who Guards All Living Things," chanted Master Li.

Screams overhead made me look up to see the most terrifying of all creatures, the three winged servants of the Patron of Pestilence who had once allowed a cavalier to love her, the Queen Mother Goddess of the West. Those who know the lady would say that her claws had touched the cavalier but lightly. Now from the Mountain of the Three Dangers had come the Great Pelican bearing upon its back the Pestilential Hag, Yu Hua-lung, and the Small Pelican that carried Tou-shen Niang Niang, the Plague Queen, and the Green Bird that carried Ma Shen, Patron of Pustules and Pockmarks. The three Death Birds swooped low, screeching, and for one heart-stopping moment I thought I saw an immense tiger claw rip through the sky from horizon to horizon, but then I realized it was a claw of Yellow Wind.

The scarf was signaling and the clapping boards sounded. Down, shove, up . . . wait . . . wait . . . down, shove, up, and both boats made the turn evenly, with the yang boat still leading by ten feet, and my liver turned cold. That last rock was marked with yang symbols from one end to the other. It was the last gnomon marker, half a year, and the strength of yang must now give way to yin if the earth wasn't to burn and plague and pestilence run rampant. As our boat had swung wide I'd been able to look ahead. I'd seen a white streak of sunlight cutting straight across the path of the music water, and the course narrowed as it approached the finish line, and squarely in the center, suspended in air, hung a shimmering ring. It was *pi*, symbol of the harmony of Heaven, seamless continual circle of yang and yin, and the tips of the two long slim dragon horns thrusting from the prows began to glow with the same shimmering light. Master Li and Envy flung both scarves wide, and drums and clapping boards pounded like giant heartbeats, and the rowers made great gasping sounds as they put every ounce of strength into their strokes.

"Lady of Solace, Lady of Purging—"

Whatever goddess Master Li had in mind had better hurry, I thought, because the rowers on the yang boat were equally strong and the gap was getting no shorter. I was flying around trying to achieve perfect balance with the oar as the boat bucked and bounced and skidded over great waves, and when the water boiled between our boat and Envy's and something lifted from the depths I was too busy to really see it at first. Then I did see it, and in a flash I understood that Master Li had not been praying to a goddess at all. Right from the start he had been invoking a priestess, a healer, a shamanka, and lifting through the rainbow water was the head of Yu Lan.

The puppeteer's beautiful daughter looked at me for a long moment. Her lips parted and I saw the glitter of fangs, and one of her claws lifted through spray and fell back. Two of the drops that trickled slowly down her face weren't music-water. Then she dove. Yu Lan disappeared beneath the waves and I was never to see her face again, but I did see something else. Ahead of us and to the left the water boiled in front of the yang boat, and then a great shining fish tail lifted into the air. Harsh sunlight blazed on the scales, and it whipped around with tremendous force and smacked squarely against the prow.

For an instant the yang boat paused as though tied to a leash that somebody had jerked, and when it moved forward again the gap had gone. We were dead even, or perhaps we even had a bit of an edge in that the smooth strokes of our oarsmen hadn't been disrupted, and Master Li began to roar like a volcano.

"On, First Doer! On, Ancestral Intelligence! On, Lungs and Stomach! *Hao! Hao!* Rising and Soaring, Seizer of All, Sharpener and Amputator! On, Husky Lusty One! On, Extreme and Extraordinary One! *Hao! Hao! Hao!*"

Bounding and Rushing pounded his drum with all the force he had, and Gliding Sliding One smashed his clapping boards, and the rowers strained to match the strokes of the lead oars. Master Li's right hand was out and I waited for the scarf to uncoil and shoot back. It came. Down, shove, hold steady, aim, lift just above the surface and wait for the scarf . . . Down, hard left, up . . . Down, soft right, up . . .

We had a slight lead and had cut across the path of the yang boat, oars were scraping oars, wood was screeching against wood, the long, slim, glowing horn from the prow of our boat was reaching out—and then it plunged through, and the shimmering pi ring was snugly around the tip. In an instant the finish line had vanished, and the banks had vanished, and the rowers leaned back and hauled in their oars, and two great Dragon Boats floated side by side in a soft mist.

Master Li turned slowly to the puppeteer. Envy turned at the same time and they examined each other for a moment, and then—at a cost beyond my comprehension—the glorious sunrise smile lit up the garish ape face.

"Poetic justice is a bit too neat for my taste, but I have to admire its effectiveness," Envy said. I realized that his boat was turning transparent, and so was the crew, fading into the mist. Only the puppeteer remained as before, and he bent down and came up with the last cage he had taken. "There's a way to get the key without releasing the creature inside, you know," he said matter-of-factly. "It's time for you to meet the last of my brothers, but have no fear. It would be a poor cavalier who accepted a challenge and resorted to murder when he lost."

He did something with his left hand and there was a bright flash, and when I could see I was looking at the last demon-deity. The God of Sacks was surely the final creation of a dying race, Master Li later told me, surely the clearest statement of what it means to lose an entire civilization. It's a shapeless bag, that's all. Its father was Chaos and its mother was Nothingness, and it has no reason for existence, no beginning, no end. The great cavalier I had known as Yen Shih reached out tenderly and embraced his brother, and the bag opened for him, and then they lifted into the air and fluttered like a blind moth, flapping this way and that, Envy and Anarchy, aimless and inseparable, flying away to find nothing in nowhere.

The yang boat and crew had vanished. The yin boat I stood on seemed to be becoming translucent, but somehow I wasn't afraid of melting away. I left the oar and walked past the resting rowers to Master Li.

"Look, Ox," he said softly.

The mist ahead of us was breaking up, and we were floating

gently forward and then nudging to a stop at a long gray dock, and the ghosts were waiting for us.

The dead were in a festive mood as they climbed on board. They seemed to take up no space, no matter how many walked up the gangplank that Gliding Sliding One and Bounding and Rushing slid out, and I somehow understood that my job was done, and so was Master Li's, and from now on the experienced crew would take over. The dock finally emptied. The lead oarsmen shoved off, and the boat began moving forward again into mist. I was standing with Master Li on the high prow and I could look back over the stern, past my steering oar, and see ghosts leaning out over the water, beckoning and calling. I turned to Master Li with questions in my eyes.

"The dead are trying to coax lung dragons to follow the boat and bring rain," he said quietly. "You see, Ox, it's a pact made long ago. At the Festival of Graves we bring summer clothes and food and wine to the dead, and clean the graves and make them comfortable. At the Hungry Ghosts Festival we feed spirits too unfortunate to have family to care for them, and we pray for their souls. At the Festival of All Souls we bring the dead paper money so they can redeem their winter clothes from the pawnshops of the Land of Shadows, and we bring new clothes when necessary and supplies of everything they might need for the winter. In return the ghosts help bring rain, and fight disease and illness, which no longer have any power over them."

We had passed through the mist and were gliding out on North Lake. Fear had kept the crowds from the banks, but the old woman called Niao-t'ung, "Chamber Pot," and the old man called Yeh-lai Hsiang, "Incense Which Comes by Night," meaning the smell when he removed his sandals, were not going to be denied a ritual they'd performed since they were children, and they painfully hobbled to the water's edge. Puzzlement was apparent in their gestures as they shaded their eyes and looked at us, and then right through us. The authorities had said there would be no boat race this year, but instinct told the two tottering wrecks that there was indeed a boat race, and they nodded firmly to each other and placed their little paper *sung wen* boats in the water. The boats carried the diseases their families might encounter during the next six months, and Incense Which Comes by Night tossed a pocketful of tiny dogs made of clay as well. The dogs would bite any diseases that slipped out of the paper boats and keep them from swimming back on shore.

Paper boats are drawn in the wake of racing ones, and the ghosts were calling and beckoning, and the little bobbing things drifted out and turned obediently to follow the gentle rippling trail behind us.

The boat was vibrating like a tuning fork. On the shore I saw buildings shake and loose tiles fall. The great Yu was sounding the final notes to announce the precise second of the solstice, and a gauzy graceful waterspout was lifting into the air on the port side, higher and higher, spreading dragon wings, forming a cloud. Another dragon followed, and another, and they turned on the dirty fingers of Yellow Wind and began chasing them back into Mongolia. Clouds were spreading across half the sky, just in time to catch the light of the setting sun, and rain began to fall, and a cool fresh breeze washed the city, and people began pouring out, running to the water carrying their families' paper boats.

"Ox . . ."

I turned and cried out as two ghosts came through the crowd of the dead. My mother embraced me, and my father smiled and twisted his hands together awkwardly.

Hundreds of ghosts were greeting Master Li. A huge flotilla of disease boats was following us now, bobbing up and down over gentle waves, glowing in the sunset, and when I looked up from my parents I saw some kind of dark barrier like a wall of low fog, with a shining open archway in the center, and the water that led into it was woven from the colors of the sky.

"But, Mother, Peking really isn't all that much different from the village," I said. "You shouldn't believe all the alarming things you hear . . ."

The ghosts around Master Li had stepped back, bowing to the deck, and the sage was walking forward with a big smile of greeting on his face, and eight hooded gentlemen closed around him, and I could see hands lift and gesture in an animated conversation.

I laughed and pointed. "Look, that's Master Li," I said. "How could I possibly get into trouble working for a sweet little old man like that?"

The boat glided silently through the glittering arch. Ahead was the great looming shape of the Jo tree, where the goddess Kan-shui would catch the sun and bathe it and send it down the underground stream to the other side of the world, so it could climb branches of the Fu-sang tree and again reach the sky. The flowers of the Jo tree were beginning to open and form the first stars of night, and the water around us was gloriously woven from the glow of sunset.

"Ox!" cried Master Li. "Bring your esteemed parents and come say hello to some friends of ours!"

"Yes, sir," I said.

About the Author

Barry Hughart is the highly acclaimed author of *Bridge of Birds*, which won the World Fantasy Award, and *The Story of the Stone*. He lives and works in Tucson, Arizona.